'You're a real woman, and you need a man in your life, and in your bed.'

Trembling, Zoë whispered, 'What makes you think that?'

'This does . . .' he said softly. He reached out and took her shoulders firmly, pulling her towards him, and into his arms.

Zoë gasped, 'No, Quentin, please don't . . .' knowing that this was what she had feared would happen, though she had tried to pretend it was not so. She had feared it when she knew he had been drinking, feared it every time he came near her.

She made one wild, desperate effort to escape, twisting in his arms, but she was not strong enough and fell back on to the turf. Quentin's body blotted out the stars and crushed her beneath his weight, as his mouth closed possessively over hers, ignoring and stifling her cry of protest. She pushed at his chest with both hands, trying vainly to thrust him away. But instead her hands slid round his powerful body, and an unbidden yearning sprang up inside her, a longing to yield to that brutal embrace, here beneath the veil of velvet darkness cast over them both by a Chinese night.

Ann Hulme was born in Portsmouth and educated at the Royal Holloway College—part of the University of London—where she took a degree in French. She has travelled extensively, and it was the fascination of the various countries in which she made her home—France, Germany, Czechoslovakia, Yugoslavia and Zambia—which made her begin to write. She now lives in Bicester, Oxfordshire, with her husband and two sons.

The Garden of the Azure Dragon is her eighth Masquerade Historical Romance.

THE GARDEN
OF THE
AZURE DRAGON

Ann Hulme

MILLS & BOON LIMITED
15–16 BROOK'S MEWS
LONDON W1A 1DR

First published in Great Britain 1986
by Mills & Boon Limited

© Ann Hulme 1986

Australian copyright 1986
Philippine copyright 1986
This edition 1986

ISBN 0 263 75478 2

Set in 10 on 11 pt Linotron Times
04–0886–78,300

Photoset by Rowland Phototypesetting Limited
Bury St Edmunds, Suffolk
Made and printed in Great Britain by
Cox & Wyman Limited, Reading

CHAPTER ONE

THE STEAMER *Empress of Cathay* had made her way overnight through the Pearl Delta, and dropped anchor just after dawn. Zoë came up on deck in the cool early light to find the ship floating gently in the midst of a log-jam of other craft, loading and unloading, and took her first eager sight of the Middle Kingdom. It was fascinating, noisy and colourful, but no one could have called the scene beautiful. Half the population must have come down to greet the *Empress of Cathay*, from either necessity or curiosity, and she wondered whether there would be anyone able to direct her to the British Concession. She had a letter of introduction to some people called Linton, with whom she was to stay briefly in Canton before travelling up country. But she knew nothing about them, other than that Mr Linton was a representative of a British firm who had been out East some years.

The greasy, grey-green stretch between the steamer and the shore was littered with sampans and junks, ferries, fishing boats and floating homes. Rubbish of all kinds was freely jettisoned and floated on the surface. The combination of the noise and the smell was indescribable. On one of the sampans Zoë could see a small toddler, no more than three, balancing with ease on the narrow side of the boat. These Cantonese water-babies were born acrobats.

However, what drew Zoë's interest more than anything else was a flapping rope ladder which hung down the side of the *Empress of Cathay*, and trailed in the water slurping about the rust-spotted hull. Sooner or later, and each passing moment made it sooner, she would be forced to descend by that ladder to one of the sampans jostling near by, to be borne ashore. Her heart sank at the prospect of the climb down, and she tried to concentrate on other things. There was no point in dwelling on it. Besides, she reasoned, visitors had already swarmed aboard by this risky route. Through the porthole of her cabin she had glimpsed a European customs' officer with two Chinese, an official and a clerk. Shortly after had followed a second European, a very tall and strongly-built man in a crumpled white suit and a panama hat with a wide brim. All had made the ascent rapidly and with a sure foot. It was probably not so difficult.

After breakfast in her cabin, she came up on deck again. The visitors were still all closeted with Captain Hansen. Despite the early hour, Zoë had noticed, with disapproval, the steward taking along a tray with glasses and a bottle of whisky. Some while later, the customs party emerged and disappeared down into the hold. But the tall European remained in the captain's cabin. Once, muffled and indistinct, Zoë fancied she could hear their voices, raised in some argument. The captain was a cheerful, even-tempered man, and any discord must have been introduced by the newcomer.

It was now just before ten, and getting very hot. Zoë ran a finger round the high collar of her striped blouse, made stickier and more uncomfortable by the tie that went with it. Under the blouse she wore a corset and a cotton camisole. Beneath all this highly unsuitable clothing the perspiration ran in rivulets down her skin. She was beginning to think the corset a particularly bad mistake, even though it was one of the latest, straighter models, a far cry from the wasp-waisted horrors now blessedly going out of fashion. But, uncertain who would meet her, she had made a resolve to arrive looking correct.

The breeze blowing across the water snatched at her

straw boater, perched jauntily atop her curled chignon of dark brown hair, and she caught at the hat to prevent it being swept away. There was a chair under an awning on deck, and as there appeared to be nothing she could do, she retired thankfully to sit in the shade and re-pin her hat firmly to her hair. Her luggage was neatly stacked on deck, awaiting the order to be lowered over the side. There was quite a lot of it, though one trunk and a portmanteau sufficed to contain her clothes and personal belongings. The two sturdy crates contained new school-books, and half hidden, as it lay on its side behind the crates, was her bicycle. A faint pucker creased Zoë's finely-arched dark eyebrows. She had insisted on bringing the bicycle, sure it would be useful. But the curiosity it had already aroused in the Chinese crew made her suspect that riding it about the local countryside would not be without incident.

As she surveyed her luggage, footsteps scraped on the deck, and the European customs' officer appeared. He was short and stocky, sweating profusely, and a chewed black cheroot protruded from the corner of his mouth. Without removing either his hat or the cheroot, he pointed at the boxes and asked briefly, 'All yours?'

'Yes, school-books,' Zoë told him.

He scribbled something on a pad of forms in his hand, then paused and ran a professional eye over her. 'Missionary . . .' he said in a resigned voice, and began to write this on the form. It was not a question, but a statement.

'No,' Zoë said firmly. 'I'm not a missionary. I'm a school-teacher, that's why I have school-books.'

He eyed her, and moved the cheroot from one corner of his mouth to the other by a complicated movement of his lips. 'Same thing . . .' he said laconically, and to her chagrin, completed the word on his form. 'Going up country?' he asked next, without much interest, adding discouragingly, 'they've got the smallpox up in the hills.

Dropping like flies, I hear.' He walked off, calling back as he did so, 'Send your baggage ashore when you like.'

She was sure the statement about the smallpox had been made purely to put her in her place, and wasn't true. But it wasn't very cheering, all the same. Zoë sat back and heaved a sigh.

She was a tall young woman of twenty-five. Though not conventionally pretty in the 'chocolate-box' style much fancied at the time, she had a clear skin, good teeth and large hazel eyes, and was generally held to be a 'handsome girl'. She had been born late in her parents' marriage, and twelve years separated her from her elder sister, Eve.

Their father had been a celebrated master at a well-known school, but by the time Zoë arrived unexpectedly in their midst, he was already retired. As a consequence, he had endless time to devote to his little daughter. The bright, precocious toddler had played about the leather armchairs of his study, while he showed her the pictures in the great heavy books she could not lift, and gravely explained them to her. She had listened spellbound as he read to her of ancient travels, and fabulous monsters, and magical lands beyond the sunset, peopled by ruthless warriors, and beautiful but treacherous enchantresses. Lands where the gods walked and talked with mortals, changing into unlikely disguises, so that one was never quite sure who a stranger might be, or what role he might play in one's life. As he talked, he planted in her infant heart a yearning to see all these things for herself some day.

As she grew older, he took personal charge of her education, giving it a scope and setting a standard few then thought necessary for girls. At eighteen, she had left his hands a self-possessed, well-educated and determined young woman of strong opinions, which she was prepared to defend with energy and obstinacy. It had seemed only natural that she should become a teacher and follow in the footsteps of her elder sister Eve, who at that time had just gone out to China with a Dr and Mrs Morton. The Mortons were to found a mission in the interior, and Eve a girls' school to accompany it. Both sisters agreed that far too few women had the chance of an education such as they themselves had received, and meant to put this right, in so far as they were able. China, still only opened up to Westerners for some thirty years, lured them both with a siren song. But when Zoë had suggested enthusiastically that she should join Eve in China, she, to her immense surprise, had written in the strongest terms, refusing to allow her sister to come out East. Zoë, Eve had insisted, must stay in England.

Hurt by the apparent dismissal of her services, Zoë had begun to teach in England, while still secretly dreaming of China. Until, that is, she had met Philip, and a whole new purpose had entered her life, unsuspected before.

Zoë closed her eyes and ears to the sights and sounds around her on the deck of the *Empress of Cathay*. In her mind she could see Philip's handsome, boyish face. Nothing in her father's books had taught her about love; nothing had warned her that algebra and physics were no substitute for a knowledge of the complexities of human behaviour, and the pain of loving. All the knowledge she had gained before was as nothing to the hard, cruel fact learned on that fateful day when Philip, unusually flushed and awkward, had explained to her just why he would not be marrying her, despite his protestations of ardour, but someone else.

'You see how it is, Zoë,' his earnest English voice echoed painfully in her ears. 'I've *got* to marry money. Father spent the lot on wine, women and song, and didn't leave us anything but debts. The whole estate is in a hopeless mess, and needs huge sums spent on it. You do understand, don't you? Others depend on me: my mother, my sisters, all the tenants . . . Frances isn't . . .'

well, she isn't *you*, Zoë, but she'll bring me the money I need. It sounds cold-blooded. Dammit, it makes *me* sound so blasted cold-blooded!' He had shaken his head wretchedly. 'But I don't have any choice. You'll meet someone else. I wish—I wish it could have been different.'

'If you had told me you loved her,' Zoë had replied quietly. 'If you'd said you loved her, I'd have forgiven you, Phil . . . I'd have wished you well and happy. But for money! You wrong both of us, me and your heiress. I don't feel sorry for you. You feel sorry for yourself. I feel sorry for poor Frances, who will be married to a man who wants her only for her fortune. Does she know that, Phil? Have you been as honest with *her*?'

His handsome young face had reddened and he'd muttered, 'I have to have the money . . .'

'You could earn it!' she had shouted at him, not angry for herself, but because he had suddenly appeared so weak and ignoble. He had been her idol, but her idol had feet of clay and had fallen. 'I would have helped, worked too!'

'I don't know how to work, Zoë,' Philip said wryly. 'I was born into a family of landed gentry, and I only know how to give orders to others. Besides, there's too much of the old man in me. Society's butterflies, Zoë. I know you don't understand, but that's how it is.'

So that was indeed how it was. For some weeks afterwards she had not known what to do. Her life had seemed, for the first time ever, without purpose. Then, out of the blue, Eve had written. Dr and Mrs Morton were forced to close the mission and return to England because of Mrs Morton's failing health. But Eve meant to stay on and run the girls' school, singlehanded if necessary.

It was like a lifeline to a drowning person. China had been Zoë's original goal, and how stupid she had been to be drawn from it by a foolish affair of the heart! There was nothing now to keep her in England, and she wrote to Eve immediately to say that now, at last, she would be coming out to join her, and would not be stopped.

She was jolted from her daydreams as three Chinese crewmen appeared and, chattering cheerfully among themselves, began to organise the lowering of her luggage over the side. They had attached her trunk to a frayed-looking rope, and now it swung perilously above a sampan that bobbed on the river below, waiting to receive it. As it began to hurtle downwards, shrieks of protest arose from the sampan. Perhaps the ferrymen feared, as did Zoë, that the trunk would go right through the frail craft unless its progress was slowed.

'Not worry, missee!' the Chinese crewman beside her assured her with a grin. 'Luggage very safe, you see.'

Zoë trusted his optimism was well founded. Indeed it proved so, for the trunk, by some miracle, was caught and manhandled deftly aboard the waiting sampan without mishap. The crewmen prepared to lower the rest of her luggage towards the gesticulating figures below. They reminded Zoë of the tiny fishermen on a willow pattern plate. But it seemed that her luggage was in good hands, and the moment was drawing inexorably near when she herself would have to descend that greasy rope ladder. The truth was, she did not like heights. Just standing on a step-ladder to knock in a picture nail made her uncomfortable. But that was something no one here must know!

The sound of European voices broke in upon the others. At first she thought it might be the customs returning, but looking up, she saw it was the tall man, who had at last emerged from the captain's cabin and was coming towards her, accompanied by Captain Hansen himself. The man's long shadow, cast across the sun-drenched deck, seemed somehow ominous.

As they came up, the Captain exclaimed jovially, 'Well, well, how goes it, Miss Hammond? You'll soon be on *terra firma*, and glad of it, I dare say.' He indicated his companion. 'May I present Quentin Farrell to you?'

Zoë raised her eyes to take in the newcomer properly, and beheld an extraordinary figure by any standards, even here, among so many strange sights. He was a giant of a man, even taller than she had realised, towering over Captain Hansen and dwarfing the Chinese sailors. He must have stood at least six feet four in his socks, and was very powerfully built, with long arms and legs and broad shoulders. He carried not a pound of spare flesh, so that at first glance he appeared gaunt, but a closer look took in the sinewy frame and solid muscle of a man in the peak of fitness, accustomed to lead a very active life. Yet an otherwise impressive figure was marred by a general neglect of personal appearance. It was so much at odds with his superb physical condition that Zoë could only conclude that it was not the result of a slovenly attitude, but of contempt for the social conventions adhered to by others. 'You may take me as I am,' announced that creased and dusty white suit and battered panama hat, 'or not, as you wish. It makes no difference to me.'

His blue eyes, screwed up against the sunlight, seemed to be studying and assessing whatever object they regarded, and just now they regarded her, very disconcertingly. On either side of a wide, straight, unsmiling mouth, two long lines scored the sunburned cheeks, and a pugnacious and unshaven chin thrust itself aggressively towards her.

As if he accused her of some crime, he demanded truculently, '*You* are Eve Hammond's sister?'

Already ruffled by her brush with the customs, and sick with apprehension at the prospect of the descent by ladder, she felt that his tone put the finishing touch to her unsettled mood. She flushed, and bridled. 'Indeed I am, Mr Farrell.'

'But you're younger than she . . .' He appeared to

realise how ungallant his words were sounding, and amended them, belatedly, to 'You are younger than I had expected.' That was not very polite either, but then, she suspected, he was not concerned with being polite.

'*You* had expected?' she asked coolly.

He ignored her question completely and turned his back to her, to address Captain Hansen. 'I don't like it,' he said bluntly. 'I told you in the cabin I didn't like it, and now I've seen the girl, I like it even less!'

'Perhaps,' said the Captain nervously, seeing the light of battle leap into his passenger's hazel eyes, 'you should explain . . .'

'Oh, yes . . .' Farrell muttered. As an afterthought, he dragged off his panama hat in a belated gesture of courtesy. The sun beat down on a wild mop of auburn hair in which the copper glints gleamed like fire. Unbidden, there leapt into Zoë's mind one of the pictures in her father's books—mighty Hector, standing on the walls of Troy, the sun shining on the burnished bronze of his helmet.

She closed her eyes briefly, and shook her head to erase the illusion. When she reopened them, the disreputable form of Quentin Farrell had replaced the heroic vision. He clapped his hat back on his head, his brief tribute to good manners over, and announced laconically, 'I've come to escort you up country, Miss Hammond, to your sister.'

'I'm to go up country, with *you*?' she asked disbelievingly.

Captain Hansen, evidently fearing that introductions were getting off on a bad footing, broke in hastily, 'Mr Farrell is a trader, and does much of his business in the district which includes your sister's school. He's by far the best person to advise you.'

That this gigantic, unkempt, dishevelled and wildly unreliable-looking figure should prove a whisky-swilling trader did not surprise Zoë. But the thought of accepting advice from such a source, about anything at all, left her temporarily speechless.

'Don't fancy the idea, is that it?' Farrell demanded, seeing her face. 'Well, that makes two of us, because neither do I!'

'Then perhaps I'd better make my own way to join my sister!' she retorted, finding her voice. 'Why on earth should I agree to go with you?'

'Because you have no choice,' Farrell replied with quiet irony, 'any more than I do.'

For a brief moment they stared at one another in a silent battle of wills. Determined not to lose it, Zoë tilted her chin, fixed her hazel eyes on his face and set her mouth firmly.

A curious expression flitted across Farrell's highly individual features, as though he knew what was in her mind. The hard line of his mouth softened imperceptibly and he gave her a little nod, as if he conceded the point to her, not out of gallantry, but because he humoured her as one does a petulant child or someone not quite in possession of her wits.

Then he thrust his hands into his pockets, hunched his broad shoulders as the breeze blew across the estuary, and, after exchanging a meaningful glance with Captain Hansen, went on more reasonably, 'See here, Miss Hammond, you've chosen a devil of a time to come out to China. The country is on the verge of revolution. I keep telling Eve—telling your sister—that she should come down to Canton and stay in the British Concession for a while, where she would be safe, and could take a well-earned holiday. But she's so confounded obstinate, and now I'll have the two of you to worry about.' He scowled at her.

'Well, I'm sure both my sister and I appreciate your concern, Mr Farrell,' Zoë said crisply. 'But I dare say Eve knows what she's doing.'

'I'm pretty sure *you* don't!' he retorted frankly.

'All your luggage seems to have gone ashore, Miss Hammond!' Captain Hansen interrupted with loud, forced joviality.

'Not all, Captain. My bicycle is still aboard.'

Farrell, who had half turned aside, spun round and exclaimed incredulously, 'Bicycle?' Then he repeated in a stentorian roar which made the Chinese crewmen look up in alarm, '*Bicycle?*'

'Yes, I'm afraid I've brought you a lady cyclist, Farrell,' the Captain admitted, throwing in the towel. Let them argue it out. As soon as the girl was off his ship he wouldn't be responsible for her any longer. Farrell seemed to be reasonably sober, for once, and had come to take charge of her. Let him get on with it.

'You can't go pedalling a blasted bicycle around rural China!' thundered Quentin Farrell. 'I knew it! I knew you were going to be nothing but trouble. Eve deliberately misled me about you. She told me you were a responsible woman. "Capable" was the word she used. She let me believe you were much of an age as she is, and in similar circumstances. I came here, expecting a middle-aged schoolmarm with a Bible and an umbrella —and I find I'm landed with an emancipated Amazon on a bicycle!'

'How old are you, Mr Farrell?' Zoë asked sharply.

He looked a little taken aback. 'Thirty-eight,' he said, after a moment when the narrowed blue eyes searched her face suspiciously.

'And you would describe yourself as "middle-aged", would you, Mr Farrell?'

'Ah,' he said, relaxing. 'I take your point, Miss Hammond. Your sister is a fine woman, whom I've known for a number of years. Don't misunderstand me. I've the greatest respect and admiration for her. I was using the term "middle-aged" figuratively, as it were.'

A cry of awe from the sampan below broke the air. Dangling majestically above the water was a lady's bicycle with large, narrow-rimmed wheels and a dress-guard, being lowered imposingly towards the amazed ferrymen. With reverence they caught it, and lifted it aboard their bobbing craft. For a moment, all three surrounded it, silent in wonder. Then one of them ventured to give the front wheel a push. It spun round, whirring. Immediately a torrent of excited comment burst from them, and they shouted the news across the water to neighbouring sampans.

'The news of the "flying wheel" will reach shore ahead of us,' Quentin said wearily. 'By tonight, all of south China will know of the foreign lady and her bicycle. Time for us to go ashore, Miss Hammond—unless you have any more surprises to spring upon me?'

'Farrell tells me you will be staying at the Lintons tonight,' Captain Hansen said. 'So I shall be seeing you at dinner, and we do not have to make our farewells yet.'

The moment had come to descend the greasy, swaying rope ladder. Zoë eyed it, unable to conceal her apprehension.

'Do you think you can climb down there?' Quentin asked her irritably. 'Or have we to sling you down in a hammock?'

'I am not a piece of livestock, Mr Farrell. I can climb down the ladder!' She was by no means certain of this, but had not the slightest intention of allowing him to see her doubts and fears. He was the very last person who must know of them.

'Hmm,' he said. 'I'll go first. Just follow me down.' He climbed athletically over the side and disappeared from view.

Captain Hansen helped his passenger to climb on to the ladder. 'Don't hold the sides, Miss Hammond. That will cause it to belly out. Hold the centre of the rungs, and then your own weight will keep it hanging flat. And don't look down.'

Zoë nodded, her heart sickening. On the ladder she

felt horribly vulnerable. It shook and quivered as Quentin completed his descent. She could hear his voice calling to her from below. Taking a deep breath, she began to climb down. The wind, blowing strongly across the waters of the estuary, caught at her fluttering skirts, but she could not free a hand to control them. Down, down . . . every rung closer to the bottom, where a tricky jump had to be made down into the sampan.

The *Empress of Cathay* lurched and rocked on a sudden swell in the water. It was not much of a movement, but on the rope ladder it became exaggerated. The ladder swung away from the ship's side, Zoë clinging to it, and back again. For a horrible moment her foot, searching for the rung below, beat on the empty air before finding its perch, and she feared she would plunge into the water.

'All right, it's steady now, keep coming down!' shouted Quentin's voice from below.

But Zoë couldn't move at all. Paralysis gripped her. Her hands were set so tightly on the rungs that nothing could have prised them loose. She was as incapable of climbing up as down, so remained where she was, her eyes shut, clinging to the ladder.

It was shaking again, as Quentin climbed back up towards her. Suddenly his voice came from quite near at hand, about the level of her ankles.

'Now, you listen to me,' it said icily. 'If you cannot get down, try and go back up. And when you get back on board, oblige me, and everyone else, by staying there until the ship sails and takes you back to England! If you cannot even get off the boat unaided, you won't last five minutes in the remoter parts of China . . . and there is no point whatsoever in my taking you there!'

Whether he intended his scornful words to spur her into activity and break the steel band of fear which bound her motionless, she did not know, nor did she care. But fury swept over her and momentarily swamped her panic. Forgetful of all else, of her precarious grip on the ladder, of the sampan below, of Captain Hansen watching anxiously over the rails, and above all, of the fact that she was a responsible, educated lady teacher of five and twenty, Zoë hissed in tones of concentrated rage, *'Shut up!'*

There was a moment's silence. 'That's better,' Quentin said. 'Right, I'm going back down, before you kick me, accidentally or otherwise, in the teeth. I expect you to follow me and no more of this nonsense, do you hear?'

He scrambled down again, and she managed to follow him somehow or other. At the bottom, she flung a look over her shoulder and saw him balanced on the sampan, and holding out his arms to catch her. 'Come *on!*' he shouted at her impatiently.

She swallowed, and jumped, landing in his embrace with a jolt which sent them both stumbling back to sprawl in the tiny craft among her luggage.

'Allow me to give you a word of advice,' Quentin said, retrieving his hat which had fallen off. 'Never claim to be able to do something if you know you cannot. People take you at your word and rely on you—and inevitably you let them. In an emergency, Miss Hammond, that can prove fatal.'

'I do not require a lecture, Mr Farrell!' she spluttered.

'Oh well,' he said, suddenly relaxing his mood in a disconcerting way. 'I shall have to take you up country, I see, because there is no way I shall ever get you up that ladder again.'

He was laughing at her! Insults could be fended off, but mockery is the most wounding of weapons. Zoë, humiliated and embarrassed, but more than anything angry with herself and her own weakness which had betrayed her to her opponent, snapped, 'I have come to China to stay!'

'Have you, now?' Suddenly he swept a long arm

towards the wharves of Canton, across the crowded water, dotted with bobbing sampans. 'Then there is China, Miss Hammond, the last surviving empire of the ancient world.' He turned his blue eyes on her, the look in them violently hostile. 'And you've come to change it all, have you, my dear?' he said softly. 'You'll get no help from me!'

As running feet sounded noisily on the wooden staircase of the tenement building where he lodged, young Li Kim's heart leapt up into his mouth and the calligrapher's brush dropped from his hand. But the feet passed by his door, and Kim rubbed the perspiration from his brow with a shaking hand. At nineteen, it is impossible to admit to others that you are afraid, but there is no denying it to yourself. For the past week, ever since he had been given secretly the little stock of revolutionary pamphlets, printed on cheap paper in Chinese and English, which lay in the drawer of his desk, the youngster had been expecting Manchu agents to burst in the door and drag him away to an unwelcome appointment with the public executioner.

Kim took up the calligrapher's brush and was pleased to see he had not flicked ink on to his paper in his panic. While he waited for his trembling hand to steady—the drawing of Chinese characters requires control—he read through his poem. It was a love poem. Nineteen is an age of deep passions, when falling in love, and rebellion against authority, go hand in hand. Li Kim did not know which made him the more apprehensive, raised the greater hopes, caused the greater pain. Well, his love caused the greater pain, and offered him few hopes. In the poem, he had compared Green Jade's skin with the blossom on the apple tree, and her hands with the petals of the lotus. But he knew it was unlikely that she would ever read it, because he would always be too embarrassed and too shy to send it to her, even if he finished it to his satisfaction—and was not arrested today.

Every day, Li Kim said to himself on rising, 'Perhaps I shall be arrested today . . .' In a curious sort of way it helped, accustoming him to the idea until it became a familiar and marginally less frightening one. And every day he thought, 'Green Jade will be in the garden, by the peach trees.'

Kim uttered an exclamation of disgust and set down the brush in the little pottery jar. What was the use of trying to write of your love when your heart thumped in agony—not from passion, but from simple fear? He let his mind drift to when he had last seen Green Jade, in her father's garden, and a bitter-sweet calm stole over him, a kind of gentle melancholy which was sad, but pleasant.

He had gone there to bring home his younger sister, who had been on a visit, for their families were related. He had found both girls in the garden, among the peach trees, feeding the fish in the pond. They were laughing at the antics of a fat old carp which jostled the other fish for the titbits, and quite unaware that Kim observed them.

Once the girls had seen him, he had been obliged to come forward and greet them. There he had stood, before Green Jade, with an expression on his face much like that on the face of the carp, and with his mouth opening and closing soundlessly, just like the fish, as he struggled in vain to find something to say. Green Jade had treated him with all the customary deference due to a male guest—but he was sure she must have thought him quite witless. He had since begged his sister to speak well of him to her friend. Nevertheless, despite his sister's efforts, and although it was the desire of both their families that he and Green Jade marry, Li Kim was convinced that the girl had him marked down as a prize idiot. He knew for a fact that she did not want to marry him, because his sister had told him so. He had tried to pretend she had told him it to tease him, but he was gloomily certain it was true.

Li Kim sighed, and remembered the stack of pamphlets. He retrieved them from the too obvious drawer and hid them hurriedly in a chest of his clothes. Walking back to his unfinished poem, he glanced through the open window which afforded a view of the Canton waterside basking in the early morning sunshine. A steamship was newly arrived overnight and lay off the busy wharves, a British ship. Kim picked up the telescope the Englishman, Farrell, had given him, and put it to his eye. He could make out the name painted along the bow—*Empress of Cathay*. Despite his gloom, the name brought a dry smile to his youthful face. If he and his friends had their way, there would soon be no more emperors or empresses in China. But he must find a safer place to hide his stock of republican literature.

However, in the meantime, there was his poem, still unfinished. Li Kim walked determinedly back to his desk, took up his calligrapher's brush, and as an encouragement to himself, painted in the characters of the dedication: *To the lady Green Jade . . .*

Despite his last words, delivered with such a chilling unfriendliness that Zoë had been quite unable to find a reply, she had to admit she could not have managed her disembarkation without Quentin's aid. He organised porters for her luggage, and gaily-painted sedan chairs to carry them both to the Lintons' house. In a very little time, she was seated in a chair and being carried at a remarkably fast rate through the narrow, crowded streets.

She was glad to be away from the wharf so quickly. Within moments of setting foot ashore, she had found herself the centre of a crowd of curious onlookers, who whispered together concerning her appearance, which was obviously extraordinary to them, and a little amusing. It was her clothing, Quentin said casually, which attracted attention, adding, as one or two of the women ventured close to put out a hand and twitch the material of her blouse and skirt, that it was polite among the Chinese to show interest, and such close examination was by no means ill-mannered. In fact the women's manner was more shy and inquisitive, like children's, than it was rude, so Zoë smiled and bore it all patiently. Nevertheless, she was glad to gain the relative sanctuary of the sedan chair, away from curious eyes and prying fingers.

She had never imagined that streets could be so crowded. The open-fronted shops, overhung by shuttered balconies, were dark and tiny, so that, not surprisingly, a great deal of business was being conducted in the street itself. The men all wore the pigtail imposed on them as a sign of their subservience to the ruling Manchu dynasty, but some of them had wound the long braid round their heads, not unlike the way in which German or Scandinavian peasant girls did, and which, to Zoë, appeared very odd. The front area of the skull was kept carefully shaved, and the barbers were plying a brisk trade, in the street naturally, their clients seated on rickety wooden chairs, pedestrians milling about them.

No attempt was made to protect from the dust the food offered for sale, and it distressed her to see the poor chickens, hung trussed upside-down, in some cases ready plucked, but all quite alive, awaiting a purchaser. Even more did she pity the songbirds in their tiny cages. Every shop-front was adorned with a paper image of a god, to avert the demons, and within the cramped interiors, joss-sticks smouldered before the family altars, offering respect and homage to gods and ancestors alike. Several times Zoë glimpsed a statuette of a fat, smiling figure, clasping what looked like a silver brick to his portly stomach. It was the money god, with his silver ingot, especially venerated by shopkeepers.

At last they passed over the bridge on to the island which housed the British Concession, and into a different world. There were plenty of fine houses here, surrounded by well-kept gardens, and before one of them they stopped. It was a white-washed building surrounded by a wooden veranda and with balconies at the windows above. They clambered out of their chairs, and the porters deposited the luggage. Zoë moved away and looked about her. It was a beautiful house, but she had already discovered that Farrell was also a guest here, and it impaired the enjoyment which she would otherwise have felt at being liberated from her cramped quarters on the *Empress of Cathay*.

A shout roused her, and looking up, she saw, striding briskly towards them, a stocky, red-faced man with a thick neck and the self-confident, swaggering manner of a habitual bully. He seized her hand before she had offered it, exclaiming loudly, 'Edward Linton. So you're Eve Hammond's sister. By Harry, I hadn't expected such a fine-looking woman, and I don't suppose Quentin did, eh? You're more than welcome, my dear, more than welcome!'

Quentin turned aside without comment to pay off the porters and chairmen. As soon as he had done so, Linton shouted to the men to be off. The coolies, who had been laughing and chattering happily, and who had performed their tasks with the utmost efficiency, withdrew in a changed, sullen silence. Zoë fancied that Quentin cast their host an unfriendly glance. Linton still clasped her hand in a hot, sweaty grip, and she was forced to free her fingers by jerking them forcibly from his hold

'We don't get too many pretty women out here,' he insisted, leaning towards her. 'Eh, Quentin, what do you say?' He treated her to a roguish wink.

Entering the conversation for the first time, Quentin

said curtly, and a little enigmatically, 'There are better places for them!'

Linton's red face grew a shade darker, and he moved away from Zoë reluctantly. 'Come inside and meet Emily,' he said brusquely. 'She'll be pleased of a chance of some female chatter and news of home. Tell her what the latest fashions are, eh?'

Zoë became aware of eyes watching them, and looking up, saw a woman standing on the veranda, waiting. She was probably, she thought, in her early thirties, and running to a not unbecoming plumpness, flattered by a well-made blue silk gown with a lace ruffle on the round bosom, giving her something of the appearance of a pouter pigeon. Pale but sharp eyes in a pretty, vapid face watched their approach and swept over Zoë appraisingly. For a moment the eyes were enlivened by an extraordinary expression, almost of shock, and then resumed a curious lack-lustre appearance, before the gaze moved to Quentin and rested on him. Her husband was ignored.

'Come and have a drink,' Linton urged Farrell. 'Let the women get acquainted.'

Both men disappeared into the house. Emily's pale eyes followed them, or rather, followed Quentin; then she turned back to Zoë and indicated a pair of cane chairs. 'Would you like some lemonade, Miss Hammond?' Her voice had a strange, plaintive quality. 'I'll get them to bring some, and it's pleasanter out here.'

As a teacher, Zoë had occasionally heard that tone of voice in pubescent girls, prey to the self-pity which goes with strong emotional upset. But this was no young girl. Zoë eyed her hostess curiously, as Emily Linton began to talk in a rapid, nervous way—almost urgent— stringing together questions, comments, complaints and bursts of information about herself in a jumbled, illogical manner, which some people might have described, unwisely, as 'chattering brightly'.

'Have you brought the latest copies of the *Illustrated London News*?' was her first, eager demand, leaning forward, lips parted. When Zoë, startled, confessed she had not, Emily sat back, obviously disappointed. 'One is so cut off here, one never knows anything. Did you "come out", Miss Hammond? I had a London "season". It was such fun, so many parties and balls. I had eight ball-gowns, besides the white one for Queen Charlotte's Ball . . . and everyone thought I should make such a fine marriage . . .' Emily's voice trailed away peevishly.

'I'm afraid I wasn't "brought out",' Zoë said firmly. 'My father disapproved of the whole thing. He believed it encouraged idleness and vanity. "Addling young girls' brains", he called it.'

Puzzled disbelief crossed Emily Linton's face, and she began to quiz Zoë on her family and circumstances. She soon had the feeling that Mrs Linton found her eccentric. Certainly she was quite unable to comprehend that anyone should *want* to be a school-teacher!

As for herself, she had left three children behind in England, either at school or in the care of relatives, and since coming out East had given birth to another, a little girl referred to only as 'Baby', so that Zoë began to wonder whether the child had a Christian name at all. Nor was Baby to be seen, being shut away in the nursery in the care of a Chinese ayah.

It was obvious that Mrs Linton, by virtue of her status as a married lady and the mother of a family, to say nothing of having had a London season, considered Zoë in some manner deficient, and saw her duty as extending to poor, unmarried, school-teaching Miss Hammond a condescending friendship. It was all the more tiresome because it expressed itself in a litany of self-centred complaints, which Emily probably intended as confidences.

With hardly a pause in the stream of brittle chatter, she informed Zoë that it was unusually hot, and the humidity gave her a headache. She had felt quite sick for the past two days. The servants were lazy. The milk had gone sour in the kitchen through negligence on the part of the cook, who naturally blamed the weather. It was very dull in Canton just now. Most of the other European ladies, together with their children and attendant ayahs, had escaped the humid heat by taking the steamer down the coast to Portuguese Macao, to benefit from the sea breezes. There were missionary ladies in plenty left, but they were always handing out tracts and exhorting one to give a good example. She seemed to think Zoë should stay at least a week, purely in order to keep her company. As an inducement, she offered to introduce her to such members of the Canton Ladies' Circle as were not holidaying in Macao—an offer Zoë had no difficulty in declining.

'You understand, Mrs Linton,' she managed to say in a break in Emily's flow of gossip and chatter. 'I haven't seen my sister for some years, and I'm anxious to join her without delay. For the past year, she has been struggling on at the school alone, since the Mortons left.'

'I can't think why Eve Hammond wants to bury herself up country,' Emily responded in a querulous way. 'I can't think what she does for good servants. I'm sure there aren't any. I shouldn't think there's even a decent dressmaker. Chinese dressmakers are very good, Miss Hammond.' (This was the first time Emily had expressed any satisfaction with anything.) 'It is such a shame you didn't think to bring out the *Illustrated*. It's always so out of date when we get it here. The dressmakers can copy anything, and lengths of silk are to be had very cheaply. I do recommend you to have some silk dresses made up while you are in China, Miss Hammond.'

'I doubt I shall need silk dresses up country!' Zoë said briskly, adding with a touch of sarcasm, 'I'm only a schoolmarm, you know.'

'Yes, so you are, so I don't suppose you will,' agreed Emily, apparently without the slightest intention or awareness of any insult. 'I'm sure you will find it very dull.' She heaved a sigh and stared blankly at Zoë, as if not sure what could be done about so hopeless a case.

In return, Zoë contemplated Emily Linton in a frustrated silence. Here was a woman living in a country of great diversity, stupendous scenery and ancient culture, and knowing less of it than did the average English schoolboy. Neither did she show any curiosity to learn anything of it, either its past or its present. Her sole concern was for her own comfort, and her one aim to reproduce in Canton an upper-middle-class English drawing-room. She had met no Chinese, other than her own servants, with whom she communicated in a limited 'pidgin' English. Yet she blandly, and with a complacent smile, assured her, 'Please ask me anything you wish to know, Zoë dear. For, as you see, I'm quite an old China hand!'

As she lay on her bed after lunch in her camisole and drawers, Zoë felt an unaccustomed mood of depression settle over her. This was not how she had envisaged China. It was a poor reward, after a long and uncomfortable sea voyage, to find nothing but hard-drinking Eurpeans and their spoiled women. No one seemed to think it worth her while to join the school, and for the first time she felt an element of doubt concerning her own suitability. Quentin thought her too inexperienced in local ways. Linton saw in her just an unsuspecting newcomer to seduce. Emily—she was not sure how Emily saw her. At first Zoë had imagined she simply found her an oddity. But over lunch she had caught Emily watching her closely. She had become even more gushing and confidential, a sure sign she was trying to find something out. But what? She had even sensed an underlying antagonism in her hostess which she was at a loss to explain.

Zoë wriggled in the humid heat. Perhaps the school, set in the foothills of the mountains to the north, would enjoy a more congenial climate than here on this flat coastal plain. That evening she would make it her business to enquire of Quentin what sort of country it was to which they would be travelling—and who would be going with them. In view of his stated disinclination to take her, it was quite likely that he would refuse to divulge any information at all. He would take pleasure in being awkward, and his surly and antagonistic 'You'll get no help from me!' echoed in her head, which buzzed from the heat, just as the solitary fly which was pinned against the wire screen of the window buzzed monotonously, too drowsy to seek any other way of escape.

Quentin was prepared to take her to Eve, to do no less, but certainly no more, than what was required of him. She wondered why he was prepared to do even that.

Perspiration trickled across her scalp, the fly buzzed, but intermittently, either exhausted or sleepy, Zoë slipped into a fitful doze.

A knock at the door awoke her. Thinking it might be the ayah, she sat up and called, 'Come in!'

To her horror, it was Edward Linton who came into the room quickly and furtively, closing the door quietly behind him.

'What are you doing here?' Zoë snapped. Realising she wore only her underwear, she jumped up from the bed, and lacking any other suitable covering to hand, dragged off the sheet and threw it round her like a sarong.

'Now, don't panic, my dear,' he said placatingly, and came towards her, smiling.

There was something so pathetic about the man, as he sidled up so hopefully, that she could almost have laughed, had she not been so angry. Not too angry, however, to see that the situation could turn very nasty.

'I don't know what you're doing here,' she said evenly, 'but you'd better go.'

'Oh, come now,' he wheedled. 'This isn't England. Everyone here makes the most of having a little more liberty. Have a little fun, eh?'

'Get out!' she ordered flatly.

He stared at her with his bloodshot eyes, the whites yellowed either from whisky or from past attacks of fever. Some of these long-resident Europeans looked upon alcohol as a life-preserver, and drank heavily to ward off tropical diseases. He still had that foolish smile on his red face, so that she wondered whether he was drunk now, though it was mid-afternoon. Yet she felt rising anger at his conceit, to be so confident that she would encourage such unattractive advances.

'You've made a mistake!' she said coldly.

He began to look sullen. 'Well, what's a man to think? Fine-looking young woman, emancipated they call it, don't they? Travelling about the world all alone. You must know a thing or two . . . Nice girls stay at home with mama, or did in my day.'

'Perhaps they did in your day, whenever that was,' Zoë said icily. 'But you've been out of England too long, Mr Linton. This is nineteen-ten, and times have changed. I may be emancipated, as you term it—but that doesn't mean I have no morals. You're confusing me with another sort of woman, one you probably know quite well!'

'Phew, you've a sharp tongue!' he said. He chuckled maliciously. 'Waiting for Quentin, are you? You'll have your chance with him, when you go up country.'

'I said, *get out*!' In her anger, she gave him a push, but it was a mistake.

He seized her wrist and twisted it painfully. 'Come on,' he invited hoarsely. 'Just a kiss never harmed anyone . . .'

She hit him then, as hard as she could, and in her fury

it was a solid blow. She had to release the sheet to do it, because he still gripped her other arm, and it tumbled to the floor. But she was less concerned with modesty, now, than resolved to get rid of her unwanted admirer.

He had not expected such a violent response and for a moment he gaped at her stupidly. She seized her chance, tore her wrist free, and ran past him to the door, wrenching it open.

Linton stood for a moment in the middle of the room, still staring at her foolishly. Then he recovered his damaged composure, and walked slowly past her, out of the room. 'Let me know, if you change your mind!' He grinned at her insolently, and thrusting his hands into his pockets, strode off jauntily down the corridor.

As he went, Zoë fancied she heard another door close, near at hand. She spun round, looking accusingly at the other bedroom doors, but there was no sound of movement from behind any of them.

Zoë went back into her own room, and wiped the perspiration from her forehead. She was shaking now, by way of reaction. 'Is that what they all make of me?' she asked herself in wonder and despair. 'Is that what Emily thinks? What Farrell thinks? That because I'm young, and travel alone, and am not a missionary, I automatically enjoy easy virtue?' She tilted her chin and shook back her loose brown hair. 'Well, they'll find differently!' she promised aloud.

CHAPTER TWO

THAT SAME afternoon, in a small town on the lower slopes of the far-off mountains, the regional Controller of the Salt Revenue, Wu Feng, was sipping jasmine-scented tea from a tiny porcelain bowl, an expression of satisfaction on his plump face. He was a wealthy man. Collectors of the salt taxes were seldom poor in imperial China, but Mr Wu was not a particularly corrupt official. He performed his duties with a quite exemplary justice, and was a by-word for incorruptibility. His wealth was based on revenues from his considerable estates.

Such a man should be happy and satisfied, but Wu Feng had one abiding sadness. He had no son. It was a matter of the utmost seriousness, for he himself was scrupulous in paying due obeisance to the shrine of his ancestors. But who, in the future, would perform the rites which would enable *his* earthly spirit to rest in peace? He had frequently contemplated taking a second wife. But there was a problem. His first and so far only wife, for whom he had much affection, was a Christian, and to bring another wife into the house would cause her offence. She would not have objected aloud, but she would have grieved in silence—and Wu Feng did not wish that.

He had, however, a daughter, and Green Jade was a great consolation, beautiful, dutiful and clever. She was a boarder at the school of the English lady, Miss Eve Hammond, and good at her studies. And now Wu Feng had just agreed a marriage for her, with the son of an old friend and colleague, the military commander of the district, General Li . . . the same who now sat drinking tea with him.

Wu Feng rose from his carved laquered chair and gave a titbit to a pet parrot in a cage above their heads, holding out the morsel with his long, pointed fingernails. He was an important man, and such men did not need trimmed, workaday nails.

'Yes, my dear friend,' he said benignly. 'It gives me much satisfaction to know that our families will be united. I have, as you know, no son . . . and only the one piece of silver. But I give her to you with a happy heart.'

General Li made some suitable reply, and then looked glum. 'Sons can grieve the heart more than daughters. My own son I sent to the foreign school in Canton, to learn English. There he has learned a host of other things, and comes home full of the words of the revolutionary, Dr Sun Yat-sen, and a mass of fanciful ideas which might yet cost him his worthless head.'

Wu Feng sat down again, and folded his hands in his long silk sleeves. He eyed General Li thoughtfully. They had been boys together, roaming over the hillsides. Their respective grandmothers had been sisters, so Li was a cousin as well, although on the female side. Li was a hard-headed, shrewd-thinking man, and Wu Feng respected him.

'You think a storm wind gathers in China?' he enquired delicately.

'It is my unworthy opinion that a revolution brews in China!' Li returned with military brusqueness.

'That has happened before.'

'This time it will sweep away the Manchu, and send them back to their Tartar homeland!' Li growled.

The parrot squawked impatiently, but Wu Feng did not heed it. 'It is your enlightened opinion that one should give a cautious support to this Sun Yat-sen?' he asked diffidently, as if the answer were really of no great interest, but his eyes watched General Li carefully.

'A wise man keeps his counsel,' Li said. 'But he marks which way the storm wind blows, too.'

Wu Feng stared out of the round window which gave on to his garden. He was fond of his garden, and had a fancy to be buried in it. A geomancer had assured him it was a favourable spot, with the correct proportions of the male and female forces of nature, rising land behind it and a pool of water—all good signs. In the earth beneath, the elemental forces were balanced nicely on either hand, so that the garden lay between the Azure Dragon and the White Tiger, which slumbered beneath. Yes, he would be buried there. But who would burn the joss-sticks before his tablet? No son . . .

'Before that storm wind comes, another may break upon us!' he said suddenly. 'I hear the bandit Yang has moved his rabble towards us.'

'I knew Yang when he was a miserable lieutenant in a flea-bitten garrison,' Li said with a snort of disgust. 'And now the wretch calls himself a warlord!'

'I should perhaps remove my family to safety?' Anxiety touched Wu's voice.

'Yang would not dare to enter my district,' General Li growled. 'His heart is craven, and he cannot rely on his men.'

'That is good,' Wu Feng said in relief. 'Honoured cousin and guest, may I not invite you to view my humble garden?' He waved one hand, tipped with its long, silvered nails, towards the garden door. 'I have recently restocked my fishpond, poor thing that it is, and I would value your respected and informed opinion.'

The general was a man who had no interest in fish, unless they were served up grilled on a bed of rice, and he was well aware that Wu Feng knew this. But his cousin's transparent eagerness to show off his new fishpond filled Li with indulgence, and he followed his host out into the garden, where it was cool beneath the trees.

General Li had had many worries of late. Yang, the self-styled warlord, hovered on his boundaries, and he was by no means so sure he could be kept out—as he had indicated to Wu. As if that were not enough, revolution threatened in China as a whole, and in the prevailing state of anarchy men like Yang did as they pleased. Even worse, Li's own son, Li Kim, whom he had sent to study in Canton, had become infected with new and dangerous ideas. The Englishman, Farrell, whom Li respected because Farrell had himself once been a soldier, had been pestering Li to provide an escort of foot-soldiers for yet another English lady who wished to travel to the region. As if there were not enough English and American ladies already striding about China, all as tall as giants, and with enormous feet and extraordinary garments made out of what looked like tent-cloth. They all had loud, strident voices, and lacked even a vestige of female modesty. They marched aggressively up to perfectly strange men, and thrust printed tracts into their hands, dealing with sin . . . as if immodest women were not in themselves an affront to a decent man!

However, today was a day of rejoicing, and in the pleasant sweet air of the garden, Li's heart lightened. He watched his old friend throw scraps to the gold and silver fish that were darting about the pond—which was the eye of the Azure Dragon, watching, from beneath the earth, all that went on. Had they not concluded a first-class marriage for his erring and undutiful son? A marriage which gladdened Li, not only because it was to the daughter of his old friend and cousin, but because he suspected it would please the boy, Kim—and with luck, keep his mind off revolution. There was nothing like a new bride to keep a young man at home. Li recalled his own wedding day, and the veiled bride they had brought to his father's house in her red robes and pearl-encrusted head-dress. How proud he had been, and anxious, lest she prove ugly. That she had the tiniest of bound feet he had known, for a paper outline of the bride's foot had been sent to him, to prove how small it was. How nervous he had been on his wedding night, and how his hands had trembled . . .

The general shook his grizzled head. Girls seemed different now. Many did not even have bound feet, and all of them liked to have their photographs taken, just like westerners. The girl, Green Jade, was pretty, but had received a western education at the foreign woman's school. On the face of it, it had been a good idea to seek a bride for his son who had also received the foreigners' schooling, but western teachings had a trick of making the young people dissatisfied with the old ways. He had seen it in his son, who, to his inexpressible horror and alarm, had arrived home last time with short hair, just like an Englishman. Perhaps the girl also had learned new and undesirable ways.

But no, that was not possible. A young girl of such good family, the Salt Controller's daughter, no less. What could she be but a lotus blossom, like his own daughters? Carefully brought up to obey, to look beautiful, and to bear a male child, a woman's duty.

A contented smile crossed General Li's dour, weather-beaten face. With complete honesty, he said loudly, 'Your garden is truly a place of great happiness, and a man can be at peace in it.'

Wu Feng smiled modestly.

But perhaps the dragon in the earth stirred, and stretched his silvery sky-blue scales, as this conversation filtered down to find him. Perhaps he looked up through his fishpond eye, and wondered that two such wise men could be so foolish as to imagine they understood women.

It was the entry of the ayah which awoke Zoë fully. She had been so agitated, after Linton had left her room, that she had not expected to fall asleep again. But the soporific climate had won, and she was startled to find that she had slept all afternoon, and it was time to dress for dinner.

After a long sea voyage, Zoë's luggage, as might be expected, consisted mostly of laundry, and nothing remotely resembling a dinner-gown. She opened her trunk and took out the first clean dress she came to. It was quite pretty, in white lawn, with a deep square frilled yoke, patterned in *broderie anglaise*. Emily Linton would be disappointed to see her guest in what was more a garden-party dress than a 'London fashion', but that could not be helped.

The ayah was a thin little woman with laughing eyes and hair scraped up into a topknot, out of which protruded several silver and jade pins, like knitting-needles out of a ball of wool. She took the gown away, smiling and nodding, and returned it shortly, beautifully pressed and quite transformed. Zoë, meantime, had been struggling with her long brown hair, which in the humidity refused to curl or to stay neatly pinned. In the end, exasperated at her repeated failures, she solved the problem by piling up the top and side hair, and leaving the back hanging loose and long, in the American fashion. The ayah helped her to dress, her dark sloe eyes alive with curiosity. The corset seemed to fascinate her especially.

'Chinese lady bind feet and breasts to make small and very beautiful,' she pronounced suddenly. 'English lady do same for small waist.'

'Yes, I suppose you're right,' Zoë admitted, struck by this novel view of it. But she noticed that the ayah had feet of natural size, and learning quickly the Chinese custom of showing her curiosity, she remarked on this.

The ayah sighed and explained sadly that she, alas, did not have feet like 'celestial lotus-buds'. She had been abandoned as a baby by poor parents, and brought up in a foundling home run by the China Inland Mission, which was strongly opposed to binding the feet of girl children. She seemed to regret that the enlightened and kindly missionaries had spared her the painful and crippling deformity of three-and-a-half-inch feet, rotting steadily in the compressing bandages, deprived of the blood-flow to keep the flesh alive. 'You would be astonished,' Eve had once written to her sister, 'at the stench of putrefaction which arises from the "feet like golden lilies".'

When she was ready at last, Zoë went to the window and opened the shutter. A glowing crimson sunset bathed the garden, and tinted the sky with indescribable shades. She stood watching it spellbound until it disappeared and night darkened the sky. Then, fearing she would be late, she hastened downstairs.

In fact, she was early, and the main downstairs rooms were still deserted. In the dining-room, the table was laid for an elaborate dinner, but no one was in sight. However, louvred doors of varnished slats stood open on to the covered veranda, and her ear caught the faint scrape of a chair. A little hesitantly, she went to the open doors and looked out to see who was sitting outside to enjoy the early evening coolness.

The sky was now an extraordinary blue-black, and the sultry air, made more agreeable by the night, was yet heavy with the scent of the camphor trees on the lawn. Coloured paper lanterns hung in their branches to light the approach from the main gate for callers, and chirping crickets filled the air with their tiny, melodious refrain. Somewhere in the distance, Chinese voices were raised, probably in the kitchen, but they seemed no more than a background noise. Very faintly, floating on the night air came, the curious persistent tone of some stringed musical instrument which she could not identify. The doubts, inspired by Quentin and the Lintons, that had seized her earlier were dispelled instantly, and Zoë thought, 'I'm glad I came. I truly think that this country could cast a spell over me.'

It was Quentin who lounged in one of the cane chairs on the shadowy veranda, one foot propped up on the other knee. With the stronger light from the dining-room behind her, it must have been as difficult for him to make out the details of her face as it was for her to see him, until her eyes adjusted to the dimness. To him she must have appeared, quite unexpectedly in the yellow light of the doorway, as a dark silhouette, a slim girl with long hair, in a white dress.

It was obvious that he had not heard her approach. He looked up, startled, and very quietly, in a voice in which disbelief mingled with a sort of hope, he whispered, 'Alice?'

'It's Zoë,' she said awkwardly, because she had the feeling something had happened which she had not understood.

He shook his head, as if to clear it, and passing a hand across his brow, muttered, 'Yes, of course. I'm sorry. I was wool-gathering.' He hauled his long frame out of the creaking cane chair. 'Good evening, Miss Hammond. Please, won't you join me? Linton is talking business with Captain Hansen. I am sure that both of them will arrive shortly. As for our hostess, I dare say she's engaged in some piece of domestic organisation.' His tone was faintly dismissive. 'Please . . .' He held out his hand to indicate a chair like his own.

Zoë went out and sat down reluctantly. Something had disconcerted him, and he was covering his temporary loss of composure—a state rare in him, she was sure—by talking fluently and rapidly, and with unusual courtesy. This last, alone, showed how shaken he was.

'I didn't mean to disturb you,' she apologised, strangely embarrassed.

'You don't!' An impatient note sounded in his voice, contradicting the spoken words. But she was relieved to see he had regained his normal assured and forthright manner.

She could see him properly now. He had changed his clothes, bathed and shaved, and looked quite different from the dishevelled figure who had climbed aboard the *Empress of Cathay* early that morning. The improvement in his general appearance, as the light from the open dining-room doors fell in a long, bright shaft across him, emphasised his strong and highly individual features, too expressive of the personality behind them to be conventionally handsome, yet making a powerful impression, not easily forgotten.

Zoë fought off an inexplicable unease which had gripped her, saying briskly, 'I'm very glad to have the opportunity of a word with you, Mr Farrell.' He raised an eyebrow at this, but made no reply, so she plunged on nervously, 'I was wondering whether you would tell me something about the area to which we shall be travelling? Also, who will be travelling with us.'

'The first part of the journey we shall make by boat up the river,' he said in a clipped, businesslike way. 'That should not give any problems. The more difficult part will be made by pony—including some pack-animals for those wretched books of yours, and that confounded bicycle. Coolies will carry the rest.' Quentin leaned back in the cane chair which creaked again protestingly under his weight. 'In fact, I've been to considerable trouble to arrange our journey. I would make it myself in any case, because I conduct most of my business in that area, and I have a house there. I'm taking you along in order to oblige your sister. I don't do it as a favour to you, Miss Hammond, and I wish to make that quite clear.'

'I was under no such illusion,' Zoë told him calmly, adding drily, 'and I had been wondering why you were so kindly burdening yourself with me.'

'The circumstances of our journey are unusual in more ways than one. In normal times, I would inform the *yamen* of the local magistrate of each district through which we pass, of our intentions, and he would send one of his men to act as runner and escort us through his area. This is so that he may say he's done his best by us, and if some mishap befell us, it wouldn't be his fault.' He gave her a very direct stare.

'However, these are not normal times. So I sent word—and a box of Havana cigars which I know to be his particular weakness—to General Li, the military chief of the district to which we are going. I courteously requested him to provide us with a soldier escort for the latter part of our journey. He was a little loath to part with any of his men, because he is faced with possible trouble on his doorstep, but eventually he agreed. I still can't guarantee that the escort will meet us at the appointed spot, but I've found Li to be a man of his word in the past—when he can be persuaded to give it. He is a canny old warrior who takes a long look before committing himself. His son is a student here, in Canton. He's a nice youngster, with a head full of wild ideas, and just at present suffering the pangs of unrequited love. What it is to be young!' Quentin grimaced.

'No other Europeans come with us?' A sinking feeling assailed Zoë as she anticipated his answer.

'Just you and I, Miss Hammond.'

'I see,' she said awkwardly.

'Look, Zoë . . .' Quentin leaned forward to lend urgency to his speech. 'I'm glad to have a chance of a word with you, too. I don't suppose Eve has explained anything of what is happening in China just now. The trouble with her is that she's so wrapped up in running that school that she doesn't see or hear anything else. But China is on the verge of revolution. The present Emperor is a four-year-old boy, and power lies in the hands of the warlords. The Manchu dynasty cannot survive, and when it falls—as it must—so too will fall four thousand years of empire. The Manchu are not China's most glorious dynasty by any means, but they will have the dubious distinction of being its last imperial rulers! The loyalty of the army is in question. It can only be a matter of months before the military governors of the provinces throw in their lot with Dr Sun Yat-sen and his followers, who will promptly establish a republic. China is like a ship whose helmsman has lashed the wheel and gone below, leaving her at the mercy of the storm. Like the ship, China has no real captain. The dead hand of tradition guides her, and she is at the mercy of every petty warlord.'

'What *is* a warlord?' Zoë interrupted.

'Oh, that is a peculiarly Chinese phenomenon,' Quentin smiled at her for the first time, and Zoë, for some reason, looked away from him. 'Imagine,' he continued, 'a robber baron of medieval Europe with his private army, and there you have something similar. In China they range in power and status from imperial princes, with real political power and an eye on the celestial throne, to little more than powerful bandits. The one *you* have to worry about, Miss Hammond, is a thoroughly unpleasant gentleman by the name of Yang. He operates in an area to the north of the district where I have my house and your sister has her school. He was originally an officer of a local garrison in a small and somewhat overlooked area that no one thought important. So small and neglected was it that Yang had little chance to line his pockets, either by the time-honoured expedient of drawing pay for imaginary soldiers, or by claiming his share of provincial taxes. So he seized control, made the soldiers into his private army, and has controlled the countryside around for several years. He raises his own taxes on the unfortunate peasants, and indulges in murder, kidnapping and robbery or extortion to pay his men and maintain a lavish retinue of followers and concubines. He is a confirmed opium addict, and spells of peace usually indicate that Yang is "chasing the dragon", and insensible. When the opium fumes clear, he descends on the villages like a rabid dog.' He paused, and looked to see whether Zoë was appreciating his account.

'Recently Yang has grown bold and greedy, reaching out his covetous fingers beyond his territory. Probably long abuse of opium has rotted his judgment to the point where he is getting rash, but he is all the more dangerous for it. Perhaps he sees how weak central authority is now. But your sister's school is unprotected and vulnerable. I've begged Eve to close it down for a while, to come to Canton and stay in the British Concession where she'll be safe. If only you would agree to stay here, Zoë, I'm sure I could persuade Eve to join you.' He fixed his blue eyes on her face questioningly.

He seemed genuinely concerned for Eve, so much so that Zoë softened momentarily towards him. Yet the tale he had just told seemed wild and romantic enough to have come from one of her father's books. Warlords, at the head of armed bands, sweeping down out of the mists to rampage unchecked about the countryside— could such things really be? She did not express her doubts, but pointed out instead that if Eve steadfastly refused to come to Canton, even to join her sister, she would be left quite alone at the school. 'I'll do my best to persuade her to leave, if I think it necessary,' Zoë promised, to placate him, because she could see him growing restive, 'but I must join her there now. Please try and understand.'

Quentin drew a deep breath and showed his dissatisfaction at her reply. 'I'm not wasting any more of my breath on it, then, if that's your attitude. Confounded women!' he muttered savagely. 'Why can't you see what a nuisance you are to everyone, and a menace to yourselves?'

'Why should we trouble anyone?' Zoë retorted, colouring. 'Or why should Yang or anyone else trouble us? There's no money or valuables at the school.'

'Oh yes, there is,' he said with a grim smile. 'There's

money in the shape of one, and soon two, European ladies! Do you know what kind of an exorbitant kidnap ransom Yang could demand of the whole European community in China, even of the British government, in exchange for your lives?'

The volatile situation in China was also the subject of a conversation in Edward Linton's study—though for very different reasons. A haze of blue tobacco-smoke hung in the air. Captain Hansen relaxed comfortably in a cane chair, placidly puffing on a well-polished briar pipe, which had the look of an old friend about it. He took little notice of his host, who turned up and down the room with a nervous, jerky step, perspiring freely in the humid atmosphere that was only partly dispelled by the electric fan whirring softly in the ceiling.

At last Linton stopped, tossed down a glass of whisky, and turned to glower at the Captain's peaceful form. 'Confound it! You don't have to sit there as if it was none of it your concern.'

'But it is not my concern,' Hansen said placidly.

'Oh, isn't it?' Linton snapped nastily at him. 'Don't think you can just sail away from here and leave us all to sink or swim, come what may. Everything I own is here, in China. My business, my home . . .'

'My dear Linton,' Captain Hansen said in his unhurried way. He removed the briar pipe from his mouth and regarded it affectionately. 'You worry too much. It's a Chinese matter. And if there should be revolution or civil war, it will bring good business to us both.'

'I worry because I have a great deal more to lose than you!' Linton growled. Again the sight of the Captain's amiable, relaxed figure seemed to incense him. 'You damn old hypocrite, I'll bet you're an elder of the congregation in your home parish, passing out prayer-books of a Sunday!'

'No longer,' said Hansen regretfully. 'I was away at

sea so much that it was not practical—and I am a practical man. An old sea-dog, who has learned to weather the storms. So there is revolution brewing up in China like a typhoon? Batten your hatches and run before the wind. Whatever happens, whoever is fighting, they will want guns. I run them in for you, hidden among my other cargo, and you sell them to your warlords and arrange delivery up country.' He tapped out the briar with a sigh and tucked it carefully in the pocket of his spotless white jacket. 'Mark you, Linton, I'm an honest man, and that's why *I* have no fears! I bring only the best merchandise, and all the ammunition is guaranteed. No cartridges filled with sawdust or sand, such as those ruffianly gun-runners down in Macao will sell you. If the Chinese trust you, know you to be honest, no harm will come to you. All the warlords, whatever their politics, will want to keep you alive . . . and supplying them. In a situation of civil war, well, the Chinese army is so poorly armed that every general will be looking for guns, for fear of being wiped out by a rival!'

Linton leaned towards him, his red shiny face anxious. 'I'm afraid of Farrell.' He fixed his bloodshot eyes on the Captain's good-humoured countenance. 'He's been down at the *hong*, and showing more interest than I like. He's been counting up the bales of silk and chests of tea down there, and keeping some sort of tally. Perhaps he begins to think there are more chests than tea! As for you, my old "sea-dog",' Linton added sarcastically. 'If Farrell should guess the truth, he'll scupper you! He's a man who won't turn a blind eye to gun-running.'

'You don't like Farrell,' the Captain said. 'I admit that he's sadly addicted to drink . . .' He stared meaningfully at the glass in his host's hand. 'But a good fellow. Besides, he is completely preoccupied with the English ladies and their school. He doesn't want to take that very attractive young lady up country. I agree with him. It's no place for a European woman at any time. Mrs Linton, now, does she never go to England for a holiday?'

'Emily is my wife, and her place is here, with me!' Linton snapped. 'As far as the Hammond girl is concerned, Farrell can't leave with her fast enough.' He touched a small red mark on his jaw, and scowled.

Dinner was not a success, despite the contribution of Captain Hansen's jovial company. Zoë was conscious of Emily Linton's eyes on her all the time. Everything about her was carefully studied—her hair, her dress, her every word seemed of interest to her hostess.

After the meal, in a move Zoë was beginning to recognise, the men disappeared to their host's study, whence came occasional bursts of laughter and the chink of glasses. She compressed her lips tightly. It seemed that, whatever other home comforts might be lacking for Canton's foreign community, whisky was not one of those in short supply.

But as the men left the dining-room, she witnessed a curious little incident. Emily touched Quentin's sleeve and whispered something urgently. He shook his head, looking angry, and Emily's lips moved in a silent, mouthed plea. The ability to lip-read was by way of an accomplishment of Zoë's, much in use to disconcert pupils at the back of the class who imagined themselves out of the teacher's earshot. She was sure Emily's message had been, 'Later—the garden. You must.'

Now that the two women were alone again, Emily seemed sulky, as if something had happened to put her out of humour. She lay back on a wicker chaise-longue and fanned herself with a round, painted Chinese fan. Ill humour spoiled her pretty features, so that she now looked like a spoiled child who had failed to get her way and was working herself up into a tantrum.

Zoë said how much she had enjoyed the dinner and Emily replied that it was difficult to buy any fresh meat other than pork, and she was thoroughly tired of it. After a few more desultory attempts at conversation, both women abandoned the undertaking, and fell silent with their own thoughts. Zoë was wondering how long politeness required her to sit here before she could decently retire to bed, when, in the quietness, a child began to wail dismally somewhere on the upper floor of the house.

Emily fidgeted and exclaimed petulantly, 'There is Baby, fretful again. Teeth, I suppose.' She snapped the painted fan shut irritably.

'If you want to go and see,' Zoë suggested, 'I don't mind being left alone.'

Emily's pouting mouth took on an obstinate set. 'Oh, my dear, the ayah will see to her. She's very good, and doesn't play tricks with opium. Or, at least, I've told her she mustn't.'

'Opium?' Zoë asked, puzzled.

'Oh, sometimes, you know, when a child is fractious, the ayahs have a trick of putting a little opium under a fingernail and giving the baby the finger to suck. It's very bad for children, though it does send them off to sleep,' she concluded casually.

I'm not surprised! thought Zoë, in considerable alarm.

But Emily Linton had something else on her mind. Quite brusquely, she began, 'I don't see why you and Quentin have to set off so early tomorrow. It's most tiresome and quite unnecessary. Quentin knows it very well. But no one can argue with him, and I suppose he cannot wait to get away, as usual!'

She scowled behind the fan, and Zoë wondered whether Emily's ill humour might not arise from some dispute with Farrell. But why should Quentin quarrel with his hostess?

'Quentin—Mr Farrell,' Zoë corrected herself quickly, but not quickly enough. A momentary gleam showed in Emily's pale eyes. 'He has a house, I believe, near my sister's school?'

Emily smiled thinly. 'More a Chinese pleasure palace, if all reports of it are true. I haven't seen it, but Edward's been there and says it's past description, and thoroughly Chinese. Quentin has a lot of money, you know. Some of it comes from his business affairs—and some of it doesn't.'

Zoë dearly would have liked to ask Emily just what she meant by this curious statement, but her hostess had said all she meant to, and was staring at her appraisingly. Zoë had already realised that to show too much open interest in Quentin might not be wise. So she returned Emily's stare with an enquiring look, and waited. Baby had also fallen silent.

'You're quite an attractive woman, Zoë,' Emily said suddenly in a grudging voice. 'I hope you won't mind my saying so. May I ask how old you are?'

Nettled, Zoë told her.

'So few single women come out to China,' Emily continued. She shrugged. 'Marriageable ones, anyway. Plenty of flat-chested spinster missionaries with steel-rimmed spectacles and dowdy dresses. But you hardly fall into that category, Zoë! Canton and Shanghai are full of lonely European bachelors.' An almost vicious note entered Emily's voice on the last words. But then she added cajolingly, 'Why don't you stay here for a little? I could introduce you to quite a few single men, and I promise you, you could have your pick.'

'Thank you!' Zoë said sharply. 'If I were husband-hunting, I shouldn't have come all the way to China to do it.'

Only a fool would have thought Emily was concerned for the newcomer's marriage prospects, and Zoë was no fool. She understood perfectly that Emily wanted Quentin to leave Canton alone, not because she wished for Zoë's company, but because she resented her being in Quentin's.

As if to confirm Zoë's conjectures, Emily said obstinately, 'I don't think you should go up country with Quentin. It's hardly respectable, and it's not as though you were plain.'

Again a fretful note entered her voice, but a burst of laughter reached their ears at that moment, coming from the study. Edward Linton's voice echoed more loudly than any other.

'You are quite right not to marry!' Emily said suddenly with quiet bitterness. 'Marriage is a confounded bore. Men are all the same, selfish! They care for nothing but themselves, and the worst mistake a woman can make is to let a man see she cares.'

She became aware of Zoë's startled expression, and a little smile crossed her round face. 'Oh, don't be shocked, dear Miss Zoë, and don't, whatever you do, fall victim to Quentin's charm, will you? Just because he chooses now to act like a bear with a sore head, that doesn't mean he can't be very persuasive, if he sets his mind to it. I don't know if they have locks on the doors of Chinese inns, but I do recommend you to bolt yours!' Emily gave a brittle little laugh.

'I'm sorry,' Zoë replied coolly, rising to her feet. 'It's getting late, and I'm rather tired. Perhaps you'll excuse me, if I go up to bed.'

As bad luck would have it, Edward Linton was at the foot of the stairs. His florid complexion even redder through whisky and heat, this time he was obviously drunk. 'Leaving us so soon, my dear?' He moved clumsily, blocking her path with his thickset body.

'We make an early start.' Zoë tried to step past him, but he had not left her enough room to squeeze by, so she was forced to wait, as he leaned towards her, smelling of whisky and breathing hoarsely.

'Oh yes,' he said, widening his round, bloodshot eyes

in a grotesque expression. 'Going up country with Quentin Farrell, and all unchaperoned!' He chuckled huskily. 'Why don't you stay here a while, my dear, with us, eh? Keep Emily company.' He placed a hot, clumsy, sweating palm on her shoulder. 'I like to see a pretty girl about the place . . . You're not bearing a grudge, are you, now? On account of our little misunderstanding this afternoon? See here, a woman likes to be admired, don't she?' He swayed slightly, and his eyes glazed as they ogled her.

There was a faint noise and a movement by a door into the hall. Distracted, Linton looked round, giving Zoë a chance to slip quickly past him, out of reach of his clammy, possessive hand. The scrape of a foot which had attracted Linton came from Quentin, who lounged against the door-jamb, watching them idly, something like amusement in his face.

'If she doesn't come with me tomorrow,' he drawled, 'she'll have to take herself up country alone. I can't wait about here while missie indulges in tea and gossip in Canton!'

'I shall be ready in the morning!' Zoë told him furiously. She turned her back on them both unceremoniously, and ran upstairs to her room.

When she had disappeared from sight, Linton lurched across to Quentin and stood before him, hands in his pockets and swaying slightly. 'Fifty pounds,' he said. 'Fifty pounds says you'll get nothing from the ice-cold school-lady! I wager fifty that you won't succeed . . .'

'I'll pay you now,' Quentin said curtly, turning aside. 'I don't intend to try!'

The ayah was waiting in Zoë's room. She held up a neatly-pressed garment and indicated that she had been busy ironing her sadly crumpled clothes.

Zoë thanked her, and asked a little anxiously, 'How is Baby?'

'Girl-baby sleep very well,' said the ayah cheerfully. She picked up one of Zoë's hatpins which had a blue glass knob, and turned it curiously in her fingers, before putting it down carefully.

'Please,' Zoë said, picking it up and handing it to her. 'For you.'

The ayah's eyes sparkled and she carefully added the hatpin to the silver pins already protruding from her knob of black hair. Friendly relations having been established, she was now disposed to chatter. 'Girl-baby very nice, fat baby. Next time, maybe, come boy-baby. Boy-baby good.'

'All baby good,' Zoë said firmly.

The ayah considered this. 'All baby good. Boy-baby better!' she pronounced.

Zoë sighed. With traditional attitudes such as these, Eve must have experienced any amount of frustrations. If the women did not believe in their own value, how to persuade the men of it? 'Tomorrow, early,' she said. 'I'll come to nursery, to see girl-baby.'

The ayah nodded. 'Very nice baby. Tall Englishman with red hair already come to see her.'

Zoë's fingers had been buttoning her nightgown. She stopped in mid-movement, and exclaimed. 'Mr Farrell? Came to the *nursery*?'

'Always come,' the ayah said. 'Always come to see Baby.'

Zoë frowned, and finished buttoning her nightgown in silence. But she was so tired that Quentin Farrell and the entire Linton household went out of her head as soon as it touched the pillow, and she fell instantly into deep slumber.

She awoke, thinking she must have been asleep a long time, but the moonlight enabled her to make out the figures on her alarm clock, and she saw with surprise that she had been asleep only some hour and a half. She was very hot, and her nightgown damp with perspiration.

Throwing back the sheet and climbing out of bed, she went to the louvred balcony doors and opened them. The sky still sparkled as if a lavish hand had sprinkled jewels across a swath of black velvet. Zoë went out onto the balcony and leaned on the rail. A blissfully cooling breeze ruffled her hair, and she breathed deeply. It seemed so quiet and peaceful that the unexpected sound of voices made her start. Someone was whispering urgently, in the garden below.

Alarmed, her first thought was of thieves approaching the house. But then she realised one voice was a woman's—Emily Linton's. It grew louder, as the speaker became more agitated.

'I'm sick of it all, I tell you! I hate Canton, I hate China, and I want to go home to England! Edward keeps promising, "next year" . . . But next year never comes. I've been over three years, almost four, in China. There's nothing to do, nowhere to go. I see the same people, day in and day out . . . I really think I shall go mad.'

'What would you do in England but see the same people, day in, day out?' It was Quentin's voice, and somehow, Zoë was not surprised to hear it. Instinct had told her who it would be. 'You're well off here, Emily, and you know it. Edward draws twice the salary he'd earn at home. In England you'd be lucky to have a maid of all work who could manage a little plain cooking, and perhaps some wretched little skivvy to scrub your floors. But not a full staff to run your house as you have here, while you sit about looking pretty.'

The last words were spoken drily, and the tone not lost on Emily. 'I won't even have *that*,' she burst out fiercely, 'if you behave again as you did this evening. I told you before, you don't have to show such interest in the child! Edward will get suspicious. His brain isn't so pickled in whisky that he can't see what you make so obvious. Why on earth did you have to go the nursery?'

'I had a fancy to see my daughter!' Quentin said sharply.

So . . . Zoë's fingers tightened on the balcony rail.

'If Edward ever finds out,' Emily said in a dead little voice, 'he'll divorce me. How can I go back to England, a divorced woman? He would never let me see any of my other children again. Even my own family would shut their doors in my face!'

'I've told you,' Quentin replied stonily. 'If that ever happens, I'll support the child.'

'Oh, the child . . .' Emily repeated bitterly. 'But not *me*. You wouldn't marry me, if Edward divorced me.'

'No, I wouldn't,' Quentin agreed evenly. 'I accept your word that the child is mine, but I'm not the only single man passing through Canton who has stayed here—and enjoyed the favours of his hostess!'

'You're a swine, Quentin,' Emily hissed in a quiet but perfectly audible voice. 'The lowest scoundrel I ever met!'

'Very likely, my dear,' he told her calmly.

There was a rustle of a woman's skirts, and the sound of running feet. Emily Linton's form burst out of the darkness of the shrubbery and ran wildly into the house. After a moment, Quentin appeared and stood below the balcony, lost in thought. Zoë knew she ought not to have stayed, but feared to move now. Then, suddenly and without warning, he looked up and saw her. He uttered an exclamation, and dashed into the house.

Zoë backed away from the balcony, and stumbling into the room, fumbled with trembling hands to light the oil lamp on the dressing-table. She knew he was on his way up to confront her. She had just managed to get the little lamp burning, filling the room with a yellow glow, when the door burst open peremptorily and Quentin strode in.

He kicked the door shut with his heel and stood, his hands thrust into his pockets and his feet planted astride, before her. 'How long were you out there, snooping?' he demanded harshly.

Shaken by the blazing anger in his voice, and the aggressive stance of his muscular figure towering over her, Zoë forced her voice to hold steady and clear. 'I went out for fresh air. I didn't realise anyone was out there, at first.'

'Then you saw someone was, and stayed to eavesdrop?' He moved closer towards her deliberately, and she automatically backed away, putting out a hand to ward him off.

Noticing her alarm, a flicker of scorn crossed his lean features. Then he asked brusquely, 'You heard?'

It would be pointless to deny it. She drew a deep breath, stood her ground, and said firmly, 'Mr Farrell, whatever situation you've got yourself into here, I'm sure you're more than capable of getting yourself out of it. It is, in any case, no concern of mine.' Seeing the set of his mouth tighten, she burst out, 'Oh, for goodness' sake! If you want to know what I think, I think that your affair is despicable and sordid, and you and Emily are equally at fault. But I don't suppose my opinion worries *you*, and you may be quite assured I won't be indiscreet, so Emily needn't worry either!'

'I'm so relieved to hear that!' he retorted mockingly. 'What a sanctimonious old maid you are, Miss Hammond, to be sure.' He walked over until he stood directly before her, and she could see the pulse beating in his sunburned throat through the unbuttoned collar of his shirt. He stared down into her face for a moment, then abruptly turned aside and threw himself down on to a wicker chair by the bed. Propping one foot across the other knee as was his habit, he leaned back and surveyed her thoughtfully. 'What are you running away from, Zoë?' he asked in a voice which was direct, but without the usual aggressiveness.

She flushed at the question, but puzzled, replied,

'Nothing. Why should I be running away?' Despite herself, her voice held a defensive tone.

Quentin shrugged his broad shoulders. 'You're young, and a fine-looking woman.' His eyes ran appraisingly over her figure, clearly outlined beneath the cotton nightgown. 'And you have education, and spirit. Don't blush, my dear—it doesn't become a woman past seventeen. Edward's marked you down already. You can't have failed to notice that, or pretend that you don't know what's on his mind. Why should a woman like you come out to China, if it's not to escape something, or someone, at home? Which is it?'

Very quietly, Zoë said, 'If I were to tell you I really believe in what I'm planning to do here in China, you'd only mock at it, and at me. So I won't tell you that. But I'll tell you this, and you can believe it, because it's true. I don't run away from things, Mr Farrell.'

There was a long silence. Quentin broke it at last in a soft, chill voice. 'We all run from things, Zoë, sooner or later. There's always something in our lives we don't want to face. You don't even have to move from place to place to run. You can stay right on the spot, and still be running.' When she did not answer, he got to his feet, and went on in an altered, milder voice, 'You can think what you like about me. It won't cost me any sleep. But don't think badly of Emily.'

'My thoughts of Emily are better not expressed!' Zoë retorted imprudently.

Immediately she saw his expression harden again. 'You don't need to!' he said swiftly. 'You don't trouble to hide your opinion of any of us, that was plain enough to read on your face all through dinner. You're free, with no ties and no doubts, so it's easy for you to despise the weaknesses of others. Emily hasn't your good fortune. She is separated from her children, her relatives, her friends and all that she enjoys, not because she has chosen to be so, but because she was rash enough to make a bad marriage to a man who drags her down with him, and after him, wherever he goes. There are still tribes who drive out their unwanted members to perish or survive, if they can, in the desert. Edward Linton and I, and a thousand like us, find ourselves in China, or India, or Africa—or a dozen other places about the globe—because our own people have exiled us! I'm luckier than most, because I like it here. Emily doesn't. She hasn't your commitment to the welfare and advancement of others to sustain her. She's a lonely, not very intelligent, woman with a husband who is a womanising lout. Not all people, you see, can fill the gaps in their lives with a crusading mission, as you have done. Some people just have empty lives. Emily goes from lover to lover, having nothing else to do. She combines it with an extraordinary hatred of men, which is understandable. I was sorry for her, and stupid enough to . . . Well, that's not your concern, as you rightly said. But you, Zoë Hammond, of all women, do not have the right to despise her!'

Shaking, Zoë almost shouted, 'I'm not filling my life with a crusading mission! Nor am I running away! By your own admission, *you* are the one who is doing that! It's my *opinion*, Mr Farrell, that you have an uneasy conscience!'

His face darkened. 'You know nothing about me! And since we're collecting opinions, here's mine. You are a frustrated and embittered spinster, without a jot of understanding for others, no experience of a world outside books, a set of multiplication tables for a brain and a lot of worn-out moral platitudes where your heart should be! You were created, Miss Hammond, to rule over a school-room!'

He turned to the door and flung it open. It would have to be, Zoë reflected, fuming, Edward Linton who was passing in the corridor just at that moment. She had a brief glimpse of his red, surprised face before Quentin, stepping out into the corridor, slammed the door. Through the panels, she heard Linton's voice say, with his hoarse chuckle, 'Well, you sly devil, perhaps I shall have to pay up my fifty pounds after all!'

She did not know what he meant, and did not hear Quentin's reply. She turned down the oil lamp, and watched the flame flicker and go out. She was leaving here tomorrow. It could not be soon enough! But to be leaving with Quentin Farrell . . .

Emily Linton, sitting before her dressing-table in her nightgown and wrap, rubbed cream into her skin and patted nervously at the tell-tale streaks about her eyes. Her gaze focused on the form of her husband, reflected in the glass as he stood and watched her, and her hand grew still. Seeing the hostility in her eyes, Linton grinned at her with malicious enjoyment.

'Think I don't know?' he asked mockingly. 'He's finished with you, hasn't he?'

'You're drunk!' Emily said scornfully.

'Oh, I know, all about Farrell, my dear,' he went on, ignoring her. 'Just as I've known about all the others!'

'Divorce me if you want!' she retaliated savagely, twisting round on her stool to face him. 'Divorce me, and make an end of it. You don't have to torment me like this!'

'No, I'm not going to divorce you.' He came up close behind her and put his hands on his wife's shoulders, either oblivious of, or enjoying, her shudder of distaste. 'You should be grateful to me, my dear. Saving your reputation.'

'It's more than you ever did with my money!' she burst out viciously. 'You spent all that, and now we're forced to live out here!'

'That's it,' he agreed equably. 'You're forced to live out here with me, Emily, because you can't find anyone to take you away—although you've tried hard enough!

Oh, don't entertain any lingering hopes of Quentin. I've just seen him coming out of the school-teacher's room.' Linton grinned, and she could read the triumph in his bloodshot eyes. 'You've really lost him, Emily! Lost him to little Miss Prim-and-Proper, who isn't so prudish as she'd like to pretend. You'll have to make do with me in your bed, after all . . .' He chuckled, his grip tightened on her shoulders and stooping clumsily, he kissed her neck.

Emily closed her eyes tightly and bit her lips to prevent herself screaming. 'Damn you, Quentin Farrell,' ran through her mind in a throbbing refrain. 'Damn you . . . Take the school-teacher, take her and make her as wretched as you've made me. Be the death of her, as you were of Alice Theydon . . .'

CHAPTER THREE

'So we are delayed for twenty-four hours. It's not my fault,' Quentin said loudly and belligerently. 'I was promised that your Chinese travel documents would be ready to collect early this morning. They aren't. But they will be ready by tonight. We shall have to set off at first light tomorrow, that's all.'

Angrily, Zoë burst out, 'But I don't *want* to spend another day and night in this house!' That was honest, if nothing else. She saw him look slightly surprised at her forthrightness and raise a questioning and sardonic eyebrow. 'It isn't fair on the Lintons,' she added, by way of excuse.

'The Lintons don't mind. Emily's lonely, and Edward thinks you're attractive. But, as it happens, I don't want to hang about here any more than you do. It just can't be helped.'

I'm sure you don't want to stay here, a rebellious Zoë thought, but did not dare to say aloud. Not here, where your sins are coming home to roost! I'm sure you'd like to be a hundred miles or more away.

'You need a Chinese travel pass,' Quentin was saying obstinately. 'If we run into some local official who doesn't read English and doesn't like foreigners—and there are plenty of those—it won't be any use pushing British documents under his nose. We should be held up while he telegraphed for instructions. You'll just have to be patient.'

Zoë gave a hiss of frustration, and plumped herself down in a cane chair on the Lintons' veranda and glared at him.

Quentin stood before her, his hat in his hands and the

morning sun glowing in his auburn hair. 'Sulking won't help,' he said coolly. 'Nor will losing your temper with *me*. I thought lady teachers were models of calm.'

'You never lose your temper, of course!' she snapped.

'Yes, I lost it down at the passport office for a minute or two. Now I'm resigned to waiting. Don't worry, the papers will be there tonight. The Chinese are slow but thorough; eventually everything will seep through the system and come out right.'

He was quite right, of course. Zoë sighed. 'Yes.' She obliged herself to add with forced politeness, 'I'm sorry I shouted at you. It isn't your fault, and has given you a lot of trouble and held you up. I apologise for being the cause of the delay.'

He leaned back on the veranda rail and stared at her appraisingly. After a moment, he scratched his mop of hair as if this aided inspiration, and offered, 'I'll take you out to see the city, if you like.' He could not be said to sound enthusiastic. Like her, he was being polite.

'No, thank you.' She was going to be thrown together with him for the next three weeks, and that was enough.

He looked relieved. 'Fine. It's probably better if you stay here and talk to Emily.'

Talk to Emily? What about, for goodness' sake? She got up and marched indoors. It was wrong to vent her resentment on him, but something about the man upset her. He made her feel entirely out of sorts, at odds with the world and herself. She had not yet seen Emily that morning, so his instruction to go and talk to her hostess could not be put into effect, in any case.

There was a clatter from the hall, and Zoë went out to find the ayah about to set off with Baby on a morning airing. She had come downstairs with the child balanced on her hip, and smiled and bowed at the sight of Zoë. A western perambulator with high-sprung carriage and large wheels stood incongruously in the hall, being given a final polish by a houseboy. The child might have been royalty, for all the fuss being made.

Zoë held out her arms, and the ayah smiled more broadly and nodded, lifting the little figure off her hip and passing her into the girl's embrace. The baby didn't seem afraid of a stranger. She was immaculately dressed, overdressed if anything, in crisp frilled white garments and a large sun-bonnet. Red curls escaped rebelliously from under the bonnet, and two round blue eyes stared up at Zoë solemnly.

'Very nice Baby,' the ayah said proudly.

'Very nice.' On an impulse, Zoë kissed the plump cheek. A beautiful baby, surrounded by adoring Chinese servants, fussed over and pampered by them. But no mama had appeared to tie the strings of the starched bonnet. Emily probably hadn't even seen the child today, and Linton probably hardly ever saw her.

'Where is Mrs Linton?' Zoë asked.

'Sleep still.' The ayah looked past Zoë. 'Go walk now,' she said to someone behind them.

Zoë turned, still holding the child, and saw that Quentin had unexpectedly followed her in from the veranda. He was staring moodily at them both. Baby knew him, and laughed, leaning forward and holding out one plump arm to him, asking to be transferred to him. He stretched out one finger, and the tiny hand grasped it tightly. Zoë found it curiously moving to see this huge, untidy, aggressive man behave so gently with a tiny child.

'I came to say that I'm going down to Linton's warehouse,' he said, not looking at Zoë, but still contemplating the child morosely.

She felt ashamed of her own hostility towards him, but a perverse instinct to compound her error made her blurt out, 'I trust you don't intend to sit drinking all day, Mr Farrell.'

She handed Baby back to the ayah, who deposited her

in the baby-carriage, adjusted a sunshade to shield the occupant and set off in a stately progress for the walk.

Alone in the hall with Zoë, Quentin demanded in a low, fierce voice, 'What does it matter to you, if I do? What does any of it matter to you?' He turned and strode away.

Left to her own devices, and feeling unwontedly depressed, she went slowly upstairs. It was getting late in the morning, and she was rather surprised that Emily should be sleeping still. She wondered if her hostess were not well, and paused before the closed bedroom door. After a moment's hesitation, she tapped softly.

'Come in!' ordered Emily's querulous voice.

Zoë pushed open the door. The room was dimly lit, because the shutters were still fastened and sunshine entered only in narrow strips. It was in an incredible disorder. The crumpled, stained bedclothes were dragged into twisted heaps and the pillows tossed on the floor, as though some kind of wild pillow-fight had taken place. The air was stale and stuffy. Emily sat in her nightgown in a chair, seeming to be doing nothing but stare into space. She hadn't even brushed her fair curling hair, which tumbled on to her shoulders.

As she crossed the room, Zoë felt very much a trespasser in this marital bedchamber. 'I came to see if you were all right.' She frowned, and bent over Emily. 'Are you?'

Emily looked up, her pale little eyes hostile. 'You're going to take Quentin from me, aren't you?'

The question, put so unexpectedly and with such quiet hatred, shocked Zoë. 'No! Why should I?'

'You're young, fresh out from England. You haven't lost your looks with child-bearing and this confounded climate. Edward said that Quentin was in your room last night.'

So that was it. Linton, bearing malicious tales. Zoë drew a deep breath. 'Yes, he was, for a few minutes only and not for *that* reason. He—we had a little argument about something. Frankly, I find Mr Farrell very rude and unhelpful.' Seeing the disbelief on Emily's face, Zoë wondered why, after all, she was explaining this. Emily might believe herself to have some right to criticise what Quentin did, but she certainly had no right to quiz her on the matter.

Emily stirred in her chair and pulled her nightgown round her, but not before Zoë had noticed a bruise on her neck. For a single appalling moment, it crossed her mind that Quentin might have done that, last night, in the garden. But then Zoë's eye fell on the havoc of the bed and she realised that it was Linton himself, and the true nature of what had taken place here burst upon her, so that she felt herself redden in embarrassment and in a kind of horror.

Emily was still hunched in the chair. 'I hate this place,' she said dully. 'But no one cares how I feel. Nothing ever happens here, and no one can live in any style. I try my best. You've no idea how many servants have been through this house. I try to find good ones, but they don't mind me, and insist on doing things their own way. Edward is all day at the *hong*, or drinking, and when he's home . . .' Her eye fell expressionlessly on the bedclothes.

That she was telling all this to a virtual stranger did not seem to trouble her. Her mouth had taken on a sullen, obstinate set. Zoë said nothing, recognising the symptoms, just as she had been forced to recognise them in Philip. Emily was incapable of standing alone. She needed a prop, someone to lean on, someone who would take her troubles away and solve them all for her by magic. Inevitably, she looked for it in the wrong places, plunging into passing love affairs which never helped and only exacerbated her situation.

Zoë wanted to say, 'If you'd only stop pitying yourself, and pull yourself together, try to stand on your own feet. Perhaps even your husband would come to respect you.'

But it was no use saying it, because Emily could not have been brought to understand it. She was locked into a descending spiral of self-pity, rancour and spite. Such people were utterly ruthless in their self-centred search for survival, spreading their own unhappiness like a contagious disease.

Yet, at this moment, Zoë felt only pity. 'Would you like me to help you to dress?' she asked gently.

Emily looked up, and a sudden energy transformed her pale face. She gripped the arms of the chair, and hissed vehemently, 'I shall escape from here somehow! I shall find a way! You—and Quentin—can stay here in this godforsaken country. I hope you're trapped here with him for ever!'

It was not until they set off on their long and arduous journey that Zoë truly realised the vastness of China and her inaccessibility. They began it by travelling by river, upstream against the current, a slow process. Sometimes the Chinese crew poled the boat along like a large punt, and sometimes they sprang ashore and towed it, calling to their aid casual workers who waited by the river banks to be hired for just such a purpose. And this incredibly painstaking and hazardous journey took them almost two whole weeks.

At first she was interested to sit and watch the river banks glide by, a moving picture of Chinese life. Water-buffalo, often in the charge of tiny boys perched on top of the huge patient beasts, plodded through the shallows. Women brought down their washing, and the pails to fetch water for the family soup. Villages of wretched shacks straggled down to the water's edge, occasionally a temple, and from time to time a vast graveyard in which the buried mingled with the unburied dead, for no Chinese could be laid to rest until a geomancer consulted

by his family had decided the propitious day and hour.
The body, sealed in its coffin with mortar, might lie for
up to a year to await the lucky date. Those with larger
houses kept the deceased in a spare corner of the
living-room. The poor took their coffins to the graveyard
and deposited them there, to lie above ground until the
time came. Even those who had died of contagious
diseases often lingered unburied in this way.

After the first twenty-four hours, however, Zoë took
to spending much of her time cooped up in a tiny
compartment rigged up for her amidships with matting
panels. It was uncomfortable, hot and cramped, and
swarmed with insect life varied enough to satisfy the
most enthusiastic entomologist. But it was reasonably
private, and the particular charm of this refuge was that
it kept her from having to talk to Quentin.

Quentin was drinking. She hadn't exactly caught him
doing so, but she knew he was. There was a distinct aura
of whisky about him, and once or twice he exhibited
discernible signs of being somewhat the worse for alcohol, which amused the crew greatly. He was never
exactly drunk—he probably had a hard head and a
cast-iron stomach. Neither was he entirely sober.
However, they had reached a mutual, unspoken, working agreement to be polite to one another, whatever
their respective private opinions. Quentin's manner had
grown more relaxed since quitting Canton, and it was
not all due to whisky. He had, after all, Zoë recalled, left
behind him in Canton a complex emotional involvement
of which he had tired and wished to be free . . . or did
he? He was not in love with Emily—she herself recognised that—but he seemed to have an affection for her
based on old memories, perhaps, and long association,
and she claimed he was the father of her child. This was
her hold on him, though the affair was dead.

But as they progressed on their river journey, Zoë's
self-imposed seclusion became well-nigh unbearable.

The matting panels were home to fleas and cockroaches, and after she had spent four whole days in her 'rabbit-hutch', as she privately termed her accommodation, she emerged, gasping, to enjoy some fresh air.

Quentin sat on the planks of the narrow deck, in the shade cast by her 'rabbit-hutch'. He was bareheaded, the breeze ruffling his hair, and looked more than usually disreputable. A blue and white handkerchief was knotted around his throat in lieu of collar or tie, and his chin sported four days' growth of beard. He looked completely at home, even to be enjoying himself, and for a moment she envied him. He glanced up at her, leaned his arms on his bent knees and narrowed his blue eyes against the bright light behind her.

'Come out of the sun,' he ordered.

Zoë edged into his patch of shade and scratched her elbow where something had bitten her. She felt hot, sticky, dirty and miserable, but she adopted as brisk a tone as possible. 'Mr Farrell, my—cabin—is full of beetles.'

'You choose to spend all your time in there,' he pointed out. 'Air's fresher out here, and there's more to see.' He raised one sunburned hand and indicated a fishing boat near by. The fishermen plied their skills with the aid of cormorants. The birds plunged into the water to scoop up the fish, but were able to swallow only the very smallest, because of a cord tied round their necks. The larger fish were quickly retrieved from their beaks, and the fishermen then released the unfortunate birds to try their luck again, doomed to endless frustration.

The sunlight dappled the water, which sparkled, dotted with sudden pinpoints of radiance like the glitter and flash of a string of diamonds. Zoë almost ached to plunge into its cool depths and wash away perspiration, grime and insects.

'Mr Farrell, there's very little washing water. I know the men will always draw up a bucket from the river, but what I really need desperately is a bath. I was wondering, out here in the country, if we found a sheltered spot, perhaps we could draw into the bank, and—and you could keep everyone away and I—I could bathe in the river.'

She made this request with a distinct nervous tremor in her voice, and waited for his response. He raised his eyebrows. 'If you insist,' he agreed, after a moment's reflection. He got to his feet and went to speak to the boat's captain.

In due course they moored at an attractive spot where the river turned in a horseshoe loop, and the bank was shaded by willows.

'Right,' Quentin said, after everyone had scrambled ashore, and the crew, in the manner of workmen everywhere given an unexpected break in their toil, had set about brewing themselves tea. 'You just go through the trees, my dear, and wash down in the water. No one can see you from here. They are busy,' he pointed to the crew who crouched, chattering and laughing, around their kettle, 'and I've told them you're not to be disturbed.'

'Thank you,' Zoë said awkwardly.

'Who keeps *me* away?' he asked impudently, grinning at her suddenly.

'I assume you to be a gentleman, Mr Farrell.'

'Hah!' he muttered. He scratched his red curls and turned his back on her to wander off along the bank in the opposite direction.

Zoë collected a fresh set of underwear, concealed it carefully in a towel, and made her way to her secluded bathing-spot. She divested herself of her blouse, skirt, petticoat and corset, shoes and stockings, unpinned her hair, and descended gingerly into the river in a set of knee-length cotton combinations with a camisole bodice, which made a fairly good, if improvised, bathing-costume.

It was bliss. It was heaven. Nothing could be so wonderful! No paradise could hold out such a reward. The cool water lapped at her sticky skin and she spread out her arms and slid into the grey-green embrace of the river.

She was a good swimmer. Her father had believed it healthy exercise, and insisted on his daughters learning when both had been quite small. Now she swam strongly against the current up-river, and then turned, and holding a floating branch, allowed the stream to waft her gently back with no effort on her part to her starting-point. She felt she could stay there all day.

Alas, her peace was soon shattered, for having swum up-river yet again, she saw, when she turned, that she was being closely observed—with amazement bordering on stupefaction—by a boy on a buffalo, from the shallows by the river's edge.

Where he had come from, goodness knew. He and the beast might just have dropped from the heavens. But there both were, and so startled was she that Zoë automatically gave a loud cry of surprise.

The result was immediate and alarming. The buffalo, startled also, and scenting an intruder and stranger, snorted and lowered its massive head threateningly. She shouted again, this time in real alarm, for a water-buffalo is a very large beast. In response, there was a crashing as a body hurtled through the trees, and Quentin burst into view, clasping a rifle, and skidded to a halt. 'What is it?' he yelled at her.

Zoë stumbled out of the water, dripping wet, her cotton combinations clinging to her body and her long hair in rat's tails, and shrieked, 'It's going to attack!'

Quentin put down his rifle and said in tones of deepest disgust, 'It is *not* going to attack! Do you mean to tell me that you brought me running to save you from a domestic farm animal and a six-year-old boy?' He turned to the boy and buffalo, and waved an arm at them, shouting something. The child and his cumbersome mount turned and waded out on to the bank, and plodded away out of sight.

'I'm sorry,' Zoë said, ashamed. 'I didn't know it was there, and the child looked very small to be in charge of it, and control it.' Conscious that he was eyeing her, not without interest, she backed towards the river and crossed her arms over her breasts.

'Go and finish your bathe,' he said abruptly. 'I'll sit over there, on the bank, and ward off any more interlopers. Don't worry, I won't watch.'

He went back up the bank, gathered up his rifle, and sat down by her neatly folded heap of clothes. Despite his promise, he did watch her as she waded back into the river. Principally, he told himself, it was to make sure she was all right. He had not expected that she would go right out there in the open river, with its sparkling veil of sunspot confetti, but that she would splash about in the shallows. He supposed she could swim, so he wouldn't have to plunge in and rescue her. She seemed of an athletic, as well as a pedantic, disposition, witness that confounded bicycle. She was capable, all right, too damn capable! Quentin grimaced.

But he was also human, and she was extremely watchable at the moment. The soaked cotton combinations were far more revealing than the poor girl realised. He was irresistibly reminded of those 'art' photographs of nubile ladies, imported from Paris and hawked in the back streets of Macao. Had he wished, he could have taken an unworthy but very satisfying revenge by telling her so. But a gentleman wouldn't do that, nor would a gentleman watch: and a gentleman was what, for some reason, the wretched woman seemed to think him.

Quentin sighed regretfully, abstracted Zoë's petticoat from her clothes, folded it into a pillow and lay back, putting his panama hat over his face. It was warm, quiet and peaceful. The girl obviously knew how to swim; he could hear her splashing about in the river. He had a couple of swigs of whisky to help down the tea offered him by the crew. He dozed off.

'Mr Farrell!'

The voice, loud, imperious and so near his head, caused him to wake with a start. He removed the panama hat from his face, looked up, exclaimed, 'Strewth!' and hastily replaced the panama over his eyes.

'Mr Farrell, I want my clothes! You're sleeping on my petticoat,' said the voice in increasing fury.

'Sorry,' he muttered, as the petticoat was whisked unceremoniously from beneath him. He heard her gather up her wardrobe and stalk away. Then he sat up. He was annoyed at having fallen asleep, and at having been awakened by a shrew of a schoolmarm. His mouth felt dry and it was growing late. They had wasted far too much time on this idiotic bathe. He trusted she wasn't going to make a regular habit of it! On the other hand . . .

Quentin stared thoughtfully and regretfully at the dancing water. It hadn't been such a bad idea, and if they stopped again, he might take a leaf from her book and go and find himself a nice, quiet bathing-place. He went down to the river's edge, knelt, and scooped up water in his cupped hands which he threw over his head. It cleared his brain and made him feel better tempered. He rubbed his wet palms over his face, and sat back.

Zoë was returning already, neatly dressed and tidy, like a school-teacher on a botanical ramble. Only her hair hung long and loose, drying quickly in the hot sunshine. Not so much a school-teacher, perhaps, as a schoolgirl. She came up and sat down beside him on the springy turf, her skirts spread out round her. 'I feel better,' she told him brightly. 'I'm sorry about the buffalo.'

'I apologise for poor watch-keeping. It came from the

other direction, and I didn't see it.' He was polite, if cool.

'The water was lovely.' She gazed at it wistfully.

He stared at her profile, calm, pale-skinned, her hazel eyes fixed on the dancing silver sunspots. There was an almost luminous quality to her features as the reflected light from the mirror surface of the river played over them. 'Why, she's beautiful . . .' he thought, and was at once astonished, and angry.

Aloud, he replied sourly, 'So it might be. This is a two-week river trip. If you go on like this, it will turn into a three-week one.'

'By which time you will have a beard like an Old Testament prophet!' Zoë said sharply.

'Meaning that I should shave?'

'There is no excuse for slovenliness, Mr Farrell.' In her freshened state, Zoë brandished her newly-acquired cleanliness before him like a bullfighter his cape.

Quentin scowled at her, but in the surrounding peace, his anger melted. 'You know,' he said slowly, 'if you weren't so damn bossy, you'd be a very attractive woman.'

'That, I suppose, is meant to be a compliment?'

'Perish the thought! I know you're impervious to such frivolities,' he said irritably.

'Just as well. The last time you were moved to comment on me, you said that I was embittered and frustrated and had no understanding for others.'

'I didn't say you hadn't a splendid body. But you mistake my intention, Miss Hammond. It wasn't a compliment, it was a piece of sound advice.'

'I don't need your advice!' Zoë retorted.

'No, you know it all, don't you?'

They glared at one another. Then the breeze plucked at her long, glossy nut-brown hair, already dry, and it streamed out, fluttering, like a Chinese silk banner,

Quentin thought. He said, more gently, and before he could stop himself, 'I think it's a waste.'

She flushed, understanding him. 'I dare say you do. But *I* think the school is important. Education is important, especially for girls. It matters. I've always wanted to join Eve in her work.'

'I still think it's a pity.'

There was a look in his face which sapped at her self-confidence, and made her feel nervous. To hide it, she chose attack. 'I'm sure you have plenty to worry about without troubling yourself over me. Or perhaps you choose to forget Mrs Linton, now that we're away from Canton?'

She saw his face redden angrily beneath the tan. 'That's my business,' he snarled at her. 'Keep out of it!'

'I want no part in it. I don't care about either of you.' (There was less conviction in her voice than she would have liked.) 'But I am worried about the child. Children are my province, you see.'

'Then have some of your own,' he said dourly, 'and then you'll know what you're talking about.'

'If I ever had a child, I would hope it would be one I could own to!' Zoë flung back.

He leaned forward aggressively, pushing his face into hers. 'Don't you think,' he demanded in a low, harsh voice, 'that if I could get my daughter away from there, I would have done so? But I can't, and that's all there is to it.'

There was not only anger in his voice, but pain, too. 'He really means it,' Zoë thought. 'He truly wants that child.' It was as if a window had opened, giving her a new and unexpected view on to his personality. Aloud, and much more humbly, she said, 'I suppose so.'

'So don't tell *me* what to do!' Quentin said curtly. He got to his feet. 'And hurry along—we're losing valuable time.'

He strode away, leaving her to follow, feeling

chastened, though a flame of rebellion still flickered inside her. If he was unhappy, he deserved to be. His whole behaviour was atrocious. Everything he did. This evening, he would probably start drinking again.

She was right. He drank quite openly, with a deliberateness of manner that obviously meant he wished her to see him. But the next morning, not only was he stonecold sober, which did not surprise her, but to her real astonishment, he had shaved. She did not dare to comment on this improvement, but smiled upon him, and he continued to shave, every morning, for the rest of their trip.

Feeling a quite unwarranted inner glow of victory, Zoë turned her eye on the whisky bottle. It might prove more difficult, but that was next.

The following days passed not unpleasantly, for all the many inconveniences. Zoë sat in the shade and read, and Quentin played complicated card games with the boat's captain, which led to strings of brass cash coins changing hands frequently. Sometimes he came to where she sat and pointed out some item of interest on the bank, but when he was not chatting with the crew, he had the trick of simply tilting his hat over his eyes and going to sleep. She suspected he stayed awake at night. Certainly, someone prowled around the boat in the dark hours, and once, peeping out of her matting hideaway, she saw his dark silhouette bent over some papers, as he scribbled away by the light of a small lantern. He had adapted, like a wild creature, to his surroundings. He worked during the cool night hours, and he slumbered during the heat of the day. This topsy-turvy life seemed to suit him.

On two more occasions they stopped to bathe. This time, Quentin went for a swim, too, but well out of sight of her. 'I can't see any point in putting clothes on to go in the water and get wet through,' he said politely in explanation. 'So I take all mine off.'

'Really, Mr Farrell?' Zoë said stonily, and he strolled away, chuckling.

But gone now were the flat paddy-fields and vegetable gardens of coastal Kuangtung province. One morning, when she came out of her 'rabbit-hutch' later than usual, she saw that they had reached the foothills. In the distance could be seen the mountains. Tonight they would disembark for the last time and leave the boat to make its return journey, this time with the current and at twice the speed, while they set off by pony into the hills. Zoë felt a pang at the thought of leaving their little boat, which had become home to them, as to a family of bargees. She looked round for her travelling companion.

Quentin was standing in the bows, smoking a cigarette, his panama tipped over his eyes. She realised, with a slight start, that despite being in Quentin's company for the past two weeks, she had never seen a cigarette in his fingers before. Yet he obviously smoked, and the fumes of tobacco had mingled with those of whisky drifting from Linton's study that evening in Canton. Would it be too fantastic to wonder whether Quentin, for all his obstinate informality, had been brought up in far more formal circumstances than his present manner and appearance might suggest? Had there once been a youngster drilled in the scrupulous manners of polite society? An upper-class society, in which no gentleman smoked in a lady's delicate presence. A society living in large and comfortable mansions containing a 'smoking-room', to which the gentlemen might retire, leaving the refined air of the drawing-room to females. What was Quentin's background? He had the voice and vocabulary good schools produce, the hard head of a businessman, and the habits and appearance of a rake. Somewhere, through it all, ran a thread which drew all these seemingly contradictory features together.

He glanced over his shoulder as she wondered about all this. Seeing that she had emerged into the sunshine, he gave her a friendly smile. Zoë flushed, because she felt she had been speculating about him in a way he probably would not have liked. But he was coming to seat himself beside her, and she forced a welcoming smile in return.

'Not feeling poorly?' he enquired, and when she shook her head, he gestured with the smouldering cigarette towards the distant hills. 'Well, at least you can see now where we're making for.'

She was pleased to note that he had not, for once, been at the whisky. But his manner struck her as sober in another sense, also. Beneath the tough shell, he was worried. To confirm this impression, he added, 'I hope Li has sent that escort to meet us.'

She watched him fan himself with the panama. It was very hot, and he was in his shirtsleeves and perspiring freely, damp patches staining the material and causing it to cling to his skin. He had good hands, strong and capable, with long, lean sunburned fingers. Poor, foolish, jealous Emily Linton had certainly not been the first woman to fall for this very attractive man. Zoë wondered about the others.

She wriggled in her constricting clothing that had not been designed for this climate. To cool herself, she copied his action in taking off her hat and waving it before her face to create a breeze. It hid her features from his view as well. For some reason she felt an attack of shyness, so stupid and annoying. 'Like a seventeen-year-old who has just put up her hair and finds herself for the first time with a man who isn't a brother or a cousin!' she thought crossly.

In the far distance, the hazy mountains beckoned: mysterious, romantic, offering adventure and harbouring secret dangers, as if their little boat was poling its way laboriously into a picture in a child's story-book. She had once had just such a book, with 'pop-up' pictures. In one, a dragon, perhaps a Chinese one, emerged, snorting flames, from his rocky cave. On an impulse, she told Quentin about it.

He chuckled. 'I've never seen a scaly four-footed dragon except in a Chinese carnival. I've met a few genuine fire-breathing lady dragons in my time, though.'

'Am I one?' She looked at him over the brim of her hat, her fine dark eyebrows arched in enquiry.

He shook his tousled locks. 'No, you're something much more dangerous!' he said mischievously.

She looked away from him, back towards the blue mountain range. 'It's so beautiful,' she said suddenly. 'Like a painting on a scroll.' Turning back to him, she added seriously, 'You know, I feel as though I'm in China at last. In Canton, I hardly felt I was in China at all.'

Quentin's blue eyes ran over her shrewdly. 'You took against the Lintons, that's why.'

'I don't want to talk about the Lintons!' she said sharply.

'I thought you dealt with Edward pretty well,' Quentin said unexpectedly, disconcerting her considerably. 'Especially that afternoon when he came into your room.'

'How do you know about that?' she gasped.

'I had the room next door. Anyway, I'd been expecting him to try something along those lines, so I was lurking with an ear to the wall in case I had to dash to your rescue. I needn't have worried.'

'And you would have rescued me?' she couldn't help but ask sarcastically.

'Upon my word of honour! I was all prepared to gallop in like a knight errant, and then I heard what sounded like the crack of a very respectable straight left to the jaw, and I realised you were more than capable of dealing with poor Teddy Linton. In fact, I almost wondered if I might have to rescue *him*.' He tossed the cigarette over the side. In a complete change of subject, he went on, 'You've been in regular correspondence with Eve, I suppose?'

She was still ruffled, and replied a little curtly, 'Yes, of course!' But then she was puzzled to see how ill at ease he suddenly looked, whereas moments before he had been joking and laughing.

'She—she's told you of some of her difficulties? She was quite ill, not long after she came out here. Did she write and tell you?'

'Oh yes,' Zoë said. 'She wrote that she'd had a fever, but had quite got over it.'

Quentin said, 'Ah . . .' and chewed at his lower lip. Then he shrugged. 'Well, it's an unhealthy place for European women. Perhaps you'll change your mind, and decide to go home.'

'You know I'm determined not to do that.'

He looked at her a little oddly. 'Wait and see,' he said enigmatically. But he still looked unhappy, and she felt that the conversation had been deflected from its intended course. He had deliberately introduced the subject of Eve, and just as deliberately had changed his mind and decided to drop it again.

Thinking to prompt him, she asked how long it would take them to reach the school, once they had left the river and set off by pony. He told her 'about three days', but did not elaborate, so she was foiled.

A slight breeze sprang up as they rounded a bend in the river. It caught at Zoë's uncovered hair, dragging loose long brown tendrils which brushed across her face. She picked them free and tried to tuck them away. Knowing he was watching her, she became unaccountably nervous, and her hand fumbled at the simple task.

'Let me . . .' he said quietly, and pinned up the errant lock of hair neatly with light, efficient fingers.

At their touch, she felt a little quiver run down her

neck, and an old, familiar trembling of her heart which had once danced in this way at someone else's touch. But just at that moment, Emily's voice seemed to echo in her ear, warning waspishly how charming Quentin could be, if he chose.

So he can, thought Zoë. So could Philip. But I won't be so stupid twice. Aloud she said briskly, 'I can manage, thank you, Mr Farrell.'

'Please yourself,' he returned calmly, and getting up, regained his place in the bow of the little boat, his back turned to her, and fell to chatting with the three men of the crew. Zoë, left alone, felt herself even more unsettled.

Towards evening, they arrived at a small town bordering on the river. It was surrounded by ancient walls, and there had been a moment's anxiety that they would not arrive before the gates were closed for the night. But they need not have worried, for as they landed, a horde of sightseers descended and escorted them in a noisy procession, together with their luggage, to the main inn. Here they were received with great ceremony by the innkeeper, his wife and family. The inhabitants of Canton were used to the strange, round-eyed foreign devils, but here they were certainly a novelty, and during their progress to the inn, several small children ran screaming in terror at the sight of them.

When their food was served, interest, if anything, increased. They were surrounded by a crowd of curious onlookers. Quentin's red hair fascinated all who beheld it, and was regarded with a good deal of superstitious awe. The food was surprisingly good—strips of buffalo meat and rice, in a sauce. The meat was a little tough, but then, Quentin said, no healthy animal was ever slaughtered for food. When an elderly beast dropped dead in its tracks, it was at last butchered and eaten, but not before.

'These people,' he told her seriously, 'are among the finest small arable farmers in the world, but they live constantly on the edge of famine. Always remember that, before you raise pious hands in horror over some of the things you'll see here.'

'You love this country, don't you?'

'Yes,' he said simply. He raised his blue eyes to rest on her face. 'And I don't like ignorant do-gooders meddling with it, often causing more harm than they do good.'

'You mean me, of course,' Zoë replied immediately. 'And Eve.'

'Eve's a fine woman,' he said. 'She has been here long enough to know what can be achieved, and what can't. You haven't Eve's temperament and patience. You don't wait to find out. You charge on and cause trouble.'

'You don't know me!' she returned angrily.

'Oh, yes, I do . . .'

CHAPTER FOUR

WHEN ZOË came out of the inn the next morning, it was to discover that Quentin had been up since first light and very busy. As a result, what looked like a travelling circus was encamped in the inn's yard.

Under some stunted trees stood a group of small but sturdy Chinese ponies swishing their tails, their rolling eyes betraying uncertain tempers. As they stamped their hoofs, the bells on their harness jingled tunefully. The baggage had already been brought out and the larger items strapped to the ponies' backs. Among it was her bicycle, dismantled, so that one pony carried the frame above its pack, and another the two wheels, one on either side of the pack-saddle. The whole was in the charge of a groom, or pony-driver, an amiable-looking youngster with a squint, who sat near by and chatted with the inevitable crowd of onlookers.

Wonder of wonders, and to Quentin's obvious relief, the military escort had arrived, as General Li had promised. It was not exactly as Zoë had imagined it would be, consisting of four soldiers in unpressed cotton knickerbockers and puttees, and loose tunics. Because of the heat, they had abandoned their cloth forage-caps in favour of the traditional flat sun-hats. While waiting for the foreign barbarians to be ready, they were passing the time with playing mah-jong, and the rattle and click of the ivory tablets sounded above the men's excited chatter. They were all very young, and their appearance not very martial. Propped against a wall were their ancient firearms, all very dirty, and in one case clearly broken.

In the forefront of the watching crowd was a very old

lady in a black silk robe, leaning on a stick, and having the tiniest bound feet Zoë had seen. She was being treated with great respect by everybody, but who she was, Zoë had no idea. The soldiers around the bamboo table in the shade laughed and scraped up the mah-jong counters.

'Inveterate gamblers, I'm afraid,' said a casual voice behind her. 'The poorest coolie will bet his last brass cash coin on which of two magpies will fly up first from a fence.'

'Good morning, Mr Farrell,' Zoë said. 'Is that the escort your military acquaintance has provided? I can't say they would frighten me.'

'What would ever frighten you?' he retorted sarcastically, adding, 'I agree they probably wouldn't see off an armed warlord, but their presence gives us "face", and makes us look important persons, not to be trifled with! That matters in China.' He eyed her thoughtfully. 'Incidentally, Zoë, can you fire a rifle?'

On being told that she could not, he held up his own rifle and ran through the drill quickly. 'Got that? Never mind fancy aiming. You wouldn't have time for that, if I were shot through the heart and dropped at your feet. Just pick up the rifle, point it at the middle of the target and squeeze the trigger. You might not kill anyone, but you stand a good chance of hitting something.'

'I don't want to kill anyone,' Zoë protested, aghast.

He gave her a grim smile. 'Wait until you're faced with the alternative, before you decide on that.'

She flushed. 'Who is that old lady?'

'She is the innkeeper's mother,' Quentin told her, 'and is considered a very wise woman. She's also the local match-maker, a very important profession. She's come to tell us our journey will be favourable, for which I'm very grateful.' He fell silent and stared at Zoë thoughtfully again. Before she had time to ask him why, he suddenly lunged forward and threw one arm round her, pulling her towards him in an impromptu embrace.

'Let go of me at once!' Zoë exploded. 'What on earth do you think you're doing?'

But he had already released her. 'Go indoors and take it off!' he ordered curtly. When she gaped at him uncomprehendingly, he repeated impatiently, 'Go and take off that confounded corset! I've watched you swelter in it for the past fortnight. How do you think you're going to travel for three days by pony over rough tracks, in the heat, imprisoned in a stupid garment like that?'

He was certainly right, but in the face of his aggressive manner, she retorted, 'Mind your own business! I shall certainly not take it off—remove it.'

'Miss Hammond,' he said quietly. 'I am in charge of this expedition. Now go indoors,' his voice rose gradually in pitch and power until in a thundering crescendo, he concluded, 'and do as I damn well tell you!'

The young Chinese soldiers momentarily broke off their game and glanced over their shoulders, before falling about, giggling merrily.

Zoë stalked indoors with as much dignity as she could muster, divested herself of the offending corset and made a present of it to the innkeeper's astonished wife.

Outside again, she found that the mah-jong counters had been put away and the soldiers lounged about, rifles slung nonchalantly over their shoulders. They looked bored.

'I've taken it off,' she said coldly to Quentin, keeping a good distance from him as she spoke. 'You have to take my word on it.'

'All right, I'm not going to pinch you,' he said wearily. Beneath his breath, he added, so that she barely caught the words, 'Not much to pinch, anyway.'

The old lady in black silk had been watching them closely, and now came hobbling over. She put out a hand and touched Zoë's sleeve so gently that it was as though a falling leaf brushed against it. She smiled and made

some speech. Zoë shook her head, trying to show she
had not understood. The old dame held up her withered
hand and spoke again, this time gesturing towards
Quentin.

Quentin, who had been busy tightening the girth of
one of the saddled ponies, looked up, glanced at Zoë,
and grinned. Then he called out something to the old
lady, who chuckled, clacking her toothless gums, and
patting Zoë's arm again, hobbled away towards the inn.

'What was all that about?' she asked, with a strong
feeling she ought not to ask.

'You were being paid a compliment. The match-
maker believes you are still young enough to be married.
She was asking whether the Europeans have their own
match-maker. If not, she is willing to act for you.'

'I think,' Zoë said sharply, 'we are wasting time.'

'That is what I told the match-maker,' he agreed. 'I
told her you were much too old, and very bad-tempered,
so it would be a waste of time.' He stooped and cupped
his hands. 'Put your foot in there. Look sharp, and I'll
give you a bunk up into the saddle.'

'Thank you, I'd rather use a mounting-block,' Zoë
told him coldly.

'This is not a riding school, Miss Hammond. There
isn't one. Now, we've already been held up while you
changed your clothes, so if you don't mind . . .'

'I can still manage without your help,' she began, but
seeing a look enter his face which she was learning to
recognise and respect, she changed her mind and put
one stout, laced, Oxford shoe into his cupped palms, and
grasped the pommel of the saddle tightly.

'One, two, three—hup!' he exclaimed.

Zoë, entirely unprepared for the force with which he
flung her upwards, found herself propelled into the air
and almost straight over the saddle to the ground
beyond. Just in time she managed to grasp at the pony's
mane and haul herself safely back into the saddle.

Quentin, his head assailed by a flurry of petticoats, closed his eyes briefly against a vision of shapely black-stockinged calves and knee-length frilled cotton drawers. When he opened them again, Miss Hammond was glaring down at him.

'Do you want me to break my neck?' she demanded tightly. 'I think you are a lunatic, Mr Farrell!'

'And I think *you* have the makings of a first-rate, cantankerous old maid!' was the prompt reply.

The lady's hazel eyes blazed at him. 'Stop those men laughing,' she ordered, pointing at the soldiers. 'Why are they laughing?'

'Well, you see,' Quentin explained seriously, 'you are very tall by Chinese standards, and have large, unbound feet. In their eyes, such a cumbersome giantess makes a comical woman.' He had the satisfaction of seeing that he had temporarily silenced his adversary.

And he had one more card to play, just to complete her confusion. Before they rode off, he came up to her and handed up a beautiful Chinese umbrella of oiled paper, brand new and coloured a bright pinkish crimson.

'You may find the sun a little too much,' he said casually. 'I went out this morning and bought you this.'

'Thank you,' Zoë said awkwardly, taking it. 'It's a lovely colour.'

'Red is the Chinese colour of happiness. They dress their brides in it.'

They set off in quite an impressive procession, their four soldiers marching along in front, not quite in step, and calling dubious invitations to the village maidens whom they passed. Next, on their ponies, came Zoë, beneath her red umbrella, and Quentin, whose long legs dangled to the ground. Then the baggage-ponies with the driver whistling and shouting at them, and the bells jangling. Last came the coolies who had been hired to carry the remaining baggage. They certainly made enough noise to attract attention, Zoë thought, and news of their approach probably ran ahead of them for miles.

A movement caught her eye. Quentin had produced a battered silver flask and was taking a liberal swig from it. Zoë's jaw took on a determined set. Somehow or other, she was going to put a stop to that. He had caught a glimpse of her disapproving look, and politely held out the flask.

'Join me, why don't you? No need to stand on ceremony.' He chuckled.

'No, thank you, Mr Farrell.' Somehow she had to stop him drinking.

At mid-day they rested, and the squint-eyed pony-driver became the cook, and a perfectly able one at that, producing boiled rice, poached eggs and green tea. Quentin, who sat on the turf beside her, supplemented his share from the whisky flask, but after a while he strolled off, leaving it on the grass beside his empty plate.

There was not a moment to waste or consider her action. Zoë snatched up the flask and tucked it inside her clothing.

He missed it as soon as he came back. 'Kindly return my flask, Miss Hammond.' He held out his hand.

'I shall not,' she said firmly. 'You are setting a bad example to the Chinese with us. As they see you behave, so they will judge all Europeans.'

He appeared momentarily bereft of speech. 'Where is it?' he asked in a hushed voice.

'Concealed about my person, Mr Farrell, where it will remain, unless you choose to assault me physically.'

'Ah!' he exclaimed in disgust, 'So that's what you're hoping, is it?' He ignored her gasp of outrage and surprise. 'You spinster ladies are all the same. But you're sadly out of luck, my dear, for I'm not in the mood. Besides, I've a bottle in my baggage, so you've achieved nothing. Don't lose that flask, will you? It belonged to my father, and was the only thing the old devil ever gave me willingly.'

They spent the night in a poor and wretched inn. Its best room, which had a hole in the thatched roof, was bestowed on Zoë, and she had no idea where Quentin slept. Wherever it was, she hoped he spent a better night than she did, attacked on all sides by a myriad of bugs and flying insects.

When she came down in the morning, tired and irritable, she found everything packed up efficiently. But Quentin was in the middle of a furious dispute with their soldier escort, who were all clearly very unhappy about something, and gesticulating wildly.

Zoë went across to the laden ponies and waited impatiently. After a moment, she noticed that the pony by which she stood carried Quentin's baggage. She glanced towards the group, still deep in argument. No one looked this way. Zoë unbuckled the nearer canvas sack and delved into it. She was in luck. The whisky bottle was in this one, tucked down among his clothes. She dragged it out, wrenched out the stopper and with a furtive glance towards her companions, up-ended the bottle. The golden liquid drained out with agonising slowness and an astonishing loud 'glug-glug', the dry earth beneath soaking it up like a sponge. Just in time, she managed to return the empty bottle to the bag and buckle it up again. As she stepped hastily away from the pony, Quentin came across.

'Our escort is nervous,' he said brusquely, 'and unwilling to go on. But we've agreed a modest "squeeze", and they've agreed to stay with us.'

'Why are they nervous?' Zoë asked, more than a little nervous herself. She tried to edge further away from the pony.

'They've heard tales of the warlord, Yang. I've assured them that Yang is miles away. But they're only youngsters and have no wish to be heroes, not defending foreigners, anyway.' Farrell broke off and sniffed the air. 'I can smell whisky!' he exclaimed. He dived past her and wrenched open the canvas sack.

'I've poured it away,' Zoë told him loudly, as his hand searched for the bottle.

He froze, then slowly withdrew his hand from the bag and turned towards her. 'You did what?'

'Poured away the whisky. I do not need whisky to sustain me, Mr Farrell, and you do not need whisky to sustain you.'

Quentin leapt forward and seized her shoulders. 'You poured away good whisky?' he yelled at her. 'Do you realise how difficult it is to get it up here? Who the devil told you you could make free with my property?' And he began to shake her violently, like a rag doll.

'Stop it!' she shouted at him, 'You're hurting me!' She grabbed at his hands to break their grip, and for a brief moment they engaged in an arm-wrestling match which he must surely have won, had he not suddenly released her abruptly and stepped back, holding up his hands, as if he feared to touch her.

'You shouldn't have done it,' he said, in a strained, husky voice. He was breathing heavily, but no longer seemed angry—at least, not about the whisky. 'I didn't mean to hurt you,' he muttered.

Surprised at receiving any apology, and rubbing her sore shoulders, Zoë burst out impetuously, 'Give me one good reason why I shouldn't have done it! Your behaviour is in every way thoroughly disgraceful. These people hardly ever see a European, and base their idea of our way of life on *you*. Can you imagine what sort of a picture they are left with? I believe you to be an educated man, and one who should know better. Well, you can drink yourself into an early grave, for all I care—but *not*, do you hear, not in my presence!'

Quentin's face paled beneath the sunburn. 'You have

never seen me drunk!' he snarled at her, his anger erupting once more. 'Don't you ever dare to accuse me again of not being able to hold my liquor! What's more, I am not one of your pupils. I will not be harangued by an acid-tongued and self-righteous schoolmarm!' He pointed towards her pony. 'The slightest hint of any more trouble from you, and I shall turn this expedition round and take you straight away back to Canton. Now, get on that pony,' he concluded hoarsely, 'and don't let me hear so much as a squeak out of you, do you hear?'

They travelled on for most of the day in an unfriendly silence, until, towards evening, they saw, unexpectedly, a group of travellers coming towards them.

'What have we here?' Quentin muttered. 'Soldiers, I think.'

The approaching party came nearer, and now it could be seen that it consisted of a small number of mounted soldiers guarding a group of half-naked prisoners on foot. Each prisoner's neck was secured in a solid wooden wheel, so that the unfortunate could help himself to neither food nor drink, and each was chained to the next man. As the two parties met and stopped to exchange news, Zoë sat, her eyes riveted to the prisoners. Though they gave every sign of being illiterate coolies of the lowest order, with sullen, brutalised faces, she could not but pity their wretched condition, or the fate surely in store for them.

They moved on, and a pall of silence had fallen over their company. The baggage-coolies whispered uneasily together at the rear, the pony-driver was silent and their soldier escort looked furtive and frightened.

'You haven't quite believed me, till now, have you?' Quentin said quietly to her. 'But those captured bandits were certainly Yang's men, who foolishly strayed from the main body to do a little pillaging on their own account.'

She felt a cold prickle of fear run over her. 'So near?'

The words came whispered through her dry lips.

'Much too near,' he muttered, 'and well out of Yang's usual territory. General Li must be either unprepared, or, more likely, unable to keep him out.' He saw how pale she looked, and added more cheerfully, 'Well, a small raiding party on a village or two doesn't constitute a major force! The loss of those men may give Yang thought, and cause him to be more cautious.'

'We got to get to Eve!' Zoë exclaimed. 'Quentin, do you think we can be there by tomorrow?'

'With luck!' He smiled at her reassuringly. 'See here, in all my years in China, I've come across many incidents of bandit activity. The men you saw will be executed tonight and needn't worry you. Any at liberty will be cowardly and won't attack us. We are too many, and armed.'

'How long have you been in China?' she asked him suddenly.

'I came out here at the time of the Boxer rising,' he said. 'As a British soldier, my dear.'

Zoë turned this over in her mind. Somehow she was not surprised. So, a disgraced British officer, court-martialled, cashiered, or simply requested to resign for the good name of the regiment. She wondered which.

'You want to know why,' he said drily. Reining up abruptly, he pointed ahead of them. 'Do you see that group of trees up there? They hide a little temple. Whenever I pass this way, I stop and call on the temple guardian, a very old priest. The temple is four hundred years old, from the time of the Ming emperors, but that is recent in China's history. There is no square foot of turf in China where you do not stand on four thousand years of unbroken civilisation. It was here when Caesar's legions first set foot on British soil and found our ancestors daubed in woad. It saw Rome fall. The Chinese think us barbarians, and in comparison with their ancient civilisation we *are* brash newcomers, bent on destroying an ancient civilisation, just as Rome fell to warrior tribesmen.'

'But it's a civilisation which is a kind of fossil,' Zoë objected. 'It lacks modern hospitals and medicine, modern schools . . .'

'Yes, yes, I know!' he said impatiently. 'It needs to be dragged into a new age, but with a minimum of coercion. It wants guidance from us, Zoë, not destruction. It needs to be persuaded, not bullied. China has seen herself humiliated and dismembered. The results have been distrust, hatred and bloodshed. I was one of those who marched into Peking to deliver the besieged Europeans from the murderous intentions of the Boxer rebels. And how was our victory celebrated? By an orgy of destruction and vandalism. I saw European ladies of the highest rank pin up their skirts and scramble over the ruins of Chinese palaces to see what they could loot. You criticised me for drinking in front of those coolies. But what have we ever done to persuade the Chinese that our way is better, or that we are even civilised?'

Quentin shrugged. 'My mistake was in speaking my opinions aloud. They were badly received in such an atmosphere. It was suggested I might be happier if I resigned my commission, so I did.'

He fell silent, and not knowing quite what to say, Zoë was silent, too. Perhaps he thought she expected him to say more, because he went on to tell her of the reaction of his family to his fall from grace. Since a youngster, he had frequently alarmed them by his behaviour, and they regarded him as their black sheep. Now they were determined to rid themselves of him once and for all. Like the Prodigal Son, he was to receive his share of the family inheritance now. It had been put into a trust fund, which remitted regular payments to him. These payments would continue so long as he remained in China. If he ever set foot in any part of the British Isles again, they would stop—and he wouldn't receive a penny more. The fund would cease to exist and any money left revert to the family fortune.

Quentin told her this without emotion, but she sensed an underlying bitterness which he could not hide. She also sensed that it was not the complete tale. There was more, something he did not speak of. With a flash of instinct, Zoë found herself thinking: it was a woman. Somewhere in all this there was a woman . . .

It was difficult to imagine Quentin ever being 'in love', as most people would have understood it. Certainly his love would have been no tender passion, but rather something dark and violent. But some woman may once have loved him, loved him more than anything else in the world. He was an attractive man with a strong physical presence that even Zoë admitted she could not ignore. But what had happened? Remittance money alone would not keep him in China. He had made a fortune of his own here, and he cared nothing for other people's opinion of him. If he had wanted to return to England, he would have done so long before now, and thrown the money of the trust fund back into the faces of his disapproving family. He would have taken pleasure in doing so! But perhaps it was only, after all, some common enough, sordid little tale of some girl seduced and abandoned, an earlier Emily Linton, but without a husband to provide a refuge from her shame.

But it doesn't matter to me, Zoë thought sternly. But that wasn't true, and it did matter. Am I going to do it again? she wondered. Am I going to lose my heart again to someone who will use it and crush it and finally throw it away, unwanted? Have I learned nothing?

A wry, sad little smile touched her mouth, and Quentin, noticing it, narrowed his blue eyes thought-fully. Then he tipped his panama hat on to the back of his mop of red hair, and unexpectedly burst into song. It was not unmelodious, but it made it impossible to think. It sent their Chinese escort into fits of laughter, so that all their worries were temporarily swept away, and Zoë felt an insane desire to laugh with them.

'I am mad,' she told herself. 'Mad to have come all this way, and with him . . .'

The temple was set by a cool stream of fast running water descending from the hillside, and shaded by trees. It was well kept, and gaily painted in emerald and crimson. Little dragons in glazed pottery sported among the tiles of its curved roof, and at its corners stood the carved figures of the warrior deva who guard the gates of heaven. Though clad in armour, and their eyes bulging ferociously as they crushed demons beneath their feet, somehow these fierce temple guardians did not have an unwelcoming air. Once upon a time this temple must have formed part of a much larger complex, possibly a monastery, for among the trees stood ruined walls of a much larger compound. As the wind blew, little bells hanging in the temple eaves jangled softly.

'It is the temple of Kwan Yin, the goddess of mercy,' Quentin said, dismounting. As he spoke, the elderly priest came out to greet them.

He was so old that Zoë thought she would hardly have been surprised to learn he had been here as long as the temple he served. A straggling white beard adorned his chin, and his skin was crinkled like fine old parchment. He begged them to be seated under the trees, and after a while, an acolyte served them tea in tiny porcelain cups so delicate that the liquid could be seen through the transparent ware.

Quentin and the old priest had fallen to talking. At first the old man was curious about Zoë, and asked Quentin several questions, to which he replied emphatically in the negative. 'He has never seen a young foreign lady before,' he explained to her, 'and asks whether you are my wife. I told him that you are no man's wife, only a school-teacher.'

'Thank you,' Zoë said calmly.

A shadow of a smile passed over his face, and he turned back towards the priest. After some more conversation, Quentin grew serious. The priest was pointing into the distance, towards the hills which were their destination, and seemed to be describing something or someone.

'What is it?' Zoë asked quietly, as they took their leave.

'The old man believes Yang is coming,' Quentin said frankly. 'He says the peasants believe it, too, and are beginning to hide their valuables. When an earthquake is coming, the old man says, the snakes know it, and come up out of their holes in the ground. So, when a peasant hides his rice and his gold, the warlord approaches. No one tells them of this . . . . they know. Like the snakes, they have an instinct for self-preservation. Besides, strange horsemen have been sighted. He fears they are Yang's agents, assessing the opposition, and I'm inclined to think he is right. He says Yang is an Evil Spirit, and while he walks abroad, no man can rest. He is also right about that.'

Zoë shivered and looked up into the dusky, blue-tinged hills, over which night was creeping. Out there, somewhere, lurked the warlord and his merciless horde, ready to sweep down like locusts, leaving bare the countryside across which they passed. She and Quentin had done more than travel over many arduous miles of territory. They had travelled back in time itself, through the centuries. No ordinary bandit this, no modern wager of war, but a predatory beast in human form. The carved warrior deva, trampling on the writhing demons at the gates of the temple, would have recognised Yang at once.

Quentin's voice broke into her dark thoughts. 'We'll camp here tonight. We have tarpaulins to rig up some tents, and those ruined walls are stout enough to provide

us with some protection. Local robbers will be superstitious and unlikely to molest us within the temple
precincts. Yang, of course, would have no such scru-
ples, and burn this place to the ground and us with it, so
let's hope he's still far away!'

It was very hot in the little tent, and sticky. Zoë, who had
not undressed completely, lay tossing in her petticoat
and camisole, and dreamed a confused dream in which
temples, warlords and whisky were all muddled up
together. She awoke suddenly about midnight and sat
up, pushing back her damp hair with both hands and
struggling for breath. The atmosphere in the tent was so
stifling that she felt as if she must suffocate. Seizing a
cotton shawl, she flung it around her perspiring bare
shoulders, and scrambled out into the cool night air.

The wind was rustling in the treetops as if voices
whispered together, and from time to time it stirred the
temple bells which jingled melodiously, unseen. The
stars glittered like diamonds. Zoë felt as though she
listened to one gigantic beating heart, the heart of three
hundred and fifty million people, and an empire which
had lasted four thousand years and was now on the verge
of crashing down in ruins. For the first time she understood something of what Quentin felt for this ancient
and secretive land.

As she sat on the turf, hugging her knees, her ear
caught a new movement to her right, and without warning, the figure of a man loomed up in the darkness. Her
heart leapt into her mouth, although she knew straight
away, from his great height, that it was Quentin. He
paused for a moment as he caught sight of her, dimly
etched in the darkness against the pale canvas of the
tent. Then he came and dropped down on the turf beside
her.

'Can't you sleep?' Carefully he set down between
them the rifle he carried. It was an odd sort of gesture,

very formal. Rather like, Zoë thought, the knight Tristan, placing his sword symbolically between himself and the sleeping Isolde.

'It's stuffy in the tent.' She touched the rifle. 'Do you think we might be attacked?'

He shrugged. 'No, of course not, it's just a precaution. A walk round to check does no harm.' He leaned back, propping himself up on one elbow. 'About Eve,' he said bluntly, without any preamble, as if he took up their conversation of a few days ago on the boat. 'You do know, don't you, that she's had . . .' He broke off, and then concluded his sentence, 'You do know she's had a lot of troubles to contend with, the Mortons leaving and so on.'

'Quentin,' Zoë said gently. 'What is it about Eve you keep trying to tell me?'

'What should I have to tell you?' he replied roughly. 'You've been getting letters from her, and tomorrow you'll see her for yourself.'

The words seemed somehow to have an ominous ring to them. Zoë shivered, and pulled the shawl round her bare shoulders as the breeze stirred the trees and caused the temple bells to chime softly.

'When you see Eve,' Quentin's voice said soberly, by her ear, 'you'll understand. I hope you'll decide to take Eve with you, back to Canton, and eventually to England. Eve's given seven years of life to the school. It's more than enough. No woman ought to make such a sacrifice.'

'You—you like Eve, don't you?' Zoë asked curiously, trying to see his face.

'Yes, I like her. She's a brave woman. But you're wrong to try and copy what she's done, Zoë. You're a different sort of person. I don't mean that you lack spunk, you've plenty of that! I mean, you're a real woman and you need a man in your life, and in your bed.'

She had not expected him to express it so bluntly. Trembling, she whispered, 'What makes you think that?'

'This does . . .' he said softly. He reached out and took her shoulders firmly, pulling her towards him, and into his arms.

Zoë gasped, 'No, Quentin, please don't . . .' knowing that this was what she had feared would happen, though she had tried to pretend it was not so. She had feared it when she knew he had been drinking, feared it every time he came near her.

She made one wild, desperate effort to escape, twisting in his arms, but she was not strong enough and fell back on the turf, the shawl sliding away into the darkness. Quentin's body blotted out the stars and crushed her beneath his weight, as his mouth closed possessively over hers, ignoring and stifling her cry of protest. She pushed at his chest with both hands, trying vainly to thrust him away. But instead her hands slid round his powerful body, and an unbidden yearning sprang up inside her, a longing to yield to that brutal embrace, here beneath the veil of velvet darkness cast over them both by a Chinese night.

Quentin's grip relaxed without warning, and he raised his head. 'What was his name?' he asked, and in his voice she fancied a touch of sarcasm.

Anger, at him and at her own weakness, replaced the desire to surrender herself. Zoë pushed him aside and sat up, sweeping back the tangle of brown hair which had fallen across her face.

'Phil—Phillip . . .' she muttered, her hurt echoing in her voice. Her response to his embrace had told Quentin he wasn't the first to kiss her in that way, told him what he had wanted to know. The fact that he knew, and that she had given way so easily, made her feel cheapened.

'What happened?' His voice was expressionless in the

darkness, but required a reply, like the cold question of an inquisitor.

'He married someone else!' she threw at him. 'If you want to know it all, I hadn't any fortune, and he needed someone who had money.' Shame swept over her at the admission.

He dismissed her explanation with a grunt. 'Why didn't you make him want you more than the money? You're a clever woman.' His voice was slow, deliberate, insulting. 'It couldn't have been that difficult.'

'When I saw what he was,' Zoë retaliated furiously, 'do you think I wanted to be his wife? Even if I had wanted it, I had my pride!'

'Pride comes before a fall. Did you—fall?' The voice was still cool and expressionless.

'I wasn't his mistress, if that's what you mean!' she told him fiercely. He made no reply, and belatedly defending herself and trying to restore her dignity, she burst out passionately, 'I let you kiss me just then, but it was a mistake. I didn't know you were going to do it!'

'You knew I was going to do it,' he said in that same cool, even voice. 'You've known it for days. You've been waiting for me to do it.'

Zoë drew in her breath. 'How can you say such a despicable thing?'

'Look,' he said harshly, 'I'm not Edward Linton. I don't make passes at unsuspecting girls. I make passes at the ones who show they're interested.'

She scrabbled about frantically on the turf for her shawl, and retrieving it, threw it round her shoulders. 'I'm going back to my tent!' She hesitated. 'As—as you were *once* an officer and a gentleman, I expect you to stay out here.'

'Don't talk so stupidly!' he said curtly. 'I'm not going to burst into your tent aflame with lust, if that's what you fear. Not because I am, or ever was, what you call a gentleman, but because the game wouldn't be worth the candle. Maybe your Phillip thought so, too.'

'Emily called you a scoundrel,' Zoë said in a level voice. 'And she was right.'

'There are names for women like you, too,' Quentin said, 'of which the politest is a "tease".'

Zoë stumbled back into her tent, and for a long time lay awake, listening in apprehension. Quentin was still moving about outside. At one point she heard the click of the rifle, and her heart leapt in alarm. Was there really some threat out there, in the darkness? A long painful shiver ran the length of her body. The real threat to her peace of mind came from within, not without. If her senses were strung to breaking-point, it was not because of the wind in the trees or the click of a rifle.

After a while he went back to his own tent, and all was quiet.

In the morning, when she emerged cautiously, it was to discover that their four man military escort had decamped overnight. They must have gone just before dawn, but how they had achieved their departure so silently, she could not imagine. Now they might never have existed, were it not for the tell-tale crushed areas in the turf which showed where they had rested earlier.

Quentin was standing over the spot and staring down at the imprints. As she approached, he looked up and into the distance, screwing up his eyes against the early sunlight.

'Yes,' he said softly. 'Yang *is* coming.'

Eve had described the school in so many letters that when Zoë first set eyes on it, it seemed a familiar and friendly place. It was situated about a mile from the town, among low hills. A long, low, two-storey whitewashed building, it was surrounded by neat gardens, laid out with mathematical precision, and striped with bright green rows of growing vegetables.

No one could have wished for a more enthusiastic reception. As they rode up, the doors burst open and about a dozen girls of between ten and fourteen flew out in wild excitement, surrounding Zoë and Quentin as they made their way up the steps. Accustomed to think of the Chinese as reserved, Zoë was astonished and touched by their chorus of welcome.

A woman appeared in the doorway, and called, 'Girls, girls, please!' clapping her hands vainly to secure attention. Abandoning the attempt, she stepped forward, peering eagerly up at Zoë, exclaiming, 'Oh, my dear, I am so pleased to see you. Come inside, you must be exhausted. Quentin!' She held out both her hands to him.

Quentin took her fingertips and bowed over them gallantly. 'Well, Eve, I said I'd bring reinforcements, and here she is!'

'Eve . . . ?' Zoë whispered.

Was this indeed the beloved and admired elder sister who had left England seven years ago? Left a robust young woman with healthy pink cheeks and a ready smile—and was now this old-looking and prematurely grey woman, peering through her spectacles. Only the smile remained to make Eve Hammond recognisable to those who had known her before. Something terrible had happened to destroy those pink cheeks and the laughter in the eyes, something worse than harsh climate and isolation, strange diet and loneliness. The skin told the tale, hideously pitted and scarred. It had not been a simple fever of which Eve Hammond had been a victim, so soon after her arrival in China. It had been that most dreaded scourge—the smallpox!

CHAPTER FIVE

As FROM afar, Zoë seemed to hear her own voice stammering a reply to Eve's welcome. Even as she spoke, she could see the understanding in her sister's eyes. A sad little smile crossed Eve's careworn, scarred features, and she pressed Zoë's hand in sympathy, as though it were Zoë who should be pitied.

Zoë felt the tears burning at her eyelids, and not wishing Eve to see them, turned her head aside. Her gaze fell on Quentin, who stood apart, watching them. At the sight of her pale, distraught face, he flushed darkly and turned quickly to the pony-driver. He should have forewarned her, and he knew it. But why had he deliberately chosen not to do so? Had he simply lacked the courage? Or had he wanted the sight of Eve to be as great a shock to Zoë as possible? A shock so great that it would send her scurrying back to Canton, and the eventual safety of England?

Now he turned his back on her, and began to settle up with the pony-driver and the coolies, paying them the money owed them and the bonus of two silver taels per man he had promised if the journey were completed without mishap. The coolies loped away and the pony-driver rounded up his beasts, with the exception of one dun pony, and drove them out of the compound at a smart trot, the harness bells jingling furiously. His anxiety to begin his return journey could not have been plainer, as had been that of the coolies, who had not even rested. All believed the arrival of the warlord to be imminent.

Now Quentin came slowly towards the group of two women and the young Chinese schoolgirls. 'No news?'

he demanded of Eve. He did not look at Zoë, excluding her from his vision and his address.

Eve shook her head. 'If you mean, have we seen a desperate band of armed men? Then, no. We haven't seen a soul. Chang, the gardener, came with a lot of rumours, but no evidence, and I told him not to frighten the girls with wild tales. I suppose you've been terrifying my poor sister here with gory prophecies?' She looked at him severely.

'Oh, Zoë isn't easily frightened by that sort of tale,' he replied enigmatically. 'By other things, perhaps.' His blue eyes rested sardonically on Zoë for a moment. But before she could reply, his expression changed and he added, in a surprisingly gentle voice, and with an engaging smile, 'Well, and here is the lady Green Jade.'

Zoë turned, as a Chinese girl of about sixteen stepped forward from the back of the group and bowed politely. The child was enchanting, with a flawless skin the colour of rich cream, on which the rose-pink cheeks might have been painted by some ancient artist on a porcelain vase. Her thick, lustrous hair was coiled into a round chignon on either side of her head, and bedecked with coral and silver flower-headed pins, and the graceful lines of her traditional Chinese dress made her an exquisite work of art, yet with a shy and natural charm. In perfect English she made a little speech of welcome to Zoë, obviously carefully rehearsed for this moment. The gist of it was that the unworthy pupils were overcome by the honour done them by the well-born and illustrious teacher who had journeyed so many miles to reach them.

Zoë thanked her, quite at a loss to return the curious, exaggerated language of the speech.

'Green Jade is our star pupil,' Eve said indulgently. 'In fact, since Jessica Morton left, Green Jade has been acting as pupil-teacher. Without her help, I don't know how I should have managed.'

Merriment gleamed in Green Jade's eyes, but Zoë

could see that the young girl was pleased by Eve's praise.

'Perhaps you will be a teacher, too, one day, Green Jade?'

The laughter died in the girl's face. 'I should like it very much,' she said sadly. 'But I think it cannot be.'

'You will stay and eat with us, Quentin?' Eve urged.

He shook his head. 'Thank you, but no. My people are expecting me at home.' He went to the dun pony and pulled himself into the saddle. Tugging at the reins to turn the pony's head towards them, he added, 'You know where to find me. Send Chang with a message if—if you hear anything.'

'Thank you for your help in bringing me here,' Zoë said carefully.

He glanced at her. 'My pleasure . . .' He waved his battered panama hat at them amicably in a farewell salute, and clattered out of the compound in a cloud of dust. They had been companions in travel for almost two and a half weeks, and Zoë, despite everything, felt a wrench at his departure.

That evening, when their charges had all been sent off to bed, the sisters sat alone on the cool veranda of the school and talked, while the moths fluttered about the flame of the oil-lamp. Crickets sang unseen in the garden, and everywhere seemed very peaceful.

Eve said quietly, 'Quentin didn't tell you that I had had the smallpox?'

Zoë watched the moths foolishly hurtling against the glass shade about the flame. 'No. Why didn't you tell us, Eve?'

'And distress you? For what purpose?'

After a pause, Zoë asked, 'Was that the reason you —you wanted me to stay in England?'

Eve's hands moved nervously on her lap, her fingers twisting together. 'No, not altogether. Zoë, I've never regretted coming to China. Even if I had known how hard it would all prove, I'd still have come. But you were young, and prettier than I ever was!' She smiled teasingly, then grew sober again. 'It would not have been right!' she said earnestly. 'To bring you out here, to ask you to sacrifice your youth and beauty to this school, while you might still have met someone in England, someone you might have loved, and married, had children with, of your own.'

'I did meet someone,' Zoë said slowly. 'But it didn't work out like that. I—I made a fool of myself, I suppose. Perhaps it would have been better, after all, if I'd come straight out to China in the first place.'

Eve looked unhappy. 'I acted as I thought was best. I discussed it all with Quentin, at the time, and he was adamant that you should not come rushing out here before you'd had even a chance to see if you might settle in England with someone.'

'With *Quentin*?' Zoë interrupted angrily. 'He is the last person to give advice on matters of personal relationships!'

'No, in this case, he is the *best* person!' Eve said with such force that Zoë was stopped in mid-speech and looked at her sister in surprise.

'I should explain to you about Quentin,' Eve said firmly. 'Although it concerns his private life and, as such, normally ought not to be the subject of anyone else's conversation. But I'm not indulging in idle gossip. He is our only European neighbour. He's been a pillar of support to the school, even though he mistrusted us all profoundly when the Mortons and I first came here. He has very strong and fixed views on how China should be helped to modernise. He has a positive phobia about missionaries—and school-teachers run a close second, I'm afraid. Nevertheless, he's always been very kind and helpful, and we depend on him. He deals with the Chinese authorities on our behalf. He's well known to them, and they trust him, whereas I'm afraid they trust very few other Europeans. So, you see, I want you to understand Quentin, and not misinterpret his manner, which can be off-putting, I know.'

Eve paused and seemed to be seeking her next words carefully. 'Quentin quarrelled with his family, and has chosen to remain in China.'

'I know about that quarrel,' Zoë interrupted. 'He told me.'

'Did he?' said Eve in a tone of wonder, and stared vaguely at her sister. She had taken off her spectacles, and without them, her short-sightedness was apparent. 'Oh, well, in that case, you should know the rest. Quentin had left his fiancée in England, his childhood sweetheart, a girl named Alice Theydon.'

'Alice . . .' Zoë murmured, not intending to interrupt. 'So that . . . Oh, please go on, Eve. Don't mind me.'

'Well,' Eve continued, 'he wrote to Alice and asked her to come out to China and join him. Of course, everyone told him it was foolish to suggest such a thing to a young English girl who had no notion what was involved in such a journey, or what she would find here. In England, too, Alice's family was distraught, and tried to prevent her. But she was twenty-one and mistress of her own fortune. She and Quentin were very much in love, and, of course, they wanted to be together. So she took ship, intending to be married here, bringing everything for her new home with her. While he waited for her, Quentin built the most beautiful house. You'll see it for yourself, so I won't try to describe it. It was to be a wedding gift for his bride.'

Eve fell silent, and even the chirping crickets seemed to have ceased their song. A cool breeze touched the nape of Zoë's neck, almost as if a ghost stood at her elbow and touched her lightly with unseen fingers. 'What happened?' she whispered.

'Quentin went to meet the ship. But she had called at

Singapore on the voyage out, and there had taken on a large number of coolies, Chinese migrant workers returning home with the money they'd earned. Unfortunately, they had brought the cholera on board with them.'

Both sisters sat silent for a while. 'It ran through the crew and passengers like wildfire,' Eve said. 'The Europeans were particularly vulnerable. The bodies of cholera victims must be disposed of quickly. As they died, on the ship, they were buried at sea. Alice's body, too, was committed to the deep . . . When the ship arrived, she flew the fever flag, and when at last the quarantine was over and Quentin was able to go on board, there was not even a coffin . . . Only Alice's clothes in her trunks and all her trousseau, everything new and untouched, her wedding gown, things for the house, everything—except his bride.'

Zoë stood up and walked to the edge of the veranda, staring out into the night.

'Quentin blames himself,' Eve said gently, 'and hates the idea of any young English woman coming out to China. I'm afraid it's made him bitter. I expect you felt he was unwelcoming.'

'Yes, he was quite rude,' Zoë said. 'Although he was all right on the journey itself up here.' She glanced down at her hands, gripping the veranda railing. The fingers were white with tension and she forced herself to relax them. 'The further we got from Canton, the—the more friendly he became.'

'I think he doesn't care for the Europeans in Canton,' Eve observed. 'But he knows the Lintons well, and stays there whenever he goes down to the coast. How are the Lintons, by the way?'

'Oh, well enough, I suppose,' Zoë replied. 'I'm sorry, but I'm afraid I didn't like them much.' Suddenly she turned to her sister and burst out, 'It's a beautiful baby—the Linton baby, I mean. I went to see her in the nursery. No one offered to take me, I don't think either the mother, or—or Linton, care about the child at all. But she's so sweet, and smiled so happily when I picked her up. She has such lovely blue eyes, and . . .' She bit off her words just in time. She had been about to say, 'And a mop of red curls'. 'And is a dear little soul,' she finished, instead.

'I'm sure the Lintons care for their baby,' Eve exclaimed, shocked. 'You must have imagined it, Zoë!'

Zoë said tersely, 'Perhaps.'

Quentin's child, she thought. No one could doubt it. As soon as she had seen the little girl in the nursery, and again the following morning, she had known it was Quentin's child she held in her arms.

Quentin, too, had reached his home by late that evening, arriving just after dusk, and sliding thankfully from the saddle. Ah Ling, who rejoiced in the title 'Number One Boy', despite it having been quite sixty years since he had been anything like a boy, greeted his master gravely and with satisfaction.

'You make good journey? You not pay too much that pony-driver? He very unworthy fellow. You take bath now?' This last was less a question than a statement. Ah Ling had the bath ready.

Quentin said, 'Yes, no, no and yes,' in answer to all parts of the question and made his way to his room where the bath waited. He dragged off his dusty, sweat-stained clothes and peered at his reflected face in a mirror. Rubbing a hand over his chin, he thought, 'I look more like a bandit myself than anything. May be the girl is right, at that.' He sighed, and unfastened a gold chain from his neck, and held it up to stare morosely at the small flat locket on it. His daughter was growing fast, crawling now, the ayah said. The next time he went down to Canton, she'd probably be stammering 'mama' and 'papa'—and the person she'd be calling 'papa' would be that rogue Linton. A memory came into his mind of Zoë holding the child in her arms. 'Oh, damnation . . .' he said wearily, and put down the locket, before climbing into the bath.

Ah Ling, hovering, said, 'Why you not bring wife from Canton?'

'Because they don't grow on trees! Who wants a woman about the place, anyway?' He had—once. The sense of loss, the pain and the remorse were dulled now, but not dead.

'Man need wife. I find you concubine, nice girl, very honourable. Very small feet. You pay fifteen taels, she belong you.'

'I don't want a concubine, with or without crippled feet, damn you,' he replied mildly.

They had had this conversation several times before. Ah Ling never gave up, and was used to being sworn at, as a result. Quentin, relaxing in the water, thought of Zoë Hammond, swimming in the river. That girl had a magnificent body, like a Greek sculpture, and she hardly seemed to know it. He had become so used to seeing the tiny Chinese women, tottering on their bound feet, that it had been quite a shock to see someone who moved so freely, with such an unconscious grace. 'She's got under your skin!' he told himself wryly. She thought *he* was the Wild Man of Borneo, or so it seemed! But there had been a moment, when he had taken her in his arms that night, before she remembered to protest, when that beautiful, alabaster body had melted into one which was soft, warm, and very, very desirable. There had been something more in that brief moment, when he had caught her unawares. Hunger, a hunger to be loved. Just for a second or two there, she had wanted him to take her, no matter what she said or did afterwards.

Quentin forced away the pictures in his mind, and climbed out of his bath, towelling himself dry briskly and tying a Chinese silk bathrobe around his naked body.

'I bring whisky,' Ah Ling said, producing the bottle and a glass, neatly set on a tray.

His master stared at it moodily. 'Take it away,' he said, and for the first time ever, Ah Ling looked astounded.

Zoë was, indeed, having a very busy time. There was so much to learn, and, curious as she was to see all about her, she herself also proved an object of great curiosity to others. Nothing could have equalled her first appearance at the nearby village on her bicycle. Unwarily, she rode there to see if candles could be purchased, as they were running short of lamp oil. But as soon as she entered the village street, she was surrounded by a gesticulating throng. Though curiosity seemed their motive, she had nevertheless begun to feel somewhat isolated and alarmed, when Chang, the school gardener, appeared in the midst and took charge.

He jumped up on a water-butt and, flinging his arms about energetically, began a long speech. As he spoke, he gradually took on the manner and style of a traditional story-teller, of the kind who wandered from village to village. In response, his audience fell silent, and settled down in neat rows, standing or squatting, in the dust of the village street, to listen.

Zoë did not discover until later what Chang was telling them, and then found that it had been a highly-coloured account of her journey to China. Throwing his arms into the air, he described mountainous seas, and lowering his voice and adopting a gruesome leer, infested them with horrifying sea monsters. His audience grew pale, and their eyes started from their heads. Their chorused cries of 'Ah!' echoed their awe, whenever Chang paused for dramatic effect or to allow his hearers to comment, which they dutifully did.

The whole recital took so long that Zoë began to wonder if she were to be left standing, holding up its centrepiece, the bicycle, all day in the hot sun. But eventually Chang came to the end and, as a finale, requested her politely to ride the 'flying wheel' in a circle round the crowd to demonstrate its marvels. She obliged, and rang the bell for good measure. The whole performance was highly theatrical and exhausting, but an unqualified success. After that, she was allowed unimpeded passage through the village and on the dusty roads around. She found she could leave the bicycle unattended quite safely, for such was its prestige that although she always returned to find it surrounded by a crowd of admirers, no one ventured to touch it, or even to ring its wonderful bell.

She immediately became very fond of all the girls in the school, and was highly impressed by their quick intelligence and eagerness to learn. But to Green Jade, the eldest of the pupils, she felt herself especially drawn. There was something so haunting in the girl's fragile beauty, a wistfulness she could not explain. Gradually, through chatting of her own school-days and life at home, she found it possible to draw her out. Eventually Green Jade confided her greatest wish to the new teacher. She wanted to be a teacher, too. There was a college in far-off Hong Kong, where Europeans trained Chinese teachers, men and women. Eve had told her of it. To go there, to learn to be a teacher, was Green Jade's secret desire, but, alas, a hopeless one.

'My father would not allow it. He would not think it right for his daughter to go so far away and study.'

'Have you asked him, Green Jade?'

The girl's dark sloe eyes were sad. 'It would be no use. My father is a good, kind man—but some things he would not believe right. That is one. I am his only child. I must obey him.'

They were walking on the lower slopes of the hillside as they talked, among the stunted wild rhododendron bushes that splashed the ground with patches of mauve and pink. It was possible for Zoë to take Green Jade along with her on such a stroll, for unlike some of the other girls, she did not have bound feet and was able to walk easily. The girls who had bound feet tottered about in a spritely enough manner, but to go for a walk in the countryside, as the English understood it, would be quite beyond them. To follow an ancient fashionable fad and also to show they were of rich families and did not need to walk far, their tiny feet were crushed into the embroidered slippers which looked to a European hardly large enough to take a baby's foot. These slippers were kept highly perfumed, to hide the lingering odour of dead skin. The sharply pointed shape of the foot was due to only the big toe being left in its proper place. The remaining small toes had been folded underneath the foot and bound there at the beginning of the binding process, so that they atrophied and became useless, unseen appendages. The ball of the foot was then forced closer and closer to the heel by gradually tightening the bandages, so that sometimes the bones of the feet were even broken under pressure.

Green Jade had explained the binding process in detail to Zoë, explaining too, why her own feet were not deformed in this way—held, incredibly, to be the greatest female attraction.

'My mother is a Christian, and Christian girls do not have bound feet. So she did not wish to bind my feet. But my grandmother and aunts insisted, saying I would never get a husband, for who wants a wife with big feet?' Green Jade broke off in confusion and blushed crimson.

'It's all right!' Zoë consoled her. 'I know I have enormous feet by Chinese standards, but I'm not looking for a husband, so it doesn't matter.'

Green Jade gave her a knowing look from the corner of her dark eyes, and continued her story. 'So they started to bind my feet when I was five years old. Every time they took off the bandages to wash my feet, the pain was very great, and I screamed and cried so much that my father came to see what was wrong. He is a kind man and I am his only child, as I told you—so he was angry and threw the bandages away, and would not let them do it. Therefore I have large feet, but I don't mind—because I think bound feet very old-fashioned. Nowadays in China, even in wealthy families, it is beginning to be unpopular. You see, of the students here, about half have bound feet and half do not.'

When they returned to the school, Chang the gardener stepped out in front of them, and began explaining something to Green Jade. Then he handed over a small, mud-caked object. She turned it in her hands and asked him several questions, before she handed it to Zoë.

'The gardener dug this up in his vegetable plot. He says he has found such things before, but broken. This one is whole, and he thinks you might like to keep it.'

It was a pottery horse. Though only faint traces of its former coloured paint remained and the whole was encrusted with dirt, there was a wonderful vivacity and life about the little clay creature.

They took it indoors and showed it to Eve, who put on her spectacles and peered at it with interest. 'I'm no expert, but it looks very old. We'll keep it safe till Quentin comes next. He is a great authority on Chinese works of art, and will be able to tell us something. But we must tell Chang to dig carefully, and on no account to damage anything else he might find.'

This was relayed to the gardener, and the following morning a small child appeared, one of his numerous brood, and solemnly held up a grubby sack. When they tipped it out on a table, it proved to contain a number of fragments, all dug up by Chang in his vegetable patch at some time or other. Zoë and Eve sorted through them carefully. Many, alas, were no more than pottery shards, but later in the day a second child appeared, and handed over three figurines which Chang's children had been using as dolls since their father's spade had turned them up.

Zoë set the little clay figures out in a row. About four inches high, and wearing flowing smock dresses, they were smiling merrily and each held a different object. Though chipped and worn, close inspection revealed one such object to resemble a mandoline. Another figure held what looked like cymbals, and the third held wooden blocks of the kind popular in infant music-classes in the west.

'It's a ladies' orchestra!' Zoë exclaimed in delight. 'I do hope Quentin comes soon and can tell us more.'

Her wish was granted. The next morning, Chang appeared with a grin from ear to ear, and announced cheerfully, 'The Red Bristles is here!'

Zoë ran out on to the veranda in time to see a dishevelled figure astride the dun pony, ambling towards the school. She waved to him, as the rider came up and dismounted. Since Eve had told her of the tragic episode in his past, she had thought more kindly of Quentin, and had made a resolve to be patient with his rudeness and unpredictable behaviour. He had not behaved well towards her, and this she did not forget, but she was determined to try to overlook it. Accordingly, she smiled at him, and called out, 'Good morning!'

'Well!' he said. 'You look pleased to see me. I hadn't expected that. I thought you'd have put up fortifications by now to keep both me and the Tiger of Nan-Ling out.'

'Who's the Tiger of Nan-Ling?' Zoë demanded, diverted.

'One of Yang's many nicknames, from his birthplace in the mountains. Or have you forgotten Yang?' He raised his eyebrows.

'Yes, I had,' Zoë confessed. 'Such a lot has been happening. Oh, do come inside. We've something to show you!'

Quentin handed the pony's reins to one of Chang's

offspring, who was hopping about excitedly. 'I thought I might be offered a cold beer,' he said plaintively, 'before I'm required to admire a lot of needlework or something.'

He brushed himself off as he spoke, and clouds of red dust rose from his jacket.

'We haven't any beer, only lemonade,' Zoë said impatiently. 'And it isn't needlework.' She caught at his arm and tugged him into their little sitting-room, where the horse, the lady musicians and the pottery shards all lay waiting on a tray.

Quentin expelled his breath in a long, low whistle. 'I apologise. You *do* have something to be excited about.' He tossed his hat into a corner and ran his hands over his hair before seating himself at the table and picking up the horse. 'Go and get the lemonade,' he directed her not very politely, as he turned the horse in his fingers, examining it carefully.

The lemonade arrived. Zoë picked up the jug, poured out a glass and set it by his elbow. 'It's good lemonade, and freshly made today. It won't do you any harm.' She wished she had not sounded so admonishing, because her voice resembled that of a nursery governess, and she half expected Quentin to say so.

But he nodded, and looking up from the pottery horse, smiled pleasantly at her. 'Oh, I've been drinking a lot of that stuff lately. I'm slowly getting used to it.' The smile broadened into a grin which had a faintly conspiratorial look about it.

Zoë supposed it was some sort of joke that had to do with her having poured away his whisky on their journey. She could not really imagine Quentin, left to his own devices, sinking glasses of lemonade in place of his habitual stronger beverages. But the grin unsettled her, and gave her a peculiar quivering feeling in the pit of her stomach.

On arrival, he had looked untidy and travel-stained,

but that was only to be expected after a long pony-ride on a dusty road in the heat of the day. Now that he had brushed off the dust and wiped the perspiration from his forehead, he presented quite a respectable appearance —in fact, for Quentin, remarkably so. But then he could do so, if he wished. On the night of the Lintons' dinner party, he had looked quite impressive. Looking at him now critically, she saw that he was clean shaven, and appeared to have had a haircut. The unruly auburn curls were cropped short. His outer clothing was creased from the journey, but that, too, was a superficial matter, and the suit had almost certainly been well pressed when he set out.

He had come to call on ladies, and had obviously made a special effort. Zoë decided it was out of respect for Eve. He did respect Eve. It was one of the few points in his favour, and she did not flatter herself he had made any attempt to appear well-groomed because of *her*. However, a slight uneasiness came over her at the sight of that handsome face, with its distinctive, irregular features and sun-scorched skin. The blue eyes rested disconcertingly on her, and there was a mischievous gleam in their depths. Suspicion reared its head in her breast, a suspicion that he might just have done all this to tease her!

She set the jug down with a thump which caused the lemonade to splash over the side, and declared rather inhospitably, 'Well, you can help yourself, if you want any more.'

Eve looked startled at her sister's aggressive tone, and pushed the bridge of her spectacles further up her nose to peer curiously at Zoë, who struck her as unaccountably flushed. Eve pursed her lips and glanced across the table at Quentin. She looked thoughtful, but made no comment.

Quentin took his time examining the pieces, while the two women sat impatiently opposite, fearing to disturb him by asking questions which almost burned their lips. Zoë watched his long, lean sunburned fingers gently turning the objects this way and that. His forehead was furrowed in concentration; he was completely absorbed, and seemed oblivious of their presence. Zoë was reminded of her father, who would have been equally fascinated by the find. It was strange, she thought, to find that such an unlikely person as Quentin Farrell should have anything in common with her respectable, academic father, yet watching him now, she had a feeling that he and her father would probably have hit it off famously.

Unexpectedly, Quentin looked up and saw her hazel eyes, sparkling with suppressed impatience, fixed on him. He grinned. 'You've got a smudge of garden mud on your nose,' he informed her helpfully.

Zoë rubbed the end of her nose vigorously, and urged, 'Oh, do come *on*! Do you know what they are?'

'Well,' he said cautiously, 'I think I know what they are.' He set down the lady mandoline-player. 'I think they're tomb figures, made for burial with some important person, rather as the Egyptians used to do. Possibly the garden covers the site of a long-lost and forgotten burial. It's possible—because these are very old, at least a thousand years, and I'd guess date from the Tang dynasty. But I'd like a second opinion, and, with your permission, I could send the musical ladies and the horse down to Canton for an expert to see.' He paused. 'They could be extremely valuable. Who knows about them?'

'Only us,' Zoë told him, 'and Chang and his family. Perhaps some of the girls. Green Jade knows.'

'I'm not worried about Green Jade. But I am worried about Chang. Stop him digging. The vegetables will have to wait. These are more important, and I don't want him smashing a mattock through some larger piece which might be there. Some of these pottery shards have clean, newly broken edges. Chang's doing, I expect. Oh, and if anything more does turn up, don't try and clean it with soap and scrubbing-brush. I see you've sensibly left these. They're frail, and there's not much paint left on them. A good going-over with carbolic is the last thing they need.' He pushed the tray away. 'I've come to lunch,' he reminded them pointedly.

'I'll go and tell cook,' Eve said, getting up.

When they were alone, Quentin leaned back in his chair, and asked, 'Well, Zoë? How is it going? Possible treasure troves aside, that is.'

'Very well,' Zoë said. 'No bandits, no disasters. Everyone thinks I'm very odd, but harmless.'

'*I* think you're very odd,' he said, 'but I don't think you're harmless.'

Zoë decided to play his frank manner of comment back to him. 'You know,' she said carefully, 'since you first set eyes on me, I have had the feeling you set out to wage some kind of campaign against me personally. I can't think you are as rude to every woman as you are to me. You don't speak to Eve in that way.'

'What about you?' he returned coolly. 'Couldn't I say the same thing to you? You took one look at me and decided I was some sort of savage.'

Uncomfortably, she said, 'That was different. You looked so—wild, and were very rude, even on the ship.'

'I was surprised.' He swept the little pile of red dust from the table into a neat heap with his fingers as if this were an exercise requiring his entire concentration. 'I never said you were not a very attractive woman. I said you were a nuisance, and so you are.'

'There, you see? Why? Why am I a nuisance, and Eve not? Don't tell me it's anything to do with my being a teacher, because Eve says you've been a pillar of support to the school.'

He looked mildly embarrassed, and muttered, 'Not by choice. It was thrust upon me, as you were. Did you ever meet the Mortons? They were a pair of raving lunatics, and I was glad to see the back of them. Morton nearly got himself lynched when he first came here. I had to go and rescue the stupid idiot. Whatever we might think of ancestor-worship—calling it that for want of a better name—common sense should have told the man that it's the core of Chinese life, and it's asking for trouble to go about preaching to the locals that their most sacred traditional duty is nothing but native superstition. Disrespect for the ancestors is a crime in Chinese eyes, and here he was, urging it upon them. Though it may surprise you to hear me say this, I am not without my faith, but how a neurotic fanatic like Morton ever got into Holy Orders baffles me. His wife was nearly as bad. She kept giving me tracts on the demon drink. They both belonged to the "Fire and Brimstone" school, and came straight out here from running a mission for drunken sailors in Wapping.'

'Oh, do stop!' Zoë managed to exclaim, dissolving into laughter despite herself and wiping her eyes of tears of mirth.

'Well, well, so the lady teacher has a sense of humour, beneath that steely façade. You'll need it—especially if the Tiger of Nan-Ling gets his claws into you.' He leaned across the table earnestly, his voice and manner changing. 'Get Eve to go down to Canton with you, Zoë. It's your last chance.'

His face was uncomfortably close to hers. She could mark the lines about his mouth, and the little wrinkles round the blue eyes which seemed to look at her so directly, as if they held a message she was not sure she wanted to read.

'I don't want anything to happen to *you*,' he said softly, and the straight line of his mouth curved imperceptibly at the corners, and she could glimpse the teeth which looked so white aginst the sun-bronzed skin. 'You know I think that would be a waste.' Seeing her face alter, the mirth leaving it abruptly and the determined set of her lips, he added in his more usual, aggressive manner—which she was beginning to suspect was a form of self-defence—'I'm a normal man, my dear, and it's all a part of life—or don't any of your books deal in real life? But you know what I'm talking about, don't you?' Now he was insulting!

'I find your fashion of talking quite unacceptable, Mr Farrell. *If* I have ever given you any reason to form the curious impression of me which you seem to cherish, I assure you I did not do it intentionally.'

He shrugged. 'You don't have to intend it . . . it's there. Why do you think, that last night of our journey, that I was all set to make love to you? Because I thought, then, it was what you wanted. And I'm still not sure that it isn't.'

'You're confusing me with Mrs Linton!' was the decidedly waspish reply, and he knew he had touched on a chink in her armour. But it was a chink in his own armour, also.

'Leave Emily out of this!' Quentin said sharply. 'All right, fair enough, I don't need another lecture. You've made your feelings clear. But if you don't want *me* in your bed, I suspect you want even less to lie in the arms of any one of Yang's unwashed lieutenants. So, think over my advice.'

Zoë did think about it, and a good deal about him. He was a thoroughly irritating man, with an unsettling way of talking—even though he could, if he chose, behave reasonably well. Unsettling or not, his words had made a deep impression on her. They had received no more alarming news of Yang's horde moving any nearer to the district, yet a kind of elusive unease hovered in the air, as though the countryside and all its inhabitants waited for a storm. So she suggested to Eve that perhaps, after all, Quentin might be right. He had long experience in this country, and he felt they should withdraw temporarily to the safe haven of the British Concession in Canton. In troubled times, the Chinese were apt to turn on the foreigners in their midst, as in the Boxer rising which Quentin himself had witnessed, and before that, in the Tai-Ping rebellion of half a century before. They certainly would not take steps to protect the school, when protection of their own homes was scarcely to be guaranteed.

Eve listened to all these arguments, then took off her spectacles and shook her head decisively. 'Quentin worries. I, too, have been here some time . . . for seven years, and we've had several such scares. They are endemic to Chinese life. We've even had these bandit chiefs, warlords, come before. Not Yang, admittedly, but others like him. They demand tribute of the towns and villages. Their followers get very drunk, plunder what they can, and move on. None of them has ever bothered us here, at the school. They view all missionaries and western teachers with ill-disguised contempt. We are poor, live plainly, work hard, set store by things they despise, and have no regard for other things they find very important. They think us more than a little mad. As regards the school, they know that here we have nothing but books, which are worthless to them. Besides, they also know that the European powers send soldiers if their own nationals are attacked. If Yang comes, and I doubt that he will, he'll not bother us. I will not stop you going back to Canton, Zoë dear, if you feel unsafe here. But after seven years of alarms and upsets, I sleep soundly in my bed here at school, and I've learned not to over-react to rumours.'

So they stayed. But others were less sanguine. One by one, girls were fetched home from the school by their parents. An astonishing variety of excuses were given for removing the pupil temporarily. Not a single parent breathed the warlord's name, or even hinted at trouble. Each girl was being taken on a visit, to see an elderly relative, to attend a wedding, to escape the hot weather —the excuses were endless. But by the end of another week, only Green Jade and two other girls remained.

So occupied with this rash of departures had the sisters been, that neither had had any time to think about Chang and his discoveries. So when Quentin next rode over, to tell them he had sent the pottery figures to Canton, and to ask if anything further had been found, Eve and Zoë looked at each other in dismay and were forced to admit they didn't know. In fact, neither of them had even seen Chang for two days. A child had come to say that her father was sick, but did not need medicine. They had left it at that.

'What do you mean, you haven't seen him for two days?' Quentin demanded sharply. 'Where does he live?'

'I'll show you,' Zoë offered. 'I was intending to call there anyway, to see how sick he is.'

Quentin muttered something very rude, to the effect that he did not believe in Chang's sudden sickness, but she pretended not to have heard.

Their sudden arrival at Chang's door, however, caused such consternation that Zoë's heart sank like a stone. Something, clearly, was wrong. Chang's wife presented a picture of guilt, and even the children, normally friendly and welcoming, had scampered away and hidden as the round-eyed visitors approached. The woman made a token attempt to prevent them from entering the little dwelling, but Quentin brushed her aside, and ducking his head below the lintel, dived into the dark interior. Zoë followed, stumbling after him.

When her eyes became accustomed to the gloom, she realised they stood in a little room crammed with domestic objects. Hanging from the ceiling, on a level with Quentin's head, was the cradle containing the latest addition to the tribe of children, and on a raised bed on the far side of the room lay the immobile form of the gardener himself.

Quentin called the woman to bring a light, and when she had tremblingly handed him a rushlight, he bent over Chang.

'He *is* sick,' Zoë whispered. 'What's wrong with him?'

Chang stared up at them. His breathing seemed depressed. His eyes, though wide open, were unseeing, focusing neither on them nor on any other object. As the light flickered into them, Zoë saw how dilated the pupils were, and Chang, disturbed, rolled his head and mumbled.

Quentin gave an exclamation of disgust. 'Sick? Rubbish! He's been chasing the dragon—smoking opium. The question is, where did he get the money to pay for it? I'm afraid I can guess the answer.'

Alas, he guessed rightly. Chang, realising that the foreigners thought the useless objects he had dug up of value, had succumbed to temptation. Hastily unearthing everything else he could find, he had bundled the lot into a sack and sent if off with his eldest son to the town, where it had been sold to an unscrupulous dealer for a sum, derisory in regard to the probable value, but considerable to the gardener's poor family. The Tang treasure—if treasure there had been—was lost.

As they walked back to the school, Quentin gave full vent to his anger and frustration. 'Incompetent pair of women! You're worse than useless. Why didn't you watch the confounded man? Two days! Two days, and you accepted a feeble story of sickness without so much as a cursory check! You should have realised straight away what was going on. Anyone with half a brain functioning would have known. Call yourselves educated women? There's never been any link between intellect and common sense, and that's a fact. I doubt you and Eve have enough common sense between you to fill an egg-cup! I should never have trusted you!

'Now, just you listen to me!' Zoë broke in furiously. She stopped in the path and stood before him adamantly blocking further progress. 'How dare you speak to me like that, and blame *us*? Do you think we've nothing to do but watch over Chang? We're running a school here, and that comes first. We've been plagued all the past week by parents appearing out of the blue to take away their daughters. We've had no time for anything else!'

He glowered at her defiant figure. She stood, arms akimbo, like an avenging Fury, her eyes flashing dangerously at him, her dark brown hair tumbled loose of its pins and falling about her flushed face, and her bosom heaving with emotion.

'Hmm,' he said at last, after a considerable pause. 'Well, you're not very bright, but you look magnificent in a temper, so perhaps it's worth it, after all.'

'How dare you!' Zoë cried out, losing control of her remaining composure and her voice, which rose distressingly to a squeak of rage. 'How dare you accuse me of stupidity! You—you ignorant, womanising, ill-mannered wretch!' All her good intentions towards him crumbled, and she hit out at him with her clenched fist in her rage, striking him on the arm.

'You're deuced violent!' he exclaimed, looking down in surprise at his sleeve. 'You nearly floored poor Teddy Linton back in Canton, and now you're attacking me. I never knew a woman like you, except for a pair of lady wrestlers I saw once in Paris. That poor devil you didn't marry in England must have counted himself lucky to escape. What the hell did you do when he jilted you? Black his eye?'

'You are a hateful man . . .' she gasped.

'You mean that I am man, and you hate that,' he retorted promptly. 'I'm not surprised he ditched you. Who wants to be stuck for life with a shrewish virago like you?'

'How, like me?' she threw at him, almost choking.

'You charge about the world on your own, you ride a confounded bicycle up hill and down dale in the middle of China, you've a tongue like a fishwife, and you physically attack anyone who upsets you. What man could hope to cope with all that? You ought to *be* a man!'

'I am managing perfectly well as a woman, thank you!' Zoë shouted at him.

'A woman? I take back all I said. You haven't a single feminine quality to your name! I don't know how you ever came to take my fancy that night by the temple. It must have been dashed dark! I thought you were a woman then, but I must have been wandering in my wits!'

'For your information, a woman does not have to be forever fainting away or reading fashion magazines like Emily Linton!' Zoë yelled.

'Hah! I always suspected you were jealous of poor Emily,' he exclaimed triumphantly. He set off down the path, with his hands in his pockets, and Zoë, exhausted and temporarily silenced, was forced to walk in his tracks, refusing obstinately to hurry and catch him up. Any man with any manners would have *waited*.

After a moment, he glanced over his shoulder to where she followed a little way behind, and said, 'If Yang isn't coming, why have all those girls been removed from the school? Let's see how you manage when the Tiger of Nan-Ling gets here. I can't wait to see how you'll deal with him!'

This time, he really had silenced her.

CHAPTER SIX

'I BEG YOUR pardon for intruding, Mrs Linton. I had hoped to find your husband.' Captain Hansen waved a sheaf of bills of lading in the air as a visible explanation of his presence.

The woman on the wicker *chaise-longue* stirred and held out one plump, well-tended white hand to him in a graceful gesture. 'Dear Captain Hansen, how nice to see you once more before you leave us again. Edward won't be long. He went down to the *hong*, and will be back by half past at the latest, I'm sure.' Emily smiled up at her visitor engagingly. 'I usually take tea at this time of the afternoon. Won't you join me? If you don't, I shall be forced to take tea alone.' A plaintive note echoed in her voice, and her pretty, lack-lustre face was turned up towards him like a trusting kitten's.

The Captain flushed. 'Thank you, ma'am, I will. Kind of you . . .' He seated himself on a nearby chair and cleared his throat awkwardly.

A Chinese houseboy entered on silent bare feet and set out the tea-things. Hansen watched his hostess pour it out, her neat hands with their polished pink nails deftly handling the fragile porcelain.

'Not much in my line, drinking tea, ma'am. I'm something of an old sea-dog, I'm afraid,' he apologised.

'Oh, come, Captain Hansen! You cannot describe yourself as "old". I doubt you are above forty.' Emily raised one of those childlike little hands and shook a roguish finger at him.

He blushed like a schoolboy. He was forty-two. He sometimes told his shaving mirror that he did not look so bad . . . for a man who'd spent his life at sea. But he was pleased and flattered to hear a well-bred English lady say it, and especially Mrs Linton. He had long admired her, and he suspected she had guessed it. He was romantic enough to hope that she had, and prudish enough to be highly alarmed at the idea. She was a pretty woman who had a helpless way with her which appealed to him, for he had a sentimental streak and an old-fashioned view of what was 'feminine'. Modern women, energetic and emancipated, like Miss Hammond, for example— pleasant girl though she was—filled him with disapproval. A woman's place was in the home, not running about the world unchaperoned.

Hansen was a very moral man, and proud of it. Some people, had they known of his gun-running activities, might have been puzzled by the apparent contradiction in this. But that would have been to misunderstand the Captain's point of view. Put simply, he came of that generation which believed the European had a right to trade in the Orient as and when he liked, and in whatsoever commodity he chose. The opium-runners of the early 1800s had thought likewise, seeing nothing wrong in founding their fortunes on corruption and decay. Hansen drew the line at opium (classing it with drink as a moral weakness), but guns were another matter. The market was there, eager to buy. If scrupulous, honest men such as himself did not supply it, other, unscrupulous, traders would. If it meant circumventing the customs and the law, that was because the laws were made by politicians, a race of men for whom Captain Hansen had nothing but contempt, convinced that most of them lacked moral fibre.

For the rest, he was an easy-going man, happy in his profession, but admitting to feeling a little lonely on occasion, when his ship returned home and no one stood on the quayside to welcome him. He disliked and distrusted Edward Linton profoundly, but was obliged to do business with him. That was a fact of business life.

Mrs Linton, however, was quite another matter.

Balancing his saucer on his broad, bronzed hand, he said regretfully, 'Fact is, ma'am, I don't have a home life ashore. To sit and take tea with you, like this, is a very pleasant change for me. Very pleasant.'

'Have you no house of your own, Captain?'

He set down the fragile cup and saucer carefully. The china was painted with rosebuds, and he regarded it approvingly. Whenever he had imagined himself in a domestic interior of his own, he had seen it filled with rosebud china, polished brass knicknacks, a fire in the hearth, his favourite briar pipe, and a pretty wife clinging to him for his manly support.

'I do have a house, Mrs Linton, and a sad, empty place it is. No wife about it, you see. I've never had the good fortune to find a woman ready to wed Nils Hansen. I'm a poor catch, I suppose, being away at sea so much. A wife would be lucky to catch a glimpse of me between voyages!'

'I'm sure you would make any woman very happy,' Emily said fervently. 'You're a fine man, and any woman would be lucky.'

Hansen took out a handkerchief and mopped his moustache, damp with tea. He stared thoughtfully at his hostess. 'You don't find this a disagreeable climate, ma'am?' he asked suddenly. 'I can't say I'd care to bring a woman out here.'

'That is because *you* are a kind and thoughtful man. Edward feels my place is here. I do find the climate trying, though perhaps that wouldn't matter so much, if Edward . . .' She broke off, allowing her voice to trail away sadly, and averting her eyes from his concerned expression. 'I don't complain, Captain.'

'You need not explain it to me,' he said quietly. 'I understand your situation, ma'am. Now, I'm a frank man, and like to put my cards on the table. To come between husband and wife is not my way. It's something no man should do. But if your situation should get worse . . .'

'Worse? How could it get worse?' Emily almost screamed. 'It's already a living hell!'

Aloud she said, 'My dear friend . . .' and leaned forward to touch the back of his hand briefly with her fingertips. 'I wouldn't place my burdens on your kind shoulders, because I know you've always been a friend to me, and I appreciate it, very deeply. But you should know that my marriage is quite dead. My husband—my husband cares only for his business. I've done my best to be a good wife, but I've reached the point now where I know I've failed, and have to admit my marriage is finished. It exists in name only.'

She had made a slip which almost cost her the game.

'You and your husband have a child, twelve months of age,' he pointed out a trifle reproachfully.

He was no fool, Emily thought to herself. A marriage which produced a child had to exist in something more than name. That the child was Quentin's was something Hansen did not know. She could neither confess that, nor deny that Edward still came to her bed. She sought to repair the damage, and did it by resorting, for once, to the truth.

'When I say "in name", Captain Hansen, I am talking of affection, of understanding. Those things are part of a marriage, too. My husband has long forgotten them, but he does not forget his "rights" . . .'

The bitter note in her voice was unfeigned, a genuine note of wretchedness. If Hansen was shocked and embarrassed by the unspoken implication, let him be. No one knew what it was like, and had been like for years. Edward hated and despised her. He took his pleasure in tormenting her, and the greatest torment of all came in the form of his unwanted caresses. She cringed beneath his advances, and he knew it. Often he came to her drunk, and never in love or affection. He only ever demanded, claiming it his right, mauling her roughly about, seeking only to satisfy his own urges and never caring for her. He left her feeling used and sullied.

Hansen was staring fiercely down at the rosebud-decorated tea-things, frowning as he wrestled with the dilemma which confronted him. Linton was a brute, leading the poor woman a wretched life, forcing his attentions on her when she did not wish it. But he was still her husband . . .

He cleared his throat and looked up, and she was startled at the firmness and resolution in his face. 'See here, Emily. It's wrong you should have to suffer like this, but the man is your husband, and while he is, I'll respect the fact, no matter what thoughts I may have on the subject. I'll not take a wife from her husband. But if the rogue should desert you, or turn you out, then you have my word, you may depend on Nils Hansen. He'll not fail you.'

'Dear Nils,' Emily breathed, tears in her eyes. 'You are a tower of strength. I feel as though I have been shipwrecked, and you offer a rock to which I can cling.'

The sea-going metaphor affected Hansen deeply, as did the tears. But he had his principles, and was obstinate enough not to be shifted from them, even now. He stood up and picked up his cap.

'I sail soon. My ship is at your disposal, and any protection I may offer you. But Linton must let you go freely. There must be no skulduggery in it. He must agree.' He bowed politely to her. 'Thank'ee for the tea, m'dear.'

She watched him go in a mixture of hope and desperation. He was her last and only chance. He had meant every word he had said, *every* word. He would be her refuge, but *only* if Edward let her go. A divorce. Edward must agree to divorce her. But would he? He had often threatened a divorce when he had known how friendless she had been, how terrified of being cast out alone. But now that she wanted a divorce, it would be just Edward's fancy to refuse it. Emily lay back on the *chaise-longue*, heedless of the servant who came to clear the tea-table. And there was the child. Supposing Quentin tried to find her for the sake of his child? Suppose Hansen discovered that the child was not Linton's, but the fruit of an adulterous liaison with the most notorious remittance-man in South China?

The chance of escape was there, like a narrow channel leading to the open sea, but beset on all sides by treacherous quicksands.

When Zoë entered the classroom, two of the three remaining pupils were peeping surreptitiously through the windows, whispering together excitedly, and quite oblivious of her entry.

'Now, what's going on?' she demanded severely. 'What's so very interesting out there that you leave your desks and your books? I know that there are only three of you left, but that doesn't mean that lessons stop. Where is Green Jade?'

The two at the window turned their charming young faces, glowing with excitement, towards her. 'It is the honourable Controller of the Salt Revenue, it is the mandarin Wu Feng!' they chorused in answer to her question. 'It is the father of Green Jade!'

Startled, Zoë peered out of the window over their heads, forgetting dignity and good manners in a frank curiosity. There, before the school, stood a sumptuous sedan chair painted in red and green, the colours of importance. The carriers squatted in the shade, resting, and a solitary soldier, a token escort, loitered by the door.

'Back to your books!' Zoë ordered firmly. She had not heard the arrival of the illustrious visitor and supposed him to be in Eve's study. She sighed. So Green Jade, too, was to be taken away. She wondered what excuse the Salt Controller would give—a visit to a summer-house in the hills or a grandmother's funeral?

Zoë tried to continue teaching for another ten minutes, but her two pupils were inattentive and fidgety. They kept exchanging knowing glances. They knew, or had guessed, more about this visit than their teacher, that was certain, and something other than a simple fetching-home seemed to be in the air. Zoë clapped her hands to secure their wandering attention and then dismissed them with instructions to go and read quietly somewhere. They pattered away on their tiny feet, giggling and whispering. It was very annoying, and very mysterious.

Putting away her books, she stood for a moment in thought. Then she made her way slowly towards Eve's study. But before she had quite reached it, the door flew unexpectedly open and Green Jade appeared. She stood for a brief second, staring wildly at Zoë, an expression of despair on her face, and then ran precipitously past her without a word of greeting or explanation, and vanished into the classroom behind. Forgetting Eve and her visitor, Zoë hastened after the fleeing girl.

She found her huddled in a corner of the classroom, wet streaks of tears staining her pretty face, and her black hair tumbling loose from the silver pins which held it.

'Green Jade?' Zoë asked softly. She knelt down by the distraught girl and gently took her hand. 'What is it?'

'My honourable father is here . . .' Green Jade whispered.

'Yes, I know.' Zoë frowned. 'I expect he's come to take you home. Is that it? There's no need to cry. As soon as all this fuss and bother about—about possible trouble is over, you'll come back, and all the other girls, too.'

Green Jade shook her head. 'They will come, but I

shall not. Oh, Miss Hammond, my father has come to tell me I am to be married.'

'*Married?*' Zoë exclaimed. 'To whom?'

'To the son of General Li.' Tears began to trickle down Green Jade's cheeks. 'It is all arranged.'

'Now, wait!' Zoë urged her. 'When is this marriage to take place? Has no one asked you what you think? What about the son of General Li? Do you know him?'

'My father has arranged it,' Green Jade told her. 'I know the son of General Li. It is Li Kim, he is a student in Canton.'

A bell rang in Zoë's memory. What had Quentin said? Something about the son of General Li?

'Don't you like Li Kim, Green Jade?'

'Oh, Li Kim is all right,' she said miserably. 'And I should be grateful I am to be married to a young man and not to an old one. But I don't want to be married at all, not *yet*. I so wanted to be a teacher.'

'Now you are not to cry!' Zoë said hastily, seeing the tears welling up again. She pulled out her own handkerchief and gently mopped them from the girl's lashes. 'I shall talk to your father . . .'

Green Jade shook her head vigorously. 'You cannot. He has given his word to General Li, and I must obey. My father is a good, kind man, and believed I would be happy. But I am so unhappy!'

A scuffle at the door betrayed the presence of Green Jade's two fellow pupils, who had come to satisfy their curiosity. Zoë called them, before they could run away, and instructed them to take Green Jade upstairs and help her to wash her face and tidy her hair. Then she patted her own hair, straightened her skirts, and walking briskly to the study door, rapped on it in a businesslike manner.

Eve was seated behind her desk, a personification of a Victorian head-mistress with her straight grey hair bundled into a knot and her spectacles. The frozen severity of her features relaxed enough to betray an expression of relief, as Zoë said, 'Green Jade has gone to tidy up.' She nodded, and indicating Zoë to a personage seated opposite to her, said, 'My sister, who has come to help us here. This is the honourable Controller of the Salt Revenue, Zoë—Wu Feng.' Beneath her breath, she added, 'And a very important man!' The last words were a thinly veiled warning.

Zoë turned, and with a mixture of awe and astonishment, beheld someone who might have stepped from some ancient tale of the East. Wedged none too comfortably into a leather armchair, Wu Feng wore a round hat with his mandarin's button of rank, and sumptuous silk robes. He had been fanning himself slowly with a carved ivory fan, but as Zoë turned, he closed it in the same slow and dignified manner, and slid it into the wide sleeve of his coat. He looked so very splendid, and yet so incongruous in the setting of the little book-lined study, that Zoë could only stare at him for a moment, before she rallied and said, 'I am very pleased to meet you, Mr Wu.'

Wu Feng's eyebrows twitched a fraction but he made no reply, except to incline his head slightly in acknowledgment of her salutation.

'Does . . . ?' Zoë glanced at Eve hastily for guidance.

'Mr Wu speaks excellent English,' her sister said woodenly. She contributed nothing further. She was obviously deeply upset, but concealed it beneath an inscrutability the Salt Controller himself might have envied.

Zoë braced herself and addressed the mandarin, who still sat impassively, wedged in the leather armchair. 'I have just seen Green Jade, your daughter,' she began brightly. 'A very intelligent girl, and a great credit to you.'

So far, so good! Wu Feng's expression thawed slightly, and he spoke. 'I am honoured.'

'We, er, are honoured,' Zoë went on, searching in feverish desperation for the right turn of phrase, 'to have the daughter of such an important man in our unworthy school.'

Eve looked startled, and opened her mouth. But then she closed it again, and looked apprehensively at her sister.

Wu Feng slowly withdrew his hands from the wide sleeves of his silk coat and tapped the ends of his fingers together. His long, silvered nails gleamed in the light. Zoë was momentarily distracted enough to wonder what had become of the ivory fan, which had disappeared into the sleeve like a conjuring trick.

'I am pleased,' Wu said graciously, 'at the education my daughter has received.'

'Then you will appreciate,' Zoë went on, 'how important it is for that education to be in the reach of others.'

The mandarin's tapping fingers stilled. 'I have contributed,' Wu Feng said coldly, 'to the finances of your school.'

'Yes, and very generously, but that's not what I meant!' Zoë spoke hastily. 'Mr Wu, not only money, but teachers are desperately needed. You must know that Green Jade would like to study at a teacher-training college. She is particularly suitable . . .'

Wu Feng hissed. His whole form seemed to stiffen, and from a benevolent, rotund yet impressive figure, like a well-dressed Buddha, he became all at once a dominating and very alarming one. 'My daughter is to be married!' he said abruptly. 'It is not my wish that she become a teacher.'

'But surely Green Jade herself should be asked . . .' Zoë began disastrously.

'Zoë!' Eve said quickly in warning, but too late.

The figure of Wu Feng seemed to swell. 'I have not sent my only child to your school, Miss Hammond, to learn disobedience, or to show disrespect to the parents she should honour and obey.'

'But it isn't disobedience,' Zoë cried. 'Surely, Mr Wu, as a father, you wouldn't wish to force your daughter into a marriage against her will?'

Wu Feng rose from the leather armchair with a majesty no one who had seen how tightly his portly form had fitted into it would have thought possible. Every line of his ample form expressed outraged dignity. His eyes bulged like those of a carved warrior deva, and so little did he conceal his anger that flames might have been expected to burst forth from his mouth when he spoke. 'I shall send for my daughter,' he said icily, 'later!' He swept magnificently out of the study without another word.

'Oh, my dear,' Eve said with a sigh. She took off her spectacles with a tired gesture, and passed her hand over her forehead. 'I'm dreadfully afraid you have caused him to "lose face". His dignity has been harmed, and he'll never go back on his decision now. He cannot. A woman—and a foreigner—telling him he has been wrong! He cannot do it.'

Zoë's heart sank. 'But I didn't mean . . . Then how am I to discuss it with him, if I can't tell him my viewpoint, even in the politest way, to his face?'

Eve shrugged. 'The Chinese approached all these matters in a very labyrinthine way. In this case, I doubt we can do anything. It's a family matter. Possibly if someone else, an intermediary, could communicate our point of view to Wu Feng . . . But, even so, he will have given his word to General Li.'

'General Li!' Zoë cried out. 'Quentin! Quentin knows General Li. Quentin can help. He understands Chinese ways, and it is to the son of General Li that Green Jade is to be married. I'll ask him to intercede.'

'I really don't think it would be wise,' Eve protested.

'Well, I'm certainly not going to accept such a situation without trying!' Zoë told her vigorously. 'I'll bicycle to Quentin's house, if you will tell me the way there.'

'I'll send Chang with you, if you are so determined.' Eve hesitated. 'Zoë, do be careful!'

'I shall be very careful, but everyone knows me and my bicycle by now, so you mustn't worry. I will be perfectly safe.'

'I meant,' Eve said, 'take care how you explain it all to Quentin.'

Since his escapade with the Tang treasure, Chang had been somewhat subdued. Had the school placed accusations of theft before his own local magistrates, their reaction might well have been to slice off both his ears, so he was suitably grateful to receive a stern warning from his employers, and anxious to make amends. He trotted alongside Zoë's bicycle, keeping pace easily enough for the track was heavily rutted, and progress, even by bicycle, was slow. In fact, Zoë thought ruefully, it might be altogether easier to walk. But that would be considerably less impressive than arriving by 'flying wheel'.

It was already early afternoon and by no means the best time of day to begin any journey, however short. Zoë was soon aware that it would be late in the afternoon before she could hope to reach Quentin's house, she would be exhausted, and there was little likelihood that she would be able to make the return ride the same day. She had not thought about this before setting out, so full had her head been of her mission, but now she realised how hasty and imprudent her arrival must look, so late, without so much as a toothbrush, and an obvious requirement to be put up overnight. She had no idea whether Quentin's household was geared to the reception of single ladies who required bed and board. She doubted it. Not respectable single ladies, anyway. That was another thought which suddenly struck her and caused her to swerve violently into the road. Single European men often set up house with native concubines. Perhaps Quentin . . . No, Eve would have mentioned it, she thought.

All the same, it would have been far more sensible to have stayed at the school and sent Chang with a note requesting Quentin to ride over on his pony. But, as Quentin had rightly said, she had rushed in without thinking, and having started out so boldly, could not now turn back.

But it was a tiring and dusty ride. There was little or no shade, and very few people were to be seen. Once they passed some kerchiefed women working on the terraced fields on the low slope of the hillside, and once a pedlar travelling in the opposite direction, who set down his pack to turn and stare after her, open-mouthed. After that, they saw no one else for an hour, until they stopped to rest by a ruined shrine.

It was one of the many to Kwan Yin, whose worm-eaten wooden statue, dry and bereft of paint, still stood in the spider-infested interior. Half-burned joss-sticks lay on the dust- and bird-dropping-covered altar, so the occasional traveller or peasant on his way to market still sought to bring himself good fortune and the goddess's blessing, despite the state of the shrine. Zoë pushed the bicycle into the shade of the crumbling building and propped it up, then looked about her. A few trees, stunted and almost leafless, grew out of the rocky soil, and behind them the land rose gently in an escarpment to a long, straight ridge that ran parallel with the road. Chang had squatted down thankfully on his heels under the eaves of the tumble-down shrine and was wiping his perspiring brow with a spotted bandana. Zoë looked along the dusty road, shimmering in the heat, and lifting her gaze, let it run along the ridge on the horizon.

It was then that she saw the rider. How long he had

been there, she did not know. But he must have been sitting and watching the road below him for some minutes, quite motionless, and especially watching the progress of herself and Chang. Though he was quite a way from her, she could make him out quite clearly in the afternoon sunshine, standing as she did in the shade. He was a thickset man in a dirty cotton uniform of vaguely military style, and with his head bound in a turban. She had an impression of coarse, flat features and a skin burned nut brown by the sun, before the rider raised the rifle in his hand in a gesture which might have been either a salute or a warning, and jerking on the reins of his shaggy little pony, disappeared abruptly over the ridge.

Clearly, he had been as startled to see her, and the bicycle, as she was to see him. Alone, he was uncertain what to do, unwilling to investigate further, and had ridden off, either to relay the information or to enlist support. An unpleasant sensation of unease gripped Zoë's stomach, and a premonition of danger. The rural Chinese were by nature curious, and a *bona fide* traveller, of whatever calling, would have ridden down to inspect the extraordinary vision of a European lady and a 'flying wheel' in the middle of nowhere, and to ask a dozen questions.

She spun round and glanced at Chang. But the gardener had noticed nothing, sitting with his back turned to the ridge. 'We're going on!' she told him briskly. 'Come along, I want to get to Mr Farrell's house.'

Chang began to grumble, protesting about the heat and his weariness, but she mounted the bicycle without waiting to listen, and wobbled off down the track as fast as possible, so that he was obliged to set off after her, saving his breath for the pursuit.

At long last, he gave a shout, and pointed ahead. Zoë, who had several times glanced nervously at the now empty skyline, saw some buildings, a village of sorts, and beyond that a high wall.

'The Red Bristles!' Chang announced triumphantly. He led her up to a round gateway in the wall (evil spirits had a noted dislike of round shapes and would not pass through), and shouted for the gate-keeper.

An old man hobbled out of his cottage and stared at Zoë blankly with rheumy eyes. Probably he thought the sight of her so extraordinary that it must be a figment of his imagination. But Chang harangued him at length, and she was eventually escorted down a long, neatly raked path through a luxuriant garden. It was kept well watered by an ingenious arrangement of streams linking ponds of fish and filled from the distant river. Chang pushed the bicycle along behind her, as they wound their way through the massed rhododendrons and beds of flowers, until the bushes parted and Quentin's house lay before her.

Although she had been expecting something quite fine, she was scarcely prepared for the sight she beheld now. It was a huge, sprawling, yet graceful building, or series of buildings, for it was composed of interlocking pavilions. The roofs were curved in the Chinese style, and the sun sparkled on the coloured glazes of the tiles, turquoise and sea-green, rust and pink. Another gateway had to be passed through, with its own tiled, curly roof, surmounted by a pair of armour-clad glazed warriors, and they were in a paved courtyard, surrounded by the pavilions, cool and mysterious, with their latticed windows of intricate design. A fountain played in the centre of the courtyard, flinging its silver spray into the air, and splashing down with a musical ripple into the carved soapstone basin.

As she stood there, wide-eyed in wonder, a voice behind her said, 'Well, welcome to my home. I hadn't expected to see *you* here! I must have done something to please the gods at last.'

Zoë turned, realising that she must look very untidy, dusty and shiny with perspiration, and that her clothes were creased and damp.

Quentin's tall form was framed in a nearby doorway, looking relaxed and smiling at her. 'Come in,' he said. 'Would you like a drink first, or a wash?'

'A drink, please,' she said, adding, 'water.'

'I, too, can supply lemonade,' he said cheerfully. 'I told you. The place is awash with the stuff these days. It's coming out of my ears!'

A little later, much refreshed and cleaner, she sat opposite Quentin at the dinner-table, and between the courses of an excellent meal, related the events that had brought her. When she had completed her tale, she fell silent and waited expectantly for his comment. Outside, the sun was going down, touching the house and garden with rosy fingers. Quentin, who had sat silent throughout her recital, stirred at last and pushed back his chair with a scrape on the tiled floor.

'Why are you telling *me* all this?' There was a cool note in his voice which rang uncomfortably on her ear.

'You are acquainted with General Li,' Zoë said, a little defiantly. 'Perhaps you even know Wu Feng?'

'Yes, I've met Wu Feng. He's a most distinguished, enlightened and respected official. There are few like him in China. Would there were more!'

'Will you talk to him? To them both?' she asked. 'Explain to them that Green Jade doesn't want to be married. She doesn't mean to be disrespectful or disobedient, but she does want to be a teacher. You are the only person I know who can do it. Will you?'

Quentin drew a deep breath. 'No, I won't do it.'

Zoë's mouth fell open. 'Why?' she faltered.

'Because it's none of my business—nor is it yours.'

'It is my business!' she said mutinously. 'Green Jade is my pupil. I care what happens to her, and if she's unhappy.'

'I like Green Jade, too,' Quentin agreed. 'But that doesn't give me the right to meddle in her family affairs, nor you.' Seeing that she was about to protest further, and a warlike gleam entered her eye, he added, 'Listen to me! No—you've had your chance to speak. Now it's mine, so keep quiet for five minutes if you can, and listen. You're like every woman I've ever met, ready to talk the hind leg off a donkey but incapable of listening for a minute. So just try, will you? Arranging a Chinese marriage is a slow and tortuous business. Enormous care is taken, and the preliminaries can last ages. Detailed horoscopes are cast to see whether the two partners are compatible, and go-betweens are selected to argue out every last detail before the two families meet across the table at all. If the horoscopes agree, and if the inter-mediaries bring back satisfactory answers to all the questions, then, and only then, is the marriage arranged. By that time, much expense, time and "face" has been invested—and it just cannot be cancelled on a whim.'

'I see!' Zoë said sharply. 'So, every precaution is taken, except that of asking the opinion of the prospective bridal pair!'

'They are considered too young and inexperienced to know their own minds, and so accept the advice and decision of their elders, who are wiser and more competent to decide the match. If Wu Feng has settled this marriage for his daughter, nothing short of death, plague or war can stop it. As it happens, I know the boy, Kim. He's a fine youngster who will make an excellent husband, and I cannot see the slightest excuse for interfering. I'm certainly not going to be persuaded, by you, to abuse the friendship General Li has always extended to me, in order to wreck his son's wedding plans.'

Red in the face, Zoë exclaimed furiously, 'I have never in my whole life heard such a blatant example of—of male arrogance! So, *you* know Li Kim and *you* like him, and his father is *your* good friend, and Wu Feng, too. So Green Jade and I can just keep quiet as a pair of respectable, dutiful women should! *We* are not to have opinions. *We* are not have feelings. *We* are to have no say in the matter at all. *We* have no brains in our heads, only cotton-wool!'

'Far be it from me to say so, my dear,' Quentin replied equably.

'You are conceited and self-opinionated!' Zoë exploded. 'Worse, you are cowardly and selfish in your attitude. You will not interfere in a Chinese matter because it may cause you upset and inconvenience.'

'Be quiet!' he thundered. He crashed his fist on the table, so that all the dishes leapt and clattered alarmingly. His blue eyes flashed at her angrily and he had paled beneath his tan. 'Do you think I am the sort of man who weighs his personal advantage against what he thinks is right? If I were, I should not be here now. I should be passing the port to my fellow officers in some remote Indian hill station.'

Zoë bit her lip. It was true. Quentin had sacrificed his army career on a point of personal conviction.

'As it happens,' he went on, 'I think that *you*, Zoë, have an exceptionally good brain. More the pity, then, that it isn't allied to a little natural modesty! That, my dear, is something which wouldn't come amiss in you. *I* am self-opinionated, am I?' He tapped his chest to underline his question, and seemed ready to explode with rage. His voice rang round the room, and the drinking glasses sang in reply. 'Since I first met you, I have been deluged with your opinions on every conceivable subject, but chiefly concerning myself. You have never once asked me for my views. You didn't ask me mine on this occasion. You simply marched in here, told me your tale and requested me blithely just to run over to General Li, and tell him to call off the wedding!'

'Well, I . . .' Zoë stammered, faced with the stark truth of all this. 'I didn't mean it to sound like that.'

'Didn't you? Have you never heard the saying: "The way to hell is paved with good intentions"? So, you do not like some facets of Chinese life. There are things in China I do not like. But the Chinese have been running their own affairs for four thousand years and it does not behove either you, or I, to arrive from the other side of the world and a different culture, and, quite unasked, start telling them what to do! I warned you from the first about trying to change everything, and rushing in where angels fear to tread. You want to help Green Jade, do you? Let's see what you *have* done. You've insulted Wu Feng, an extremely honest, able and important local official. You've probably set him against not only your school, which he has generously supported until now, but everything foreign, to boot. Nothing, now, will make him reconsider his plans for his daughter. As for Green Jade, you have caused her to incur the displeasure of an indulgent father, and as for her ever studying to be a teacher—now, thanks to your efforts, that will be for ever impossible. I trust you are well satisfied, Miss Hammond, and as pleased with yourself as you generally are.'

There was a long silence. 'I wanted to help,' she said in a small voice.

Quentin groaned and ran his hand through his tousled auburn hair. 'Help?'

Rebellion surged through Zoë's veins. 'Yes, help! I admit I went the wrong way about it, but I still don't think I was wrong to try. How can it be wrong to try to help the people you care about? If no one ever tried, nothing would ever be changed for the better. It has to be better than sitting around all day, salving your conscience by drinking whisky!'

As the words left her mouth, she knew instinctively that she had made a fatal mistake. Quentin's expression changed completely. Angry exasperation had been replaced by a cold, white fury, and his blue eyes glittered hard and chill like glacier ice. He stood up and came round the table to stand beside her. Suddenly, he scooped up one of the empty glasses and brandished it under her nose, so that she started back in alarm.

'See this? It's a drinking glass, we used it tonight at dinner, and what was in it? No! Don't scramble back out of the way.' He grasped her shoulder so that she gasped in pain, and pulled her forward. 'What's the matter? Frightened of me, all of a sudden, Miss Hammond? You're not usually lost for a word, so let's have your answer now, loud and clear. What was in the glass?'

'Le—lemonade,' she stammered.

'Have you seen me take a drink of anything stronger since you arrived in this house?'

'No.' Zoë shook her head, truly frightened now, but still not quite understanding what had caused his fury.

'That's right, you haven't. Not only have I not had a drink today, but I've hardly touched a drop since I made that trip up here from Canton with you! Oh, I saw how it disgusted you, my drinking. *I* disgusted you. So, for the first time, I tried, and I fought the craving for whisky. It wasn't easy. I've been drinking for years. But I've sat here these last few weeks, in front of a bottle, and nearly wept sometimes with the sheer agony of not opening it, and of not having a drink. I stuck it out, I persevered, because *you* didn't like it! Can you even imagine what it's like actually to suffer because you want a drink of whisky and you daren't have one, because one leads to another, until you're so blind drunk you don't care any more?'

He was shouting at her now, and shaking her like a puppy with a rag toy. 'Do I really look no different from what I was? Are you blind or stupid, or do you just not want to see that I've tried, curse you? I really tried to change my ways and measure up to your impossible standards!'

Stunned, she could not find words for a moment, then she stammered, 'No, no I didn't . . . I didn't realise, I didn't know. You didn't say.'

'And you didn't even notice,' he said coldly. 'You ice-blooded little witch. You're so wrapped up in your sanctimonious, self-centred little world, organising your pupils' lives, and filling your head and theirs with some kind of impossible code, drawn from a set of books, that you haven't time to live in the real world, with the rest of us poor mortals. We just stumble along in our imperfect way, making mistakes and messing up our lives, wanting and lusting, failing and losing, despairing and struggling. But you, Zoë Hammond, you are judge and jury, you never waver, are never tempted and never fall from a state of perpetual grace!'

'That isn't true!' Zoë cried out shakily. 'I did notice things that you did to—to change your ways, but I didn't think it was for *me*! I didn't think you cared a ha'penny for anything I said!'

'Well, I've stopped caring *now*!' he said harshly. He released her and stepped away from the table. 'It's late, he said brusquely. 'You want a bed for the night, I suppose? Come along, then.'

She followed silently, not daring to speak to him, as he led her through several corridors, until they reached a large and well-appointed bedroom, situated in a separate part of the house, one of the pavilion-like structures of which it was composed. The furniture, ornate and lacquered in the Chinese style, had a pristine and untouched look about it, as though it had never been used. Yet it was all carefully dusted, and the bed was made up and hung round with mosquito-nets. Various ornaments and vases stood about, several of them probably priceless. There was a softness to this room, a mellowness of colour, not seen elsewhere in the house. Zoë thought, 'The women's quarters—this is the pavilion of a favourite wife.' And she knew then where he had brought her.

This beautiful room was designed and furnished for a woman who had never set foot in it, destined for a bride who had never come.

Quentin had turned to her and gestured at the surroundings. 'You should be all right in here, comfortable enough?' His voice was belligerent, as if he challenged her to deny it.

Pale-faced, she said awkwardly, 'Thank you,' feeling the words inadequate.

'Call the servants if you want anything.' He went to the door, and pausing there, added in a quieter voice than he had used all evening, 'I—don't mean to sound as sharp with you as I sometimes do. I have a great deal of admiration for you—for what that's worth in your eyes.' Bitterness touched his voice. He gave her a sardonic smile, and went out.

Alone, she sat down on the edge of the bed, and looked around the empty, luxury-filled room which lay at the core of this house, and perhaps at the core of Quentin's being. It represented a whole chapter of his life—but that chapter, like this room, had been shut away. It had been re-opened for her. She had dared to disturb it. Like Pandora, she had opened a box best left locked and forgotten.

It was as she undressed that she suddenly remembered the rider on the skyline. The memory of him came with quite a jolt. She had intended to tell Quentin about him, but in the evening's upset and arguments, she had forgotten. She would have to tell him in the morning, and see what he made of it.

In her petticoat, Zoë extinguished the light and made her way in the darkness to the bed, looping up the mosquito-nets out of the way, and sliding wearily into its soft depths. Tomorrow, with a new day, things might go better.

She was awoken in the middle of the night by the sound of singing. Someone, and that someone had to be Quentin, was wending his way towards her room, singing very loudly and quite tunefully, but with the haphazard abandonment of the inebriated. She sat up in bed, clasping the sheet to her, as the door flew open and he appeared, slouching at an angle in an ungainly fashion, propping himself up on the doorframe with one hand.

'What are you doing here?' Zoë demanded. 'Go away!'

He pushed himself away from the door and lurched across the room, falling in a sprawling, untidy heap across the end of the bed. She gave a little shriek and scrambled up on to the pillows, as far from him as possible. Quentin managed to get himself upright and stared at her where she sat, huddled at the end of the bed, her knees drawn up under her chin.

'Well, well, the virtuous Miss Hammond! Did I wake you up, my dear?'

'You're drunk!' she said furiously.

'Ah, yes, I'm afraid I am,' he said with dignity. 'You see, I *was* on the wagon, as they say, but I decided . . .' He paused, as drunks do, to take stock of his surroundings, momentarily losing the thread of his speech. In the silvery moonlight, the room, its contents and its occupants, looked unearthly, suspended in time and space, trapped there as in an otherwise silent and hostile world. 'I decided there was no point in signing the Pledge, after all. That woman, Mrs Morton, she was always asking me to sign the Pledge, you know, and abjure the Demon Drink. You see,' he leaned forward, determined to explain it to her, 'I'm a drunken, unshaven wretch, and a fellow like that couldn't think of laying a hand on the lily-white body of Miss Zoë Hammond! So I . . .' He fell silent, then muttered, 'Doesn't matter now. I was sick of all that blasted lemonade, anyway.' Moroseness imbued his voice and his whole being. 'Filthy stuff. Turn a man's stomach over.'

'Quentin!' Zoë urged nervously, because to attract his attention obviously carried its risks. 'You ought to go to bed and sleep it off.'

'You're absolutely right, my dear,' he agreed. He was having a little trouble with his sibilants. 'That's what I've come to do,' he added hoarsely.

'Not here!'

'Why not? Here you are, all alone—which no woman ought to be, not one like you, anyway. So I've come to keep you company.'

With that, he launched himself forward, throwing out his arms and catching her in an ungainly embrace that nearly sent them both falling off the edge of the bed together in a tangle of arms and legs.

'Now don't tell *me*,' he muttered huskily in her ear, 'that you're still harbouring all those old objections against taking a tumble in the sheets with *me*—because I don't believe it. I don't believe the half of it. Come to that, I don't believe any of it! It's all a fraud, a sham! That prissy exterior, that rigid morality, so respectable, Miss Hammond. Let's see how you behave when the respectability wears off!'

His mouth found hers in an uncompromising and brutal embrace which bruised her lips and almost smothered her. She struggled furiously, trying in vain to push him away, and knowing it had the very opposite effect to what she wanted, and that the writhing of her scantily-clad body in his arms served only to encourage the demon which had been set loose in him. He was perspiring in the heat of the night and under the pressure of his own urges, panting as heavily as she did, and so much stronger than she was that there seemed no way she could escape him.

Now they were both entangled in the sheets, and it delayed him and made him swear in frustration. He took one hand away from her to grab at the linen and rip it aside. Zoë took the chance, perhaps the only one, to fling out her hand to secure some grip. It struck against a bedside table, and her scrabbling fingers closed on some small carved soapstone ornament which stood on it. Without thinking, she clutched blindly and automatically on it, scooped up the weapon so unexpectedly put in her hand, and lunged out with it at him as he bent over her.

There was a sickening thud as it cracked against his skull. He made an odd sound between a gasp and a cry, and released her, rolling over on to his back, and was still.

The silence was oppressive, seeming to quiver with the vibrations of violent emotions. For a terrible, stomach-churning moment, Zoë thought she had killed him. She scrambled up on to her hands and knees, and bent over his immobile body.

'Quentin?'

He was breathing, thank God! She could hear him. She reached out a trembling hand and touched his hair. Something warm and sticky clung to her fingers and almost caused her heart to fail.

'What have I done?' she whispered in horror.

Quentin stirred, throwing up his arm and striking her hand away. 'Leave it!' he said faintly.

'But it's bleeding! Let me get some water!' She slid off the bed and ran across the dark room to the washstand. When she came back with a wet cloth, he was sitting on the edge of the bed, his bowed head clasped in his hands. 'Quentin, let me wipe the blood away, please,' she begged him, kneeling on the floor in front of him and trying to take away the hand he held pressed to the wound.

'I said, leave it alone, confound you!' he shouted, and

pushed her away roughly. His voice echoed about the room, ringing in the corners of the ceiling. 'Give me that cloth,' he added, more quietly.

By some miracle, he seemed to have sobered up completely, the shock of her unexpected attack restoring sanity to his befuddled brain. Silently she handed the cloth to him, and he pressed it against the side of his head to stanch the blood. 'It's nothing,' he said hoarsely. 'Only a cut on the scalp. Leave me with a sore head for a day or two, that's all.'

'I wouldn't have done it,' she whispered; 'If you hadn't—insisted. I thought, I thought you meant . . .'

'What? To rape you? That might have given one of us some satisfaction but it wouldn't have been me!' He stood up, and she cowered back instinctively on the floor. 'It's all right,' he said brusquely. 'I'm not going through all that again. I'd forgotten what an Amazon you were.'

There was a faint noise and a movement on the further side of the room, and Zoë saw, startled, that a third person had joined them. A Chinese man-servant, elderly and immensely dignified, emerged from the shadows holding a small oil-lamp. He bowed politely, seemingly oblivious of the rumpled bed and disordered dress of the two people by it, and took his master's sleeve, talking quietly and persuasively.

Quentin nodded, threw down the blood-stained cloth, and lurched out of the room. The man-servant bowed again to Zoë. 'Not worry, missee. Not hurt you. Only drink whisky very much, shout very loud, say he do many things he not do. He very wild. But not hurt you. He not hurt anyone.'

He bowed politely for a third time and went out, and Zoë could hear him escorting his master away.

CHAPTER SEVEN

'LET ME read it,' begged Graceful Willow, adding in a wheedling tone, 'please?'

'No,' Li Kim said firmly, rolling up his love poem and returning it to the bamboo tube in which he kept it.

'Pah, I shall tell Green Jade anyway. I shall tell her you have written a very long and bad poem.'

'Listen,' Kim urged his young sister, 'I want you to take the poem to Green Jade.'

Graceful Willow bit her lower lip and eyed him appraisingly from beneath her silky fringe of black hair. 'Then I shall read it together with her, and we'll both laugh over it,' she retorted.

Kim controlled his temper with difficulty. Graceful Willow had him at her mercy, and knew it. 'Then I shall keep it here, safe,' he said with dignity, 'and neither of you shall read it at all.'

Graceful Willow stacked up the counters of the board-game they had been playing. 'She doesn't want you. She doesn't like you!' she said spitefully.

'You are very badly behaved!' Kim retorted. 'Is that the respect you should show to an elder brother?'

'I think you are very unkind not to show me your poem first,' said Graceful Willow unrepentantly. 'Didn't I spend one whole afternoon telling Green Jade how clever you were, just to impress her? Not that it did, but it impressed fat old Wu Feng.'

'That,' exploded Kim, red with anger and embarrassment, 'is no way to speak of the honourable Controller of the Salt Revenue. What, exactly, did you say to him?' he added in agony.

'I can't remember,' Graceful Willow murmured vaguely, adding demurely, 'respected elder brother.'

'When the time comes that our father finds you a husband,' he said with feeling, 'I hope he finds one who is old, miserly, bad-tempered and pock-marked. I hope you are a second, or even better, a third wife, and both the senior wives make you run round all day, looking after them.'

Graceful Willow burst into tears, which she did very easily. But possibly this time with some reason, for such a situation was not unknown in China at that time. 'I shan't take your silly poem to Green Jade, so there! I can't see why you are so worried. Everything is arranged, and you'll marry her anyway.'

'No,' Kim said quietly. 'I won't.'

Graceful Willow's tears dried as if by magic, and she gaped at him.

'I won't force her to marry me,' Kim repeated, 'if she doesn't want me. I wouldn't do that to Green Jade. I—I respect her too much.'

'You can't refuse!' whispered Graceful Willow in horror, her black eyes agog with amazement and dismay.

'I won't go through with it,' he said obstinately, 'unless Green Jade wants the marriage, too.'

Graceful Willow stared at him in awe, silenced for once. A movement behind her brother caught her eye, and as she looked up, over his shoulder, an expression of panic crossed her round face. Li Kim turned hastily and beheld his father, who had entered unheard and had been standing quietly, listening to his children.

'Go and see your mother, *mei-mei*,' he ordered gruffly, and Graceful Willow trotted away with alacrity. General Li turned back to his firstborn, and asked mildly, 'And with what is it my son feels he cannot go through?'

Li Kim flushed crimson and wished that Graceful

Willow were still there. Not that she could have helped, but she was a noted pet of their father, who disliked to see her tears and seldom lost his temper in her presence. However, the moment had come when he must speak his mind or forever hold his peace.

'I cannot marry the daughter of Wu Feng, if she does not wish it,' he said baldly.

He could have uttered no words more shattering, and he knew it. Understandably, for a moment, his father did not seem to comprehend—or perhaps he simply could not believe his ears. At long last, when Li Kim was ready to faint from trepidation, General Li enquired in a hoarse voice, 'Is—is the daughter—of the honourable Controller of the Salt Revenue—not a fit bride for a son of mine?'

In agony, Kim exclaimed, 'Yes, she is! There is no one I would rather marry. But I can't marry her, if she doesn't want me.'

'Why . . .' General Li asked in the same hoarse voice which, to his own ears, scarcely sounded his own '. . . should the lady Green Jade not want my son?'

'I don't know,' said Li Kim glumly. 'She probably thinks I'm dull-witted, with no more to say than one of the fish in Wu Feng's garden pond.'

'I, too,' observed General Li heavily, 'begin to suspect that your wits are not of the sharpest. The kindest explanation I can think of is that you are feverish, and ought to go and lie down.'

'I haven't a fever,' Kim said as calmly as possible. 'What I say is the truth. How can you ask me to marry a girl who openly rejects me? It is dishonourable. To force oneself upon an unwilling bride is not a marriage, it is a rape,' he concluded. 'And I am the wretch who is being asked to perpetrate it.'

As if a cloud passed away from the sun, the General's face cleared and comprehension dawned. He chuckled indulgently and patted his dumbfounded offspring on his head of European-style cut hair. 'Ah! I see. It is the wedding night which troubles you! My dear boy, believe me, you needn't worry. The matter is not nearly as difficult as some imagine. You have but to let nature take its course. No bridegroom from this family has ever failed in his duty yet.' He cleared his throat. 'If the matter seriously troubles you . . .' he said in a low voice. 'Though I would not normally approve such a thing, possibly a visit to the House of Falling Blossoms . . .'

Li Kim closed his eyes and wished he were dead. 'That is not what I mean!'

'Then what do you mean?' the General burst out, losing his grip on his temper at last. 'I must confess myself at a loss, and beg my son to enlighten me! Is it for this that an astrologer was paid a truly heavenly sum for casting favourable fortunes for you and the bride? Is it for this that go-betweens negotiated for a whole year between our family and the Wu family? Is it for this that I sat drinking tea with my cousin and told him how happy I was that all had been satisfactorily concluded?'

'But you didn't ask me, Father,' Kim pointed out. 'If you had, I should have told you.'

'Ask you?' General Li struggled to retain the tatters of his sanity. 'Possibly my absent-minded son overlooks the fact that for most of the past year he has been frittering away his time in Canton, spending his aged father's money, and consorting with unsuitable friends in insalubrious haunts, where he has learned disobedience, rebellion, treachery and deceit!' The General's voice rose to a thunderous crescendo. 'To say nothing of bad manners!'

Li Kim, having nothing more to lose, stood his ground. 'I have not wasted my respected parent's money, and I have studied very hard.'

'I beg your pardon,' said his respected parent sarcastically. 'This misguided father was judging only by the demented ramblings issuing from his unfortunate son's addled brain.' He slapped his hand on his knee. 'Now, there will be no more of this nonsense. Good heavens, boy, it isn't as if the girl were ugly, cross-eyed, illiterate or rotten-toothed! She's a very pretty girl, and has received the questionable benefits, if such is the right word, of the dubious education—if *that* is the right word—handed out by the foreigners. At considerable expense,' he concluded bitterly. He eyed his unsatisfactory son with gloom. 'To think,' he said, 'that I planned to take you under my command, make you a lieutenant, place you upon my personal staff at a greatly inflated salary . . . In *my* day'—he was furious—'I should not have dared to humiliate my honoured parent in such a way. Do you imagine I can go to the Salt Controller and call off the wedding? It is out of the question. So kindly cease to mumble such nonsense, or you will drive me to rejoin our illustrious ancestors before my time!' He became aware of the bamboo tube in his son's perspiring hand. 'What is that?'

'It is a very bad poem,' Kim muttered.

'I am gratified that my son has sufficient education to write poetry. Is his unfortunate sire to be permitted to read this jewel of literature?'

Kim surrendered his poem silently.

The General read it through and nodded. 'Very apt. I shall convey your poem to the Salt Controller, and he will decide whether or not to give it to the lady Green Jade.' He slipped the tube and rolled poem into his sleeve and stalked away, leaving his miserable eldest son sitting with his chin in his hands, and contemplating suicide. As it happened, events were to interfere before he could execute this melancholy design.

As the first pale grey light of dawn crept through the slats of the shutters, Zoë scrambled out of bed, dressed hurriedly and sent a servant to summon Chang and her bicycle. She had spent a restless night, sleeping very little, and her one desire was to leave quietly, before she could run into Quentin.

To creep away from the house without a word was hardly the behaviour of a polite guest, but he had hardly been the perfect host, and she did not feel she could face him by the cold light of day. What could she say to him? Or he to her? She wheeled the bicycle across the empty courtyard, past the soapstone fountain, and set off on her return journey, glancing furtively over her shoulder like a departing thief. They even had to wake up the ancient gate-keeper in order for him to let them out.

Realising that this surreptitious departure must look very odd to Chang, who trotted beside the bicycle, she felt impelled to offer him some explanation. 'Mr Farrell is a very busy man. I don't want to disturb him.'

Chang shook his head and a grin spread over his face. 'Not trouble Red Bristles. He sleep.' He glanced mischievously at Zoë, and, in a gesture both international and as old as tippling itself, raised his arm, crooked, his fingers gripping an imaginary glass, and waggling it from side to side. 'Last night, Red Bristles drink much whisky. Ah Ling, Number One Boy, come find me. We put Red Bristles in bed. Ah Ling he say, happen before. Many time Red Bristles sit in room of dead wife, and after drink much whisky. Ah Ling say, one month, two month, after he come last time from Canton, Red Bristles not drink any more. Last night, begin again.'

The bicycle wobbled to a stop and Zoë put one foot to the ground. Of course, Alice, *en route* to be married when she died, would count as already Quentin's wife in Chinese eyes, and Quentin himself as a widower. She pushed at the pedals absently and rode on. She had only thought of escaping from the house, but now she began to feel as though her early morning flight had been to abandon Quentin. She had spoken to him so grandly of wanting to help people she cared about. She cared about him, but had done nothing to help him in his lonely struggle against the whisky bottle, and, worst of all, she had driven him back to it. All those weeks of solitary, agonising battle, lost. Briefly she contemplated turning back, but her departure would have been discovered by now, and to re-appear would require explanation. She sighed and rode on. It seemed as though every decision she made was the wrong one.

It was growing lighter, and in the early morning sun everything looked fresh and new. There were some women in a drainage ditch by the roadside, washing clothes. They looked up beneath their flat straw hats as Zoë passed, and she rang the bell obligingly, which set them giggling. Then they bent to their task again, dipping their washing in brackish water so murky that she fancied their laundry would come out dirtier than it went in.

It was when they reached the ruined shrine of Kwan Yin, and rested, that she remembered the rider on the skyline and the important fact that she had forgotten to tell Quentin about him. 'Bother!' she exclaimed aloud. Perhaps it was not so important, after all, she thought hopefully. Of Chang she enquired, 'Do soldiers come this way? Mounted soldiers—men on horses?'

Chang shook his head. 'All soldier in town, many *li* from here.' He waved his hand vaguely at the horizon.

'How about turbaned men?' He did not understand, and she had to mime a turban. This also brought a negative response. Turbans, it seemed, were not worn in this part of China. Chang, as a boy, had once travelled to distant Yunnan province where there were many Moslems. There he had seen men in turbans.

Zoë sifted this information as they resumed their journey. So, the man she had seen had not been a regular soldier. Neither had he been a local. He had been a long way from home, but armed and mounted. It could mean only thing—a renegade, someone forced to flee his own province to live by banditry elsewhere. But did such a man operate alone—or with others? Zoë's feeling of dread returned, and she bitterly lamented her oversight in failing to tell Quentin of the strange horseman. Now, too, she remembered the ancient priest at the temple on the last night of their journey to this region. He, too, spoke of mounted men—Yang's agents, Quentin had believed.

She began to ride faster, more than ever anxious to reach the school.

It was mid-day, and they were about two miles away, when Chang suddenly let out a wild cry of 'Ai-yee!' and pointed ahead before turning a terrified face to Zoë. But she had seen it, too, a thin black column of smoke, rising straight as a pillar into the still air.

'Tiger of Nan-Ling come . . .' Chang whispered. 'Make fire, burn school!'

'Oh, no!'

But before Zoë could fully absorb this horrific possibility, they heard a noise of some party approaching them on the road ahead. It wound here to skirt a rocky outcrop, and they were luckily shielded from the view of those approaching. Chang did not hesitate. He seized the bicycle and hurled it into the drainage ditch by the road, hurling himself after it with a supplicating 'Missee —*hide!*'

Zoë threw herself into the ditch beside him. They were only just in time. Cowering under the reeds which grew out of the foul water in the bottom of the ditch, they heard a large number of men pass by, shouting and chattering loudly. The dust rose in a cloud from tramping feet, but an acrid scent of horses told that these foot soldiers—to give Yang's men the military name they would have claimed—were accompanied by one or more horsemen, officers of some sort, perhaps including the turbaned scout—or even the notorious Tiger of Nan-Ling himself.

The men passed on. After a few minutes, Chang ventured to peer out, and seeing no sign of life, indicated to Zoë that they should take their opportunity to hide the bicycle more securely. Hastily they covered it with grass and leaves, before having to dive back into the ditch again as yet another party of men approached on the road above.

They spent the rest of the day, until early evening, crouching in their cramped, odoriferous refuge. The hot sun beating down and the damp surroundings made it like a steam bath, and the smell was appalling. In their descent, they had disturbed stagnant pockets of rotting debris, and among other things, they shared the ditch with a dead rat, its swollen body rocking gently on the brown, scum-covered liquid mud and bog. Insects buzzed about their heads, biting viciously at bare necks, faces and hands. Their feet were in the water, and Zoë's leather shoes filled like small buckets and became as heavy as lead, and her cotton stockings were no more than tepid, soggy, clinging bandages about her legs, but she dared not take them off for fear of the leeches which abounded and were attaching themselves to the bare legs of the luckless Chang.

Occasionally, on the breeze, they heard distant shouts. But towards evening these died away. Chang touched Zoë's arm. 'I go, look see.'

'It's too dangerous,' she hissed. 'Wait a little.' She, too, was wretchedly anxious to reach the school, but it was still possible that Yang's irregulars were in the neighbourhood.

The gardener shook his head. 'I go. My wife, my children . . .'

Poor Chang! He, too, was desperate to find out what had happened. Zoë made her decision. 'All right,' she said briskly, 'I'll come too.'

They clambered up out of the ditch and stood on the road. Zoë took off her waterlogged shoes and tipped them up. Brackish water poured out, and to walk in them would be impossible. She tied them together by the laces, slung them over her shoulder, and set out in her stockinged feet. Stones bruised and scraped at the tender soles as she hurried along, but she did not heed the pain. At last they arrived, breathless and drenched with sweat, and halted. Zoë's heart filled with despair. Before them lay a scene of complete desolation.

The school building was a burnt-out ruin. The framework, blackened and charred, still stood like a grotesque skeleton, smoke rising from the smouldering cinders and isolated pockets still burning like abandoned bonfires, the flames crackling within, unseen, to shoot forth unexpectedly in brief rushes of energy. The surrounding gardens, so lovingly tended by Chang, were trampled earth, a miniature wasteland. Of human life there was no sign. 'Eve!' Zoë shrieked uselessly, for only the fallen, burning beams crackled in reply.

Chang gave a cry and bolted wildly towards the hillside, running like the wind. Zoë, left alone, stood before the charred shell and steeled herself to make a search, dreading what she would find. She drew a deep breath and took a step forward. As she did, a hand fell on her shoulder and gripped it tightly, restraining her. She gave a cry, and whirled round.

'Wait!' Quentin ordered. He was panting and breathless, rivulets of sweat pouring down his skin and making pale streaks in the dust that covered his face. 'The building is unsafe and all the debris red hot. You can't go in.'

'Eve . . .' Zoë whispered. 'Oh, Quentin!' Instinctively she flung her arms round him and clung to him. 'I can't find her!' She buried her face in his shirt, fighting back the sobs of desperation.

The hand on her shoulder tightened its grip. 'I said, wait. Go and sit down over there. Come along!' He tugged at her arm and led her aside. Zoë sank exhausted on to the dry, trampled grass a little way from the ruins, and looked up at him.

'I've been scouting round,' he said, dropping on to his heels beside her. 'Someone was sent to warn me that Yang was moving this way, but you'd already left. I came as quickly as I could—as quickly as I could sober up, that is,' he added in a brief bitter moment of self-reproach.

'Yang's men passed us on the road,' Zoë croaked, her throat so dry that it felt as though filled with grit. 'Will they attack your house?'

He shook his head. 'No. My people are all armed, and I've organised a system of defence for such an eventuality. Yang knows it. Though some of his men have guns, I doubt they have much ammunition. They'll avoid organised resistance. No, he will have moved on to occupy the town. The garrison has probably fled. They won't have much ammunition, either. The officer pockets the soldier's pay, the soldier sells supplies and ammunition to make up the loss . . . so it goes here. Yang will stay for a while, "collecting taxes" and "receiving gifts", and when he considers he's milked the citizenry dry, he'll withdraw, back to his base in the mountains.'

A shout attracted their attention, and looking up, they saw Chang approaching them, leading a small party. Zoë jumped to her feet and ran towards them, hope leaping up wildly in her heart. But neither Eve nor Green Jade was among the survivors. Chang's wife and children were there, the school cook, and the other two remaining schoolgirls, who flew to Zoë's arms and burst into a stream of voluble explanation until Quentin yelled for silence. He proceeded to question them all closely and at last turned to Zoë, and wiped his perspiring forehead.

'One of Chang's sons was on the road and saw the approach of the warlord. He ran to warn his mother, sisters and brothers. They managed to get away and hide in a cave, up on the hill. The two schoolgirls were in the garden, so he grabbed them and hustled them off with his family. But before he could find Eve or Green Jade, the attackers were at the gates, and he had barely time to save himself.'

'So, Eve—and Green Jade?' Zoë gasped, dreading the reply.

'He says . . .' Quentin hesitated. 'He says he believes Yang has taken Eve and Green Jade with him. It's as I feared. Two kidnap victims so easily snared, a European lady and a girl who is obviously the daughter of some mandarin—Yang has been tempted.'

'Then we must go after them, and rescue them both!'

'No!' He shook his head firmly. 'That would be to sign their death-warrants, Zoë, and you must understand that. I know you like to rush in, but this time you must listen to me. If Yang thought his prisoners would be taken from him, he'd kill them first, out of spite. But he wants a ransom. He'll keep them safe—provided we do nothing rash—and in due course, he'll let us know his terms. All we can do is wait.'

'Where?' Zoë looked about her in despair.

'You and the two girls had better come back to my house. I'll send a message to their families to come and collect them. Come on now, you can do no more good here.'

He was right. But she was unwilling to leave the school's ruins, and moved as close to the smoking debris as she could. The ground under her stockinged feet was hot from the flames. Amid the smouldering rubble, the evening sun caught some object which glinted. She stooped, and burning her fingers, scraped aside the charred wood and dirt to retrieve it. After looking at it for a moment, Zoë turned and silently held out to Quentin the smashed remnants of Eve's spectacles.

CHAPTER EIGHT

IT HAD grown late when they eventually arrived at Quentin's house. Zoë's first concern was for her two remaining young charges. By the time she had settled them both for the night, it had grown dark.

'You should go to bed,' Quentin said to her gently. 'There's nothing you or I can do for the moment. I've sent messages to the parents of the two girls, and I've also contacted the Wu and Li families. They may well have their own ideas on how to deal with this situation and we shall have to listen to them.'

'What do you think they'll do?' Zoë sighed and rubbed her grimy hands over her face, forcing back exhaustion.

'They'll pay. They have no choice. Li may want to take some action. He's lost considerable "face" over this. Yang has snatched his son's betrothed from under his very nose, in his own area of command. He'd certainly like to stick Yang's head on a pole over the city gates.' He put his hands on her elbows and added firmly, 'You're all in. Get a good night's sleep, and tomorrow, who knows? Something may turn up. Things aren't so black as they seem. This kind of thing happens in China. There's an established routine for dealing with it, a sort of Chinese ritual.'

He meant to reassure her, and she understood it. But she did not know how much of what he said was true, and how much was an effort to bolster her flagging morale by glossing over the unpleasanter possibilities.

Zoë went to the room where she had spent the night before, and found a bath of water awaiting her. She sank gratefully into its jasmine-scented depths and washed away the dirt and grime, rubbing soap copiously into her dust-caked hair. When she had rinsed it away, she sank back under the soapsuds to consider, as calmly as she could, the calamity that had befallen them.

The life of a foreign woman had little value in Yang's eyes, except as the price of a ransom. If this were not forthcoming immediately, he would kill Eve with no compunction. For Green Jade's ransom, since she was the daughter of an important local official, he might wait longer, be more prudent. Both were in danger, But Eve's danger was the more pressing. Zoë could blame only herself. Quentin had repeatedly asked her to go back to Canton, and to take Eve with her. She had not tried hard enough to persuade Eve. She should have insisted.

What ransom would Yang now demand? How would they pay it? The school had no money. The Wu and Li families were wealthy and able to ransom Green Jade, but they might blame the school for the whole incident and refuse to pay for the release of the foreign woman who had so dismally failed to protect Wu's daughter.

Zoë remembered her last meeting with the stately Controller of the Salt Revenue. She had upset his dignity on that occasion, and he was unlikely to have forgotten. 'I'm so stupid!' she said fiercely, aloud, to the steamy room. 'I don't *think*!' But she had to think now, had to force her feverish, whirring brain to plan clearly and logically. Quentin was a rich man, and fond of Eve, and it was to him she would have to turn for the money. How it could ever be paid back, she had not the slightest idea. But that was in the future. First Eve had to be rescued from the clutches of the Tiger of Nan-Ling.

A light tap at the door broke into her thoughts. 'Zoë?' Quentin's voice came from the other side.

The bath-water splashed over the sides. 'I'm still in the bath!' she called hastily.

'It's all right, I'm not going to attempt anything dreadful,' he said, coming into the room.

Zoë put her hands hurriedly over her bosom and trusted that soapy, opaque water would veil the rest. Quentin dropped down on his heels by the side of the bath-tub, leaned his forearms on the rim, and said with a little smile, 'Don't panic! I haven't come to seduce you, only to make sure you go straight to bed and get some sleep, and don't start pacing up and down, fretting.'

'How can I not fret?' Zoë said dispiritedly, suddenly not caring whether he was there or not, because all that seemed to matter was how to rescue the captives, and she knew he understood how she felt just now. 'Yang is sure to demand a fortune.'

'You don't have to worry about that,' Quentin said quickly. 'I'll take care of it.'

He dipped his hand in the water, scooping up a shallow handful and pouring it over her bare shoulders. These emerged, or so it seemed to him, glistening and white, like a marble Aphrodite springing from the Cypriot foam. 'I was stinking drunk last night,' he said quietly. 'I'm sorry if I gave you a fright, and didn't express my sentiments in a very gentlemanly manner. That's not to say that they weren't genuine sentiments. I meant it all. Remember that.'

He smiled again, a little wryly, at the alarm in her eyes, and got up to bring her a large cotton bath-towel, which he draped over the edge of the bath. 'Stop lounging in there, or you'll fall asleep and drown! Dry yourself, put some disinfectant on those leech-bites, and get into bed. I'll turn my back. No peeking, my solemn promise.'

He wandered to the other side of the room and stood with his back turned to her and his hands in his pockets.

Zoë scrambled inelegantly out of the swirling bath-water, towelled herself dry hurriedly and dragged on her petticoat, which had dried out.

'Leech-bites!' reminded an admonishing voice from the other side of the room.

'Oh, sorry, yes.' She tipped up the bottle of disinfectant in her haste and succeeded in spilling it, so that she was barely able to save enough to rub on her legs where the loathsome creatures had penetrated her stockings.

It stung abominably, and Quentin, hearing her hiss, turned and said crossly, 'That was the last bottle of disinfectant in the house. If anyone gets hurt now, he, or she, will just get gangrene and rot. Couldn't you be careful?'

'I'm sorry,' she said. 'I get everything wrong.' She sounded close to tears.

'No, you're tired, that's all, and so am I—come along, hop in.' He pulled back the sheets and indicated the pillows.

Zoë scrambled into bed obediently and he sat on the edge, by the pillow, and put a comforting arm round her shoulders. 'It will be all right, I swear it,' he promised her earnestly, though he knew in his heart he might be promising more than he could accomplish.

Zoë leaned back against his shoulder, glad of his reassuring presence. 'Oh, Quentin, we should have listened to you.' She sighed. 'It's all my fault!' When he would have denied this, she interrupted him, 'No, it's true, it *is* my fault. There's something you don't know, something I—I just forgot!' She told him about the horseman on the skyline, and waited for his response and the explosion of anger that she could be so foolish as to overlook something so obvious and so sinister.

'You mustn't blame yourself, Zoë,' he said quietly. He lifted his free hand and brushed back her trailing brown hair from her damp forehead, and the arm he had about her shoulders gave her a little comforting hug. 'You couldn't have done anything. Yang must have been on his way, probably just over that ridge of hill. You were probably within a mile of the Tiger of Nan-Ling at that moment. If you had told me, I couldn't have got there with my people in time, still less have contacted Li and the military. If you'd turned back, you would have been captured, too, and then where should we be? Even worse off.' He bent his head and lightly kissed her soft, silky brown hair. It smelled now of bath-soap, recalling far-off, forgotten, nursery days. 'Put it out of your mind and go to sleep,' he coaxed, as one does a fretful child, and he felt her tense body relax in his encircling arm.

'Eve said that we depended on you . . .' Zoë mumbled.

Quentin sighed, and made no attempt to answer this. He leaned his head back against the bamboo frame of the bed-head, and stared into the darkness. She trusted him, that was the devil of it. She believed he could do almost anything to remedy the situation. But he was painfully aware of his own limitations. China was slipping into the chaos which precedes revolution, and often follows it, too. A foreigner, no matter how long he had lived there, or how well known he was, was never more of a foreigner than at times like these. The girl in his arms was quiet and still, and he knew she had fallen asleep out of sheer exhaustion, her head propped against his chest. The wind blew about the eaves of the house, and leaves and twigs, falling from the trees, rolled down the glazed tiles of the roof with a distant, tiny rattling sound, like the scatter of claws. There might even be a rat up there, on the roof, and it crossed Quentin's mind to send someone up there in the morning to put down poison.

'I've been too long in this country, Zoë,' he whispered to the soundly sleeping burden, warm and heavy, in his arms, knowing his voice could not wake her. 'I thought I could make a home here, and I was wrong. I thought I knew China, but I'm beginning to fear that perhaps I've never known her. That's what happens to Europeans who stay too long in strange corners of the world—they lose perspective. Before God, Zoë, I wish I could have spared you this.'

She stirred in her sleep, nestling her head against him. He glanced down. In the gloom he could make out only the white of the petticoat and the pale shimmer of her face in the dark mass of hair. Carefully he eased his arm out from under her and set her gently on the pillows, before standing up stiffly and quietly leaving the room.

In his own room, Ah Ling, anticipating his employer's wish, had left the whisky decanter ready. Quentin looked at it with a sudden loathing. Another drunken remittance-man, was that what he was? More successful in some ways, perhaps, but basically no more than that. He seized the decanter, strode to the window and flung the whisky and its cut-glass container out into the garden, where it landed with a crash amongst the rhododendrons and sent the creatures of the night scurrying away or flying up in alarm.

Ah Ling, returning to the house from the gate, looked across and saw the dark outline of his employer in the lighted window, before the shutters were slammed to, and the sight vanished. 'It is the woman,' thought Ah Ling, resignedly. Perhaps it was a good thing that the woman had come, but perhaps it would have been better for all, if the European lady had never set foot in China.

A loud crash, but of a quite different nature, awoke Zoë, who sat up in bed, her heart in her mouth, and for a second or two quite unable to grasp what was happening. It was dawn, as a grey light filtering through the latticed windows witnessed, and the house seemed to be in an uproar. The air was filled with the voices of shouting Chinese, and of running feet.

She threw back the covers and scrambled out of bed, hastily pulling on the bathrobe lying across the end of it. But before she had time to tie the belt, the door burst open and Quentin appeared, unshaven and barefoot, clad only in his trousers and an unbuttoned shirt which he must have dragged on hastily as he ran. He dashed across the room, grabbed Zoë by the shoulders and bodily hurled her down on the floor, throwing himself on top of her.

'What on earth . . . ?' she gasped, half smothered and crushed under his weight. She raised her head and tried to twist aside.

'Keep down, damn it!' he yelled into her ear, and accompanied his order by pushing her head down forcibly.

Before she could protest any further, there was a crackle from outside like a string of Chinese fireworks being set off, but these were no fireworks. With an ear-splitting crash of smashing porcelain, a large vase on the further side of the room exploded and showered fragments across the floor.

'The garden's full of blasted bandits!' Quentin shouted above the noise. 'Come on!' He scrambled to his feet, seized her hand, hauled her up and sprinted for the door, tugging her along in his wake.

They stumbled through it and raced down the corridor to the main living area, where Ah Ling and half a dozen other Chinese menservants were at the window openings, sporadically returning the rifle-fire from the grounds.

Quentin released her hand and grabbed a rifle. 'You remember I told you how to fire one of these?'

'Yes!' she managed to gasp.

'Then, here!' He pushed the weapon into her hands. 'Go over there by that wall and don't do anything stupid, such as sticking your head out. Keep by the wall and fire only when I tell you.'

Zoë ran across the floor, which was covered with fragments of glass, and crouched by the wall as bidden. Quentin broke open a box of ammunition and dropped a handful of bullets into her lap.

'They got over the wall somehow. But, with luck, they won't get into the house. A building defended by its occupants is always a difficult military objective. But keep one bullet, just in case.'

'What for?' she asked unthinkingly.

'For yourself!' he snarled at her. 'What do you think will happen to *you* if they do break in? I estimate there are about twenty of them out there, and they'll pass you round the lot of them—more than once!'

She gulped and grasped the rifle nervously.

'They come!' Ah Ling exclaimed shrilly.

The noise was deafening, as bullets splattered against the walls of the house and the room filled with the smoke of firing and the acrid stench of cordite. Then, abruptly, an eerie silence fell. Someone shouted once outside, and then there was nothing.

'They've retreated to re-form.' Quentin wiped his forehead, which ran with perspiration, and sat back, panting. Through his unbuttoned shirt his chest gleamed with sweat. Then he swore. He continued for about a minute and did not repeat himself. Most of it was totally new to her, some of it unintelligible, and some of it made her ears ring and her cheeks flame.

When he at last ran out of his colourful vocabulary, or paused for breath, she was not sure which, Zoë said accusingly, 'You said they wouldn't have guns!'

'So, I was wrong!' he rasped at her. 'Obviously some gun-runner has been selling guns to Yang.' The word 'gun-runner' was accompanied by an epithet so outrageous and unacceptably indecent that Zoë rebelled.

'*Mr Farrell!*' she shouted furiously at him. 'Kindly do not indulge in foul language in front of me!'

He stared at her, amazed. 'You mean, here I am, defending my house—and you—against a horde of bandits, probably inflamed by plundered alcohol, and I'm supposed to watch my language?'

'Yes! Please keep it within reasonable limits,' she stormed at him.

'You prissy, mealy-mouthed, sanctimonious old maid!' he yelled at her. 'Don't you ever leave that school-room behind you?' He drew a deep breath, and added fiercely, 'The men I had at the gate are probably dead, my house is pitted with holes and every piece of glass broken. Incidentally, it was all brought up river from Canton. You may have noticed, that the Chinese don't have much use for window glass. Our lives are possibly on the verge of sudden extinction. And all you can worry about is good manners! What am I supposed to do? Sit here as if I were taking tea with Queen Victoria?'

'You don't hear me swear!' Zoë shouted back obstinately. 'And, as a former British officer, I should expect you to speak in a more respectful tone of the late Queen.'

'Perhaps,' he said in a low, dangerous voice, 'you'd like me to run up the Union Flag above the house, so that we can all die beneath the colours?'

'That's a very good idea,' Zoë said approvingly, after a moment's reflection. 'Have you got one?'

'A Union Jack? Yes, somewhere. We used it for a British Trade Exhibition down in Canton a few years ago—confound it!' he roared, seeing the light of determination enter her eye. 'Don't tell me you expect me to crawl out on the roof and run up the flag?'

'Give it to me, and I'll do it!' Zoë ordered.

'You're mad. You're a raving lunatic! I'm not going to let you go out on the roof, waving a Union Jack! A sniper will pick you off, if you don't just *fall* off.'

'No, he won't. The roof is all curves and fancy tiles and pottery dragons and gods, and I don't know what else. I can't fall off it, and who is going to look up there and see me?' She turned to Ah Ling, who leaned on his rifle, following all this with rapt attention. 'Do you know where the flag is, Ah Ling?'

'Yes, missie. In attic, in bamboo box.'

'Right!' Zoë prepared to make a dash for the door.

'Now, just a minute . . .' Quentin began, seizing her arm, but at that second the bandits mounted a second charge against the house and the firing broke out again, so that he was forced to release her.

As he scrambled back to his post, Zoë took advantage of the diversion and bolted for the door. She scurried across the broken glass and spent cartridges, bent double, and raced out into the corridor.

The house was built on the long, low principle, and to reach the attics was a matter of moments. Obviously some of the staff slept up here, and she stumbled over their bedding and personal possessions, but in a corner was a large wicker box, labelled 'Trade Exhib. 1907'. Zoë tugged it open, hunted feverishly amongst its contents and came up triumphantly with a folded Union Jack smelling of mothballs.

She looked up and saw, a few feet above her head, a skylight. Tearing jagged strips from her nails but oblivious of the physical effort in the heat of the moment, she dragged the wicker box under the skylight and clambered on to it. The skylight opened easily. She threw the flag through it first, seized the frame, and then pulled herself up and on to the roof.

The fresh air struck her face pleasantly. The sun was up now, and shining down on her with warmth and brightness. She looked round and experienced an extraordinary sensation of being a trespasser, up here in a world of dragons and deva, their painted effigies rolling surprised eyes at her. The undulating glazed turquoise tiles provided easy footholds, and she scrambled across them and scuttled into a gully between two upward-curving stretches of roof and sat there, clutching the flag and having a spectacular bird's-eye view across the whole scene spread panoramically out before her.

The attackers had been driven back again and were scattered in the outbuildings and bushes, keeping well hidden. Two bodies lay sprawled and lifeless by the fountain in the courtyard, blood staining the flagstones, but she did not know if these were bandits or Quentin's men who had been trapped outside. She remembered the old gate-keeper, and wondered if he had escaped.

Zoë glanced round. On a pinnacle by a drain-opening stood an almost lifesized deva with upraised arm, flourishing a sword. What better flagpole? She slid down the gully among the dry leaves and ended up behind the heavenly warrior, shielded from the view of those below. With nervous fingers she hastily unfolded the flag and grasped the tapes on one side of it. Carefully she stood up, clasping the deva incongruously as if he were her partner in a strange dance. To fix the tapes securing the flag to his upraised arm and sword was the work of a minute, but to her fumbling fingers it seemed eternity. For a second or two, the flag hung motionless, and then a gust of morning breeze blew across the curved rooftops and caught it, so that it fluttered bravely.

Filled with pride at her success, Zoë stepped away from the protecting statue, and looked down. In an instant, the flush of triumph evaporated, and was replaced by the rising nausea of her old enemy, vertigo. She had forgotten her fear of heights in the activity and excitement. Now it returned, familiar and worse than ever before. Her heart began to beat painfully and her head to throb, a prickling heat ran over her skin and she began to perspire freely. All other sounds were replaced in her ears by a dull, roaring echo coming from within her head. The ground below began to exert a powerful magnetic pull on her which was more and more difficult to resist. It drew her down towards it, beckoning to her to jump . . . as if to jump down were the most natural and logical thing in the world. If she could only think clearly, she could fight it, but she could not, for the roaring of the blood in her ears and the swimming of her brain. If she could move backwards, up the roof to the safety of the skylight, if she could wrench her eyes away from the shimmering, swaying, enticing ground below which urged her ever more insistently to let go, to fall . . . But she couldn't move back, she couldn't close her eyes, and despite knowing how wrong it was, she began to lean forward.

Then she saw the man. One of the bandits, attracted by the waving of the brightly-coloured cloth on the roof, had come out into the open and was staring up at her, open-mouthed and perplexed. Then his face contorted in a snarl, and he raised his rifle.

'Never promise to do something if you cannot,' Quentin had warned her once. She had volunteered to come out on this roof, and now she would die here, beneath the colours, Zoë thought in a detached way, just as he said. Perhaps there would be an artist's impression of all this in the *Illustrated London News*, and Emily would see it.

At that moment a fresh burst of firing broke out, not from the house, but from behind the bandits. It broke the spell of the beckoning ground. The blood stopped roaring in her ears and racing through her veins, and now there was only amazement and indescribable joy. Men in the uniforms of the regular Chinese army were running up from the direction of the gate, led by a tall youngster in civilian, western, dress, who wildly waved a revolver and yelled like a man possessed.

The bandit who had trained his rifle on Zoë turned and fled for his life. She scrambled up the roof, back through the skylight, and raced down the stairs.

'It's all right, Quentin! General Li's soldiers are here. We're saved!'

'Cease firing!' Quentin shouted at his men. Ah Ling and the others put up their rifles, and all listened. Outside, the air was filled with screams and the report of rifle-fire. Suddenly a voice within the house itself shouted, 'Mr Farrell? Are you safe?'

'In here, Kim!' Quentin called out, and the door was flung open and the young Chinese she had seen leading the rescue hurtled into the room and skidded to a halt before them.

Quentin turned to Zoë, and stretching out his hand towards their youthful rescuer, said drily, 'And now for someone you probably consider a monster worse than any of those outside! Allow me to present Li Kim, son of an illustrious father and husband-to-be of the lady Green Jade.'

But the relief of rescue and the calm after so much chaos acted upon the last vestiges of her attack of vertigo. Loudly, clearly, and very firmly, Zoë said, 'I'm going to be sick!' and bolted from the room.

When she emerged, some half-hour later, Zoë felt much more herself. She had washed her face and dressed, and tied her long hair back with a ribbon. The house, too, was reassuming its old appearance. The servants were sweeping up the last of the broken glass, the furniture had been neatly rearranged and a pair of song-birds in a wicker cage, frightened into silence till now, began to hop about and twitter musically as she appeared.

She could not see Li Kim or the soldiers he had brought, but Mr Farrell, so Ah Ling told her, was outside, inspecting the damage. She found him standing before the house, his hands thrust into his pockets, gazing up at the roof. Following the line of his vision, she saw the flag, still brandished by the warrior of heaven, and fluttering boldly against the blue sky. Quentin was staring at it moodily, as if the sight of it conjured up old and painful memories, and even regrets.

He hardly seemed to notice her approach until she touched his arm, and then he stirred, and, without looking at her, said quietly, 'I wasn't a very good soldier.

I was a second son, you see, and marked for the army from the cradle. No one asked, everyone just assumed . . . I was always a square peg in a round hole, but I don't think I utterly disgraced the Queen's uniform, no matter what they said.'

'No, of course not,' Zoë assured him. 'Of course you didn't!'

There was little else she could say. It struck her that he seemed very lonely, an isolated person, less self-sufficient than the brash, abrasive exterior suggested, asking in an obscure and roundabout way for some form of comfort.

'I wish I'd seen you,' she said suddenly, 'in your uniform.'

'All buttons and shiny boots.' His tone was brusque. 'Like a ruddy toy soldier. All I lacked was a tin key in the middle of my back.'

'I don't believe that you have ever been a clockwork puppet,' Zoë said firmly, 'at any time. If that's what they wanted to make you, of course you rebelled. You weren't wrong. They were.'

'I wish I'd had you to speak for me then,' he said, with a touch of humour. Turning towards her, he unexpectedly took her hand in his, and said gravely, 'You deserve a mention in despatches. Conspicious gallantry under fire.'

She shook her head. 'I was petrified!'

'Yes, I know. Think I wasn't frightened? Only a fool claims he's never afraid. Fear expresses itself in different ways, that's all. *I* have been known to swear.'

'*I* heard it,' she said severely, and then she gave a muffled little moan and pressed her head into his broad shoulder. 'Oh, Quentin, it is men like those who have Eve and Green Jade. Whatever's happening to them?'

'Hey,' he put his arm round her. 'Don't break down now. We'll think of something. Ah Ling is organising breakfast, and Kim should be waiting in the house for us, so buck up.'

'I'm not going to break down. I'm all right now. I'm sorry I rushed away like that. Poor Li Kim must have thought me very strange and rude.'

'No, he thinks you very brave and resourceful, and he admires you. So do I. But you know that, don't you?'

There was an earnest tone to the question which made her look up into his face. 'I'm not a heroine, Quentin. I'm a person who rushes in and does stupid things and scrapes through with luck.'

'That a fair enough description of most heroes,' he replied, and smiled. It was what Zoë privately thought of as his nicest smile, without mockery, full of humour, kindness and understanding. It made him look very handsome, but he was a very handsome man. 'I've no medal to pin on you,' he went on. 'All I can give you is this.'

He stooped and kissed her gently on her mouth. She knew he meant to do it, and she wanted him to do it. She still had no idea what he really thought of her. Perhaps he saw her as a sort of warrior-maiden, like a latter-day Valkyrie, splendid and admirable, but not requiring to be loved or cherished. At this moment she didn't care; only wanting him to take her in his arms. Her arms slid round his neck, and the pressure of his mouth on hers and his grasp on her increased with a sudden urgency as he sensed that she wouldn't refuse—not now. 'Zoë . . .' he whispered huskily.

But then it was as though some silent, invisible, yet electrifying warning had been triggered in both of them. Quentin released her, pushing her away from him almost roughly. 'We're keeping young Kim waiting,' he said abruptly. He glanced up at the flag. 'After breakfast I'll go and take that down.'

Disappointed, and not knowing what to do about it, she protested, 'But I've only just hung it up there.'

'I know, my dear Miss Hammond,' he said patiently, 'but you hung it upside-down!' And with this demoralising retort he set off back into the house, striding out briskly and not waiting for her.

'Then leave it as it is!' thought Zoë miserably, following him. The whole world, her world, was upside-down. Comfort and security were gone. She lived in a mysterious society with unknown rules, a society itself disintegrating at the seams, and she was in love with a man who kept a fierce guard on his innermost feelings and believed his own heart to be dead.

Li Kim was indeed waiting for them with manifest impatience. No one, seeing him, would ever have believed in the 'inscrutable orient' again. He fairly trembled with suppressed passions, like a bubbling pot threatening at any moment to boil over. As they approached, he threw both arms in the air and burst into a flood of discourse, while gesticulating in agitation and hopping from foot to foot as if the tiled floor were red-hot.

Zoë had never imagined him a monster, more an awkward obstacle, and she viewed him now with much interest. He was certainly no more than twenty years of age, quite tall, a well-built young fellow with a narrow, intelligent face. She was much struck by his hair, which had been cut short in European style but not in any known fashion of the day. For a moment or two, it puzzled her. The front of it stood up like a stiff brush, about an inch long all over, but the back hair lay smooth. Then it came to her that when he had worn his pigtail, Li Kim's front hair had been shaved off bald in the Chinese fashion. Now that he had adopted a western hair style, the front had been left to grow for the first time, and so bristled up straight in this curious manner.

With difficulty, Quentin calmed him down, and persuaded him to sit with them at the breakfast-table.

'I'm very pleased to meet you, Mr Li,' Zoë said with a smile.

'I am honoured,' said Li Kim rapidly, dismissing formalities with a totally un-Chinese brusqueness. 'Where are they? My father has sent out enquiries everywhere and has received no real information at all. Yang has looted half the city and burned the other half, and his men roam the countryside in armed bands such as those who attacked you.' He crashed both fists on the table, making the crockery jump. 'When I get my hands on that low-born ruffian, I'll make him wish he was never born into the unfortunate family which owns him. I shall slice his worthless carcass into so many morsels that when he rejoins his thieves of ancestors, they won't be able to fit any of the pieces together again. The crows will pick over the remains of his opium-sodden corpse, and I shall track down every member of his unworthy clan and decapitate the lot of them! No one of his blood will survive to boast that they were of the household of Yang, the mangy renegade . . .'

'Well spoken, Kim, my boy!' Quentin interrupted soothingly. 'You're a true soldier's son. But perhaps you had better restrain your warlike ambitions for a while. Brains, not brawn, are needed here.'

Li Kim fell back in his chair dejectedly. 'If the captives are not returned, I shall kill myself,' he declared resolutely. 'The lady Green Jade and I shall make the final journey together.'

'That sounds an unsatisfactory solution to our problem to me,' Quentin told him unsympathetically. 'Turn your mind to retrieving the lady safe and sound. Have some breakfast, and keep your strength up. You'll need it.'

'I can't *eat*!' howled Li Kim despairingly, leaping up out of his chair and beginning to dance about in frustration and rage again. Suddenly he stopped in mid-attitude, like a Tang figurine, and evidently just remembering the message he had come to deliver, announced, 'My father is on his way here, and will arrive directly.' He sat down again, and propped his chin in his hands. 'And Wu Feng,' he added gloomily.

'Are they!' Quentin looked startled. 'Then I'd better go and make some preparations to receive them. Excuse me.' He pushed his chair from the table and hastened out of the room.

'I'm very sorry, Mr Li,' Zoë ventured, 'Yang has also captured my sister.'

Li Kim looked abjectly apologetic. 'Forgive me. I am distraught with grief. I had forgotten your sorrow.'

'Quentin will get them back,' she encouraged him, 'and your father and Wu Feng. Together, how can they fail?'

'Wu Feng is no use,' Li Kim said vehemently. 'He offers to pay anything, but that only makes the wretched Yang more greedy and increase his price. My father wishes to cut off Yang's ugly head. I shall request him for the honour, when we catch the wretch. I shall decapitate him with one blow and nail his head to the city gates by its large and unsightly ears.' Satisfaction crossed his face at this pleasing prospect. His revolutionary friends were all in favour of criminal reform, but no one had kidnapped their brides, and Li Kim was beginning to find an unexpected attraction in the older and more drastic forms of traditional punishment.

'Tell me,' Zoë asked him curiously. 'What exactly is it that makes you so angry? The kidnap of your bride, obviously. But is it the insult to your dignity which puts you in such a rage, or fear for the lady Green Jade's person?'

Kim stared at her, a sea of crimson flooding his youthful face. 'For the lady Green Jade I would die!' he said hoarsely. 'Do you think I care for my worthless self?'

Zoë blushed almost as dark red as her companion. 'Forgive me,' she stammered, 'it's just . . .'

'I understand,' Li Kim said quietly. He seemed very calm and in control of himself. 'It is difficult for a westerner to believe this, but there is no one I would rather marry than the lady Green Jade. In fact, if she will not be my bride, I shall take no bride. I have sworn it. But I know she doesn't want me.' The youngster looked down, obviously not wishing Zoë to see the distress on his face. 'It brings me great sorrow,' he said with touching dignity.

'I don't think it's a question of Green Jade not liking you,' Zoë tried to explain comfortingly. 'It's because there is something she would like to achieve first, before she marries.'

Li Kim nodded. 'I know. She wishes to go to the college for teachers. My sister has told me this. You must believe me, Miss Hammond. I would not prevent this, if it were in my power and the decision were mine. I want only what Green Jade wishes for herself. But you must understand, in China, it is the old who decide, not the young. For myself and for Green Jade, it is not possible to choose. But for our children, it will be different.'

This was said with deep inner conviction and impressive honesty. Zoë sat silent. Quentin had been right about this, as about so many other things. China was stirring. After a sleep of so many years, she was facing the need to modernise and to change. It could not come about overnight. Perhaps not even within one or two generations. Even revolutions do not always achieve what they so optimistically set out to do, as young Li Kim would find out. The power of tradition is strong, and there is an instinct to fear any change lest it prove for the worse. Chinese family ties were powerful and could prove irksome and even insensitive, but they were also a rock against adversity and a sure support in time of trouble. Like a somnolent dragon, the Middle Kingdom was stretching its huge head and scaly tail and turning, slightly surprised, to face a new tomorrow. Would China embrace it or would she fight it? The decision could only be hers.

Voices sounded in the air from outside, and there was a thud of running feet, and someone shouting instructions.

'It is my father and Wu Feng,' Kim said soberly. 'They have come to hold a Council of War.'

CHAPTER NINE

LOCKED IN a tiny windowless room, the only light entering through a bamboo grille in the door, Eve Hammond and Green Jade sat huddled on the bare floor and listened to the noise of Yang's soldiers carousing in the inn's main room below them. They had arrived at this place after a long, dusty, exhausting and terrifying journey by foot, and been bundled into this airless chamber, and left, together with a bowl of cold rice and a pitcher of muddy-tasting river water.

Green Jade sniffed almost inaudibly and rubbed her sleeve over her face, and Eve put her arm about her. 'Don't cry, dear! Someone will come and rescue us before long.' She heaved a sigh of frustration. 'Only I do so wish I hadn't lost my spectacles—I see so badly without them.'

'They will kill us,' Green Jade said in a cold little voice that sent a shiver running up Eve's spine.

'No, they won't!' she came back with a firmness which hid her fears. 'Why should they? They could have killed us at the school, had they wished it.'

The young girl beside her thrust her arms into her sleeves and crouched in a ball like a small, distressed animal. 'They will seek a ransom,' she said. 'They will send to my father and to Miss Zoë, and ask them for very much money. If it is not paid quickly, they will kill us. They cannot wait, in case soldiers come. If anyone tries to rescue us, as you hope, they will kill us for sure. It is always so.'

Instinctively Eve fought against the girl's bleak acceptance of their fate. 'You're very tired, my dear, and I expect hungry, too. But you mustn't lose heart.

Try and eat some of this . . .' She picked up the bowl of rice and peered short-sightedly at it. Though cold and congealed, it appeared fairly acceptable. Perhaps it was just an advantage not to be able to see too clearly.

Green Jade shook her head miserably. 'I cannot.' After a pause, she added, 'My father will be in despair.'

'So will Zoë . . .' Eve murmured. 'Thank God she wasn't with us, when they came.'

Both women, the young and the older, fell silent, remembering the dreadful moment when the school's quiet gardens and buildings had been invaded by a horde of ill-disciplined irregulars. They had turned out cupboards and desks, seeking for valuables, and finally, in pure vindictiveness at finding nothing of use to them, had set a torch to the wooden building and all its contents.

Eve had been forced to watch as her every possession, and seven years' devoted labour, were lost in minutes, as the flames leapt up the walls, licked at the window-frames and crept along the eaves. For two things she had been grateful—that Zoë was absent, and that the Mortons, her co-founders, had not seen this destruction.

She looked at Green Jade's pale, set little face and asked, 'What are you thinking now, dear?'

Green Jade put her hand to her dishevelled black locks, which tumbled over her shoulders, for Yang's men had snatched out the silver combs which had held them neatly coiled. 'I am wondering,' she said unexpectedly, 'what Li Kim will do.'

'Oh?' Eve was momentarily startled, then asked thoughtfully, '*Are* you, indeed?'

'Yes,' Green Jade looked up at her earnestly. 'Li Kim is very impatient and does not always think. I'm sure he is very brave, but that is not enough. He should think, too. I am afraid that he will want to rescue me and do something very foolish and run into danger, if no one stops him.'

'You think the young man may try and follow us here?' Eve asked slowly. 'Why do you think this, Green Jade?'

'Li Kim loves me,' she replied simply. Her eyes filled with tears. 'And I was very unkind to him, in the garden, with Graceful Willow. Because he was shy and didn't know what to say, Graceful Willow and I teased him. Graceful Willow laughed afterwards and said it didn't matter—but she is only his sister and very young, and always naughty. I was sorry, but it was too late to say so. I am older than Graceful Willow, and should have known better. I behaved very badly to Li Kim, and I wish now I hadn't.'

'Oh . . .' murmured Eve, 'I see.'

She was not to be given more time to ponder over this, however, for just then the scrape of a bolt being drawn heralded one of their guards, who lurched unsteadily into their cell—for such it really was—and stared down at them owlishly. Eve scrambled hastily to her feet and stepped in front of Green Jade, obscuring the man's view of the girl. But he was obviously fuddled with drink, and probably unable to see very much clearly at all. He shouted at them and indicated they should follow him, and lurched out into the corridor. Eve grasped Green Jade's hand tightly, and they did as he bid them.

He led them along the corridor, which was very dark and evil smelling, and down some stairs. In the darkness and without her spectacles, Eve almost fell and she stumbled badly on the ill-lit steps, so that Green Jade had to hold tightly to her arm to guide and steady her. The guard stopped, and flung open a door. He hustled his prisoners through it, and into another room.

It was much larger than the one they had left, but almost as dimly lit. A number of high, square couches ran along the wall, interspersed with little tables on which stood tiny lamps with flickering flames, and a number of pipes were laid out neatly in rows. A curious stuffy, scented odour hung in the air which made Eve feel most peculiar. Her head began to throb and her eyes to sting and water.

'An opium den!' she thought, astonished. 'Why on earth have we been brought here?'

At that moment, her unspoken question was answered, for in the far corner a shape stretched out on one of the couches moved, and assuming human form, propped itself up on one elbow.

'Come here, Englishwoman,' said a voice like the crackling of dry twigs, and a yellow, skeletal hand protruding from a cotton sleeve reached out and beckoned, like a mummified limb escaping from its bandages.

Eve moved closer, as much from curiosity as in response to the order, momentarily even forgetting her fear and lamenting the loss of her spectacles even more. At last they were surely in the presence of the Tiger of Nan-Ling, and a desire to see the face of their notorious captor overcame all else for a few seconds.

But it was dark in the corner, and Eve's poor sight could distinguish only a long, extraordinarily thin shape, and a shaven head, moving slowly from side to side at the end of a scrawny neck, like that of a large snake. The impression was enhanced by eyes of reptilian coldness, which seemed to pierce the gloom and fix themselves on the two women with ghoulish satisfaction.

'You are honoured, foreigner—and you, too, girl,' the strange, crackling tones echoed in the room. 'You are guests of the great warlord, the Tiger of Nan-Ling, and in his exalted presence. What do you say?'

Beside her, Green Jade squeezed Eve's hand urgently in a signal. Eve said, 'We are indeed honoured. We have heard of the great warrior, Yang, and his army.'

Yang gave a kind of rattling gurgle, which seemed to express pleasure. 'I am generous,' he croaked, and the snake's head moved to and fro, cobra-like, belying the words, and neither woman was tempted to take them as the beginning of some offer of freedom. 'But the officials of this district are greedy men, and corrupt. They refuse me my lawful taxes. They offer me no gifts. It is not the way to treat an important and powerful man such as I am.'

'Certainly not,' Eve agreed prudently, and with some truth.

'I have asked you no question, foreign woman,' the creaking voice said coldly, 'and you will keep silent. As I say, they are greedy men and I have been forced to come with my soldiers and take what is mine.' The dark, mummy-like figure shifted on the couch and a hiss of rage sounded from the snake's head. 'And still they cheat me. They hide their gold and their silver. They pretend they are poor men, but they shall be made to pay! That is why I have taken *you*!' The skeletal hand shot out, and a long, bony finger pointed directly at them. 'I have sent my messenger to the Controller of the Salt Revenue, that fat pig Wu Feng, who grows richer by the day and will not share his wealth with me, or so he thinks! He is a fool. He should have paid me generously when I first sent my request. He will be punished for his avarice. Now I have his daughter, and he will pay me twice as much.'

Yang creaked an order to the guard, who came forward and lit the little lamp on the table. The yellow hand picked up each of three pipes in turn, and Yang inspected all three carefully. When he had made his choice, he turned his reptilian gaze back to his prisoners. 'For you, too, foreign woman, the English will pay —even though you are old, and of no importance. It is the way of the English.' Yang shrugged at this incomprehensible foreign attitude which paid good money for a useless woman. 'They have three days to bring me what I ask. After that, I shall not wait. If it is not here, then you will die, English woman. As for the girl,' Yang paused, and the snake's head was still for a moment, contemplating the frozen figure of Green Jade. 'She is young and pretty. To kill her would be a waste. I shall give her to my men.'

The hand signalled impatiently that the audience was at an end, and the guard hustled the women back to their cell, to wait.

'Of course,' said Quentin, 'the honourable Controller of the Salt Revenue is anxious to regain his daughter, Li Kim his bride, and I to see Miss Eve Hammond safe. We are all agreed on that. But there is another aspect to this business, which it is surely our duty to consider.'

'There is no consideration greater than my daughter's safety!' Wu Feng replied sharply. He struck the folded fan in his hand on the arm of his chair in a sign of agitation. 'Whatever the rogue asks, it must be paid.'

'And the next time?' Quentin asked mildly.

'There will be no next time!' growled General Li.

'My respected friend, you know as well as I do that, if we do not prevent him, Yang will simply take his loot and the ransom money and withdraw to his stronghold in the mountains. In a few months, a year—who knows? —he'll come again. Next time it will not be the lady Green Jade, but another wealthy man's child. What father would not give his entire fortune for the safe return of his child?'

'Mr Farrell is right!' burst out Li Kim, who had been listening with growing impatience and now found himself unable to keep silent any longer. 'No one wants more than I to see the lady Green Jade safe and sound. But we cannot allow Yang to triumph over us.'

'Hold your tongue!' roared his father. He turned to Quentin and Wu Feng. 'My son has received the foreigners' schooling. It teaches the young to believe greatly in their own wisdom, and to enjoy the sound of their own voices. I believe that, given time, a western school-master could teach a puppy to make a speech, and persuade others to listen to it!'

'Li Kim speaks as I would expect the son of so illustrious a soldier as his worthy father,' Quentin returned politely, but fixing the crimson-faced culprit with a warning eye.

'Hah!' exclaimed General Li wrathfully. 'Do you think *I* wish to see that brigand escape out of my reach with his booty? This is my area of command. That upstart has usurped my authority! He has invited my men to enlist under him. He has sat in my office at the barracks, and burned my official papers. He has hoisted his banners over our walls, and above my own garrison he has flown the painted representation of the Tiger of Nan-Ling!' Li appeared about to choke in his ire. He crashed his fist on his knee. 'I will take him,' he thundered, opening out one massive hand and then slowly closing it, crooked, 'and I will wring his skinny neck with these fingers!' He paused and considered. 'No. He has flown his banners from my flagpole. I will hoist *him* to the top of it in a wicker cage—alive—and leave him there, for the crows to pick at.'

'First,' Quentin pointed out, 'we have to capture him.'

'No!' Wu Feng interrupted firmly. 'First we ransom his prisoners.'

'That means,' Li Kim muttered furiously in his corner, 'that first we sit here, doing nothing, and wait for his terms.'

'I see,' Zoë said dangerously, when this decision was communicated to her in the dining-room, where she had been left in solitary state while the men conferred in Quentin's study. 'You've all thoroughly discussed it, then? Without me, I note. You overlook, perhaps, that my sister is in the power of that fiend?'

'You're beginning to talk like a Chinese,' Quentin said, a brief smile touching his cheeks on which the lines seemed to have engraved themselves more deeply with fatigue.

Zoë was not in a mood to sympathise with him, or to be cajoled. 'Why shouldn't I talk like a Chinese? I'm being treated like a Chinese woman, and pushed into the background. What am *I* supposed to do while you all discuss Eve's fate, and what ransom is to be paid? Or is my opinion of no interest at all?'

'General Li speaks no English,' he said patiently. 'So there was no point in your attending our conference.'

'One of you could have translated, I suppose?'

'Chinese women do not . . .'

'I am not a Chinese woman! I'm an English woman, and my sister is an English woman. Tell me, am I even to be permitted to meet General Li?'

'Oh, very well,' Quentin said with a sigh. 'But, I warn you, he's quite a stern old traditionalist. Don't stare boldly at him, and don't talk. I mean that! Keep your eyes on the floor and your opinions to yourself. Promise me, or I won't take you in there.'

'I promise,' Zoë said impatiently, and he looked at her very hard.

She allowed him to usher her into the room he had just left. Li Kim was standing by the window, red in the face, silent and mutinous. Wu Feng, clearly discomposed by the situation, was enthroned majestically in a chair facing the door, and up and down the room prowled a squat, burly figure in the uniform of a high-ranking Chinese army officer. All three turned their eyes upon her as Quentin led her in, and the military personage ceased his pacing up and down and rapped out some question in an irascible tone.

Quentin replied, obviously explaining to the General who Zoë was, and making some excuse for her presence.

Zoë inclined her head graciously to acknowledge the General, whose bushy eyebrows shot up alarmingly, and then turned to the already familiar figure of the mandarin. 'Good morning, Mr Wu,' she greeted him sympathetically, thereby breaking her promise to Quentin almost at once, although she told herself that a greeting hardly counted as giving an opinion.

Wu Feng made a graceful, sad gesture with the closed fan. 'It is a sorrowful day, Miss Hammond!'

He looked so disconsolate, for all his splendour, that Zoë was moved by pity and impetuously darted forward and clasped his free hand in hers. 'Oh, Mr Wu, I am so sorry! But you mustn't worry. It will be all right,' she assured him earnestly.

Wu looked startled, and General Li observed to Quentin irritably—though fortunately Zoë could not understand it—'Can't you keep this woman of yours under control?'

'There has never been a man alive who has success-fully kept a woman under control,' said Quentin blandly to him. 'Why should I be the first?'

The General's battered features twitched. 'Possibly that is so,' he agreed gravely. 'Forgive me, I observe that the lady is very tall. Are all English ladies so? I have remarked it in the others I have seen.'

'Not all,' Quentin told him. 'But Miss Hammond comes of a very tall family, I believe. She has seven brothers, all as tall as I am.'

General Li, unable to verify this impressive claim, chose to accept it at face value. 'She has no husband?' he enquired. When Quentin informed him that she had not, he frowned. 'And you have now taken this woman into your household?'

'In a manner of speaking,' Quentin said cautiously.

General Li gave him what, in any culture, would have been described as 'an old-fashioned look'. 'You are responsible for her,' he declared firmly. 'If she has no husband, you should find her one—if you do not wish to keep her in your own household, that is. But seven brothers is a very good sign. Such a woman would almost certainly bear you male children. It might be well to think of taking her yourself.'

And indeed, thought General Li to himself, the probability of her bearing male children was her sole recommendation, for she was built like a pagoda and he was sorrowed, but not surprised, to observe that she had the inevitable large feet which always seemed to anchor western women to the ground. However, possibly Farrell did not mind this. There was no accounting for the tastes of foreigners.

'I am sure she would not wish to remain in my household,' Quentin asserted.

The General groaned mentally. Not *another* young woman bent on objecting to an eminently suitable spouse selected for her by well-disposed persons! What was the matter with the modern generation? Had they all gone quite mad?

'Then find her another husband!' he ordered crossly. 'And, in the meantime, keep her under control. Make her let go of the honourable Controller of the Salt Revenue! It does not enhance the dignity of such a man to be seized by the hand in public by a woman!'

At the sound of her husband's voice, Emily Linton started and hastily thrust the note she had been writing to Captain Hansen into a drawer. She had not expected Edward to return from the *hong* for another hour, and it was tiresome to think he meant to take an early lunch. She could hear him shouting at the servants as he entered the house. Early in the day as it was, this generally indicated he had been drinking, and would spend the afternoon sleeping it off. Emily carefully composed her features into a look of serenity which hid her disgust, as Linton threw open the door and strode into the room. He would not ask her what she had been doing. He never did.

He stood for a moment, staring at his wife, and then

muttered an oath by way of a greeting, before going to a side table on which stood decanters and glasses. He began to pour himself a drink, his back turned to her.

'Haven't you had enough?' Emily asked coldly. 'It's scarcely past mid-day.'

He glanced at her over his shoulder, and something in his bloodshot gaze warned her of an impending crisis. 'Yes,' he agreed thickly, 'I've had enough.' He gave her a sardonic look, and finished pouring out his drink.

Emily turned on her heel in a flurry of silk skirts and walked out of the room. Let him drink alone, if drink he must! She ran upstairs into the bedroom and paused to draw breath. Would she never be free of him? Never get away? Nils Hansen was clearly besotted with her, but he was an old-fashioned, decent man, deeply conventional, who would never dream of actually seducing a wife away from her husband. Only if Edward would volunteer to let her go would Nils come forward to her rescue, as he had clearly promised. In such a situation she would be alone, rejected, without support, and would appeal to the Captain's instinctive chivalry. But his ship was due to sail the next day, and it was unlikely that he would be back for three or four months. Three months was a long time in this forsaken fever-hole, and lost opportunities seldom returned.

A sound at the door caused her to whirl round. Edward stood there, in the doorway, watching, his glass clasped in his hand, and a look on his face she did not care for at all—mocking, vindictive, full of spite and a twisted pleasure. He knew the power he had over her and he enjoyed it. Yet there was something different in his face, something she had not seen there before, and Emily felt a cold finger of fear touch her heart.

He came a little further into the room and the door swung silently shut behind him. Instinctively she backed away, as he walked unsteadily forward, putting out her hand to ward him off as he stopped before her, eyeing her scornfully. 'Yes, I've had enough,' he repeated hoarsely. 'I've had enough of your running after every white man to pass through Canton!'

'You *are* drunk!' she whispered, her throat constricted in sudden fear and a cold shiver running over her.

'Not nearly drunk enough, my dear. Not nearly enough . . .' He tossed back his drink and set down his glass. 'So . . . Now it's Hansen, is it? Stupid fool, he doesn't know what a harpy has her claws into him. I pity the poor devil.'

She could have denied it, but that would have been useless. 'How do you know?' she asked in a dead little voice.

'How do *I* know?' He threw back his head and laughed. 'All Canton knows. You're the talk of the Pearl Delta! You have been for the past three years. The best-known European wanton between Port Arthur and Rangoon!'

'How dare you speak to me like that?' she hurled at him, fury replacing her fear.

'You know it's true,' he said curtly.

'And you blame *me*?' Emily retorted bitterly, her voice shaking. 'Look at yourself! Look at what you've done—to me. And if you weren't drunk now, you wouldn't dare . . .' She broke off with a gasp as he lurched forward and struck her hard across her mouth.

'What have *I* done?' He grasped her arm and shook her violently. 'I'll tell you what I've done. I've stood by and let you make a fool of me, time and time again! I've even let you bring that bastard child of Farrell's into the house to masquerade under my name! But no longer, my dear. This time you've played your cards badly, and I'm calling in my markers. Emily, my sweet, it's time to pay.' A cruel little smile touched the corners of his mouth as he saw panic invade her pale eyes.

'What do you want of me?'

He shrugged and spread his hands. 'What can you

offer, eh? You're no young girl any more, you're getting fat, a strumpet . . . No. If Hansen wants you, he can have you. If you want to leave here, go with him. He sails tomorrow. Take your chance—it may be your last. Soon no man will want you.'

Emily ran her tongue over her dry lips nervously, as she tried to assimilate and make sense of this unexpected offer of release. At the same time she was asking herself, 'Would Nils take me with him?' Her heart rising, she thought, 'Yes, he would, if Edward turns me out!' 'You agree to a separation?' she scarcely dared to breathe the question.

'Separation? No, no—I'm divorcing you!' he corrected her. 'I've instructed my solicitors in London to proceed. I'm not going to give you a penny of money, Emily. If Hansen won't marry you, you can starve in the gutter for all I care. The children have been sent to my relatives, and you won't be allowed near them—ever.'

Emily paled as she listened to him tell her openly how she had been outmanoeuvred. He had taken his time and planned it all. 'You can't prevent me from seeing my children!' she pleaded wildly.

'I can, and I will! Of course, you can take that brat of Farrell's with you'—he pointed upstairs in the direction of the nursery—'I repudiate her. She's part of the grounds for a divorce action, anyway.'

'I can't,' she stammered. 'I can't take Baby with me. I can't ask Nils to take Quentin's child. Nils doesn't know . . .'

'Doesn't know what? What a slut you are? He'll find out. But you're not leaving the child here, in this house!'

Emily thought frantically and shook her head in desperation. 'I can't, I won't!' She looked up, grasping at a straw, a way out of her dilemma. 'Quentin! Quentin's always said he'd support the child if you divorced me. Quentin has a house, money, servants . . . You can send Baby to him!'

'If Farrell wants his child, he can have her,' Linton growled. 'He can come and fetch her away at any time.'

'And you'll let me send a message to Nils?' She could still hardly believe it. 'You'll let me take my clothes, my jewellery?'

'No,' Linton said softly. 'Nothing! You can walk out of here tomorrow—now, if you wish—and sail with Hansen. But you go out in the clothes you stand up in, and not so much as a single valise more!'

'If you do that,' she said viciously, 'people will sympathise with *me*! They'll say you're behaving as no gentleman should. No matter what I've done, people will still blame you!'

He considered this, rubbing his hand over his chin, weighing this small part of his vengeance against the cold looks of the men who would no longer drink with him, if it got around.

'One case of clothing,' he conceded, 'so that it looks like an elopement. But leave your jewellery behind.'

'It's mine!' she shouted at him. 'It belongs to me. You *gave* it to me. Some of it was already mine when we married!'

'You have debts!' he said harshly. 'You incurred them while you were married to me, and it's to me your creditors will come running. You'll leave the jewellery behind, here!'

Emily drew a deep, shuddering breath. She would have to agree. However, it was a fact that the best pieces of jewellery had been sold long ago, and there was little left of real value. Perhaps the loss was of small consequence. The important thing was that he was prepared to let her go. Once she reached England, it would be her version of the story that people heard—with Nils loyally backing her up. Let Edward divorce her! She would blacken his name so thoroughly that he would never dare to show his face in London again. As for Baby, Quentin had always wanted to have custody of his daughter. Her own chief concern was for her children in England, and no matter what Edward threatened, there would be some way to find them. The family could not hide them for ever.

'All right, I agree,' she said calmly, trying to suppress the note of relief, almost of triumph, in her voice. Free, at last! It was beyond her wildest dreams. Nils would feel himself duty bound to marry her, once she was divorced. She could make a new life—with a new husband, new friends in new surroundings. 'I'll pack today and leave tomorrow!' she said, almost happily. 'I'll send Nils a note this evening, and leave in the morning.'

'That's right,' Edward was smiling at her, and it was then that she understood he meant to pursue his revenge to the last. 'Tomorrow.' He reached out and tilted up her chin with his fingers. 'And until tomorrow, Emily dear, you're still my wife—and can fulfil a wifely duty.'

'No!' She whispered the word through frozen lips. 'Not now we've agreed . . . You wouldn't, you wouldn't ask *that* of me, now!'

'Oh, but I would, Emily dear,' he said softly. 'And I do!'

He threw out his hands, and grasping her roughly, hurled her sprawling down on the bed. She tried to escape from him, but he dragged her back, tearing her underclothing in his haste, aroused by the wild excitement of conquest, and knowing that her shuddering body beneath his was utterly in his power.

About an hour later, Edward Linton was on his way back to the huge sprawling warehouse, the *hong*, which housed his office and the merchandise—legal and illegal —in which he dealt. He was in high good humour, and looked it. He whistled a jaunty tune to himself and walked briskly through the crowded streets. He even parted with a handful of brass cash coins to a beggar.

He had left his wife, crouched on the rumpled bed,

sobbing and clutching the shreds of her petticoats. If it was to be the last sight he had of her, it would be a memory which would always give him satisfaction. Stupid slut, he was well rid of her! But Hansen, too, that pious old humbug, was going to pay—literally. He chuckled to himself.

At the *hong*, the Chinese head clerk said that Captain Hansen was already waiting, in the office. The smell of the old briar pipe had already alerted Linton, however. He threw open the door and entered, rubbing his hands cheerfully in anticipation.

'Well, my old sea-dog, come to settle up, have you?'

Hansen knocked out the briar pipe on the corner of the desk. Something in Linton's manner told him that there had been some new development, and he took his time before replying, 'As usual, before I sail.'

Linton nodded, and opened his office safe, taking out a small strong-box which he placed on the desk. He took out his keys, selected the correct one slowly and deliberately, and opened the lid. There was something theatrical about his movements, as though he mimed some charade. His hands trembled slightly, and his flushed face had an excited, triumphant look about it, mixed with mockery and cunning, which made his whole aspect highly disagreeable. Hansen shifted uneasily in his chair.

Linton took a single bill from the box, and laid it carefully on the desk.

The Captain stared at it and raised his eyes suspiciously to meet Linton's gloating look. 'What's this? Some drunken game of yours? Where is the money you owe me?'

'Ah,' Linton said quickly, 'But what of what you owe *me*?'

'I owe you nothing,' Hansen replied in a slow, quiet voice which carried a hint of danger in it.

'Oh yes, you do! You have yet to pay me *for my wife*.'

He had taken Hansen by surprise. Now he felt he

could be openly superior about it, the man in control of the affair.

'Well? You want her, don't you? Take her. You can have her! I won't stop her going with you. I intend to divorce her, of course. But it is not necessary that I give you as my grounds.'

'So why should I pay you for her?' Hansen asked evenly.

'To ensure that I don't change my mind and name you in my divorce action after all.' Linton leaned back in his chair. 'I know you, my dear old sea-dog. You don't want scandal. An honest fellow like you doesn't want the word "adultery" bandied about. Tsk, tsk,' Linton shook his head in mock disapproval. 'So, if you want your name kept out of it, you'll pay. Well?' His eyes narrowed and his voice sharpened.

'It's blackmail,' Hansen accused him hoarsely. 'You're a scoundrel. I always thought it, and now I say it!'

'I'm a practical man, like you. A business man. I'm losing a wife. Out here, that's a highly inconvenient loss. I'm unlikely to marry again, unless I sign the pledge of temperance and marry a missionary, and I'm not likely to do that! I might go down to Macao and find myself a plump Portuguese widow. But, failing that, I'll have to pay a housekeeper to run my home, and pay if I want someone to share my bed. Call it compensation.'

He indicated the money on the table. 'Pick it up!' he ordered in a hard voice. 'Take it, and Emily. Or leave it there—and Emily here with me. You're perfectly free to choose. That's hardly blackmail.'

Hansen, breathing heavily, said, 'I wouldn't leave any woman here with you!' He thrust the note into his pocket, and picked up a scuffed leather briefcase, which he had had waiting, open and ready to receive his money. He snapped it shut, clicking the locks shut efficiently. 'I won't forget this, Linton. Next time, you pay me first, the whole amount, or you get no guns!'

Linton spread his hands. 'Of course, I've got only *one* wife to barter away. Come now, don't take it badly.' He stood up and patted the Captain's shoulder. 'Have a drink with me, to our future association, and business. After all, sharing a wife, we're practically related. And you were right about the Chinese generals. I'm receiving tentative enquiries about arms supplies from all quarters. They all smell civil war.'

Hansen rose with dignity and put the briefcase under his arm. 'I would sooner drink with the devil!' he said curtly, and strode out.

Edward Linton sat down again and smiled. He had hit the grasping old hypocrite in the purse—where it hurt him the most. He began to laugh. He laughed till he cried. It was the best day's business he'd ever done!

'You next, Quentin Farrell,' he promised himself aloud, as soon as he was able to control his mirth.

CHAPTER TEN

THE RESTFUL cool of the gardens was soothing to eye and mind. Zoë sat on a stone seat set in a curved semicircle of rhododendron bushes, and took stock of the situation with more calm than she had felt since events had plunged them into such disarray. Before her, the smooth green turf swept down like a velvet carpet to the edge of the stream that flowed through the gardens and tumbled at this point over a stone step, like a minature waterfall. It gurgled tunefully as it ran on to feed a large waterlily-dotted pond, dark beneath overhanging trees. Dragonflies played above the still water of the pond, darting in and out of the sunlight and shade in flashes of brilliant blue. On the further side of the stream, the lawn swept upward towards the pavilions of the house complex, of which the corner of one could be seen behind some trees. A gardener was working up there, cutting the grass with a scythe, an instrument that looked clumsy and primitive and yet which, in his skilled hands, trimmed the grass to a neat, uniform height with the precision of a surgeon's scalpel.

She sat and watched him working, the scythe moving rhythmically to and fro. It all looked so peaceful, and so normal, that she had to force herself to remember that Green Jade and Eve had been for twenty-four hours in the hands of the warlord. As yet, no ransom demand had been received, despite Quentin's repeated assurance that Yang would not waste time. Perhaps the warlord had sent a message, but something had happened to the messenger? Or something had happened to the hostages . . .

A flurry in the bushes made her jump, and a bird flew

out of the mass of dark leaves and luxuriant blooms, up and away into the blue sky, a very symbol of freedom. If only the warlord's captives could so easily be liberated! Just at that moment, Zoë saw that a second figure had joined that of the gardener on the further lawn. Quentin had come from the house and was walking towards her. He had paused briefly to exchange a word with the man, before continuing in her direction with a long, yet unhurried stride. For all his relaxed manner, something about his bearing told her he brought news at last. Her heart beating painfully in her constricted chest, she waited for him to reach her. He crossed the stream by a stepping-stone set in the midst of the glittering water, and walked up the slope slowly, to stop before her.

'It's come?' she whispered, her hands twisted tightly in her lap.

He nodded. 'Yes, I think so.' He took off his hat and wiped the back of one sunburned hand across his perspiring forehead. 'Li has sent for me, urgently. That can only mean that he's heard from Yang.'

'You're going to the town?' She could not prevent the alarm in her voice. 'What about me?'

'You will have to wait here,' he said firmly.

'No!' Zoë shook her head with equal firmness. 'I was shut out of your last conference, but I'm not going to be shut out of this one. You all seem to forget that Eve's my sister. She isn't a member of your family, she's a member of mine! Whatever is decided, you, Quentin, can surely agree only after consulting *me*?'

'Oh,' he said gently, but with a faint admonitory note in his voice, 'I don't consult young ladies on matters which can best be described as military.'

'I'm twenty-five!' she said sharply, 'nearly twenty-six, and self-supporting! I'm not some winsome drawing-room ornament, a trailing vine. I think I have enough intelligence to understand the situation.'

'More like bindweed,' he said unkindly. 'You'll be in

the way, Zoë—get under my feet and hamper my decisions. I have to be free to decide what's best. Of course, if you don't trust me to know what that is, or if you think you know more about this country and its ways than I do, please take over. Li speaks no English, remember!'

'I'm coming with you,' she repeated obstinately.

'No, you're not.' He tugged his hat over his auburn hair and thrust out his chin pugnaciously. 'I came only to tell you what happened, and that I'm just leaving.'

'I won't get in the way,' Zoë said quietly, but in a resolute tone. 'I won't argue with you in front of either the General or Wu Feng, or offer any unasked opinions. But I want to be there. I want to know what's decided.' She paused. 'I do trust you, Quentin. I promise to support whatever you decide should be done. But I want to be there.'

Quentin's blue eyes swept over her thoughtfully. 'Very well, you can come along. Just try and behave in a seemly manner, will you? I'm getting tired of apologising on your behalf to Li and Wu Feng.'

She flushed. 'You don't have to apologise for me. You're not responsible for me.'

'That's not how Li sees it!' he taunted her lightly. 'He has even given me instructions regarding you! Well, come if you must.' He shrugged ungraciously and turning, strode back down the slope without waiting for her, and jumped over the stream to the further lawn. Zoë hurried after him, but was delayed at the stream by her long, hampering skirts, which she had to bunch up in one hand before stepping on to the flat stone in the middle of it. The stone was slippery and she teetered on it insecurely. Quentin turned, and seeing her difficulty, came back. Reaching out his long arms without a word, he grasped her round the waist and lifted her effortlessly on to the grass—as though she had been no weight at all.

'What instructions concerning me?' she demanded a

little breathlessly, and with suspicion, as he set her down.

Quentin, still holding her by her waist, close to him, said, 'Li says I should find you a husband. He doesn't think it right that you should be running round on your own. I had to tell him I had more or less taken you into my household.'

'What on earth does that mean?' She stared up into his face with a frown, her hands resting on his forearms.

'It means, my dear, that he thinks you are some kind of concubine!'

She grasped his hands and pushed them away from her waist furiously. 'You let him think that! It amused you, even at a time like this.'

'As a matter of fact,' he said softly. 'I don't think it a damn bit funny.'

In the short time that had elapsed since Yang's brief occupation of the town, it had regained an appearance of normality which was astonishing. People who had fled to the countryside had returned and were philosophically counting the cost of his visit. Business flourished in the shops and on the street. Peasants had brought vegetables in to market, and stall-holders were busy ladling out heaps of steaming boiled noodles into bowls held out by hungry customers. There appeared to be no anger, or no sign of it, or of grief. The recent alarms were a part of life.

In the house of the Controller of the Salt Revenue, things were very different. The shadow of despair lay upon it. The mandarin himself seemed to have lost weight and shrunk to a travesty of his former prosperous, portly self. What was worse, to Zoë's eyes, he had sunk into a kind of lethargy, a stoical acceptance of the situation.

The Li, father and son, evidently felt differently. The General's temper had not improved, and there was a look about him that said he meant business. Clearly, between him and Wu Feng there was now some slight difference of emphasis regarding the problem. Wu was concerned only to pay the ransom and regain his daughter: the General wished revenge. Zoë sat in the corner, obediently silent, and wishing she could understand as Li spoke forcibly and at some length. Li Kim, who sat beside her and had orders to translate, had ceased to do so after the first few sentences, and sat apprehensively, watching his father and Quentin.

Quentin had been listening closely, his face growing increasingly sombre as the General spoke. At last he shook his head vigorously and made some reply, evidently in the negative. At this Wu Feng interrupted, to make what was evidently a contrary point of view. Quentin turned back to Li, and the two men exchanged glances as fellow soldiers who were faced with an unco-operative but important civilian. Li crouched on his chair, arms akimbo and hands on his knees, like a wrestler in his corner. There was a silence.

Quentin looked across at Zoë, who made signs of incomprehension, having no idea what was going on. 'If you'll permit me,' Quentin said to Wu Feng. 'I should like to have a talk with Miss Hammond for a few minutes. Perhaps you would allow me to take her out into your garden?'

Wu Feng brightened momentarily at the mention of his beloved garden, but then fell gloomy again and signalled with a resigned gesture of his ivory fan that Quentin was his guest, and might do as he wished.

'What's gone wrong?' Zoë demanded as soon as they stood in Wu's garden. 'Kim hasn't translated a word since you all three started to disagree.'

'Yang has sent his demands,' Quentin admitted reluctantly. 'They haven't quite taken the form I expected.'

'Is the price too high?' Dread seized Zoë's heart. 'Can't we raise it somehow?'

'It's not a question of the amount of the price. It's how it's to be paid.' Quentin sighed, but an obstinate expression had imbued his features. 'He wants opium, Zoë. Huge quantities of it. Yang sees that China is in chaos, and he wants some commodity valuable enough to be traded anywhere in China or the Far East, no matter what happens.' He looked away from her startled, enquiring gaze. 'I can't agree to it. I can't agree to put so much of something so dangerous and so valuable into the hands of a creature like Yang.'

'But—Eve? And Green Jade?' she whispered.

'Yes, I *know*!' he exploded angrily. 'I'm not stupid. But I can't do something so—so totally irresponsible! It would be criminally wrong, and morally indefensible.'

'Morally indefensible? He'll kill them, two innocent people!' Zoë cried out. 'He'll kill Eve and Green Jade!' When he did not answer, she asked, 'What do Wu Feng and Li say?'

'Wu Feng says, "pay". Li accepts that not to pay may well mean that we never see either of the women again; but, like me, he is appalled at the power the possession of so much opium will put in Yang's unsavoury hands.' Quentin stared into the depths of Wu's fish-pond, where the gold and silver shapes swan lazily just below the surface of the water. 'You promised me,' he said obstinately, 'that you'd support whatever I decided.'

'I didn't then realise you would set anything before Eve's safety!' she blurted.

His mouth tightened but he made no reply.

The fish had clustered on the side of the pond, near to where the humans stood, throwing their shadows across the water. To break the silence, Zoë observed tonelessly, 'The fish are greedy. They have all come over to this side because they think we'll feed them.' She felt she had to say something, anything, to relieve the tension and draw some response from her companion.

Quentin glanced sharply at her. 'What?' Then, when

she would have repeated her sentence, he signalled her irritably to silence. 'No—I heard you! You're right. That's exactly what they've done.' Suddenly a smile broke across his face as he saw the bewildered expression on hers. 'Miss Hammond, you have handed us the key to our Chinese puzzle!' His whole attitude had changed from one of dejection and frustration to one which was almost buoyant. He cupped his hands round her face, tilted it up towards his, and stooped and kissed her firmly on the lips. 'You're a girl in a million. So Yang wants opium, does he? Many a greedy fish has been hooked for less!'

'You mean . . . pay him what he wants, after all?'

'I wouldn't pay Yang a dud penny. But baiting a trap is something else. Wait here. I have to get Li's agreement, it can't be done without him!' He ran indoors, leaving Zoë, mystified, by the fish-pond.

Zoë spent the rest of the day in trying to find out what was going on. Li Kim would tell her only that a message had been sent to Yang, agreeing to his ransom demand, and that efforts were being made to collect the considerable quantities of opium involved. It was not until late in the evening that Quentin came to say that all was ready.

'Wu and Li cannot deal with Yang direct, a matter of "face" and etiquette. So young Kim and I will take the opium to Yang. We're setting off early tomorrow and meeting with Yang up in the hills. We'll go armed, but leave Li and his men a mile or two away. Yang agrees to meet us with his prisoners and a guard, but without the bulk of his private army. It's tricky. A dozen things can go wrong, but I'm hoping Yang will be so greedy to get his hands on the opium that he'll lose interest in all else.'

'You said that you wouldn't give him the opium,' Zoë reminded him suspiciously. 'And, Quentin, I've thought it over, and you are quite right about that. Eve wouldn't wish it, either, I'm sure.'

'I know what I said to you, and I hope I know what I'm doing now. If I don't, it will be an unmitigated disaster all round for everyone. Trust me, Zoë.' He hesitated, then added in a strained voice, 'I have to believe you trust me.'

Zoë stretched out her hand and touched his arm. 'You know I trust you. But I don't know what you're up to, and for some reason you won't tell me. You don't trust me, perhaps? All I know is that it's devious, and it's dangerous—and my sister is involved.'

He took her hand and held it for a moment. 'It's not that I don't trust you, Zoë, or that I'm deliberately trying to conceal anything from you.'

'Then let me go with you and Kim.'

Quentin dropped her hand and stared at her 'Do *what*? Have you gone out of your mind?'

'You see?' she said triumphantly. 'You don't trust me! You think I'm a foolish, incompetent woman who will only be in the way. I won't, I swear! Let me come along with you and Li Kim.'

'And how do you think it will impress Yang,' Quentin demanded sarcastically, 'when we arrive guarded by an English lady brandishing an umbrella? Good grief, Zoë, every time you ask me to have confidence in you, you straight away do something completely crazy!'

'It isn't crazy. If you'd only listen for a minute, I'll explain how and why!' she insisted. She ignored the cynical look he gave her, and hurried on, 'How will Yang know I'm an English *lady*? He doesn't expect an English lady or any kind of lady. As far as he is aware, he's kidnapped the only English woman for miles around —and what he is expecting is a foreign man. So why not two foreign men—or rather one man and a boy? I'm tall, and as you said yourself, I have large feet for a woman by Chinese notions. If I cut my hair and wear male clothes, why should Yang take me for anything but an English youth?'

Quentin was staring at her, dumbfounded. 'You *have* gone out of your mind,' he said flatly. 'Yes, it is a dangerous mission. All we have is Yang's dubious word that he agrees to the arrangements made. He might just decide to ambush us, decapitate us, and make off with the opium. What's to stop him, up there in the hills? We'll be armed, Kim and I, but he can still jump us. Of course you can't blasted come!'

'Let me cut my hair and put the clothes on,' she urged him. 'I'll show you that I can look like a boy. I'm a good actress. We used to act bits out of Shakespeare at school, and I always got the male roles because I was tall—and it was a girls' school, and my father took me away from it in the end, because he thought the standards too low.'

'Well, I went to a male educational establishment where it wasn't unknown for protesting third-formers to be thrust into frocks and made to act out Mrs Malaprop or some such part—but the intention was not that they go mincing round in dresses after they'd left!'

'I can do it,' she maintained obstinately. 'I'll show you!'

'Although I do not wish to be impolite,' said General Li cautiously, 'I have to say that this woman of yours looks remarkably like a young man. Well, it will fool Yang, anyway, who has seen few foreigners. But I believe it extremely unwise to take her along, even so.'

'I think the clothes suit her very well,' Quentin replied. 'Though I can't say she looks much like a man to *me*. My respected colleague, this whole expedition is extremely unwise. But if you are willing to risk your son, I am prepared to include Miss Hammond.'

Li snorted. 'If she speaks, even Yang will know it is a woman, so take care!' He went so far as to pat Quentin on the shoulder, then stomped off, pausing only to growl to his son, 'I wish to celebrate my son's wedding, not his funeral. You will follow the orders I have given and listen to Farrell. He's a foreigner, but a soldier. Do as he says, and you may return to write another poem—this time on the subject of your heroic success!'

'About that poem of mine, which you took off me, Father . . .' Kim began urgently.

The General waved a gnarled hand to cut short his words. 'I have already given it to Wu Feng. He has read it with great interest.'

'If Yang murders us all,' thought Kim resignedly, 'it won't be worse than knowing that my poem is being passed from hand to hand and read by everyone except Green Jade herself!' He drew a deep breath, straightened his shoulders and signalled to Quentin that he was ready.

Quentin turned to Zoë. 'Last chance to duck out of it. Take it?'

'No,' she said stoutly, settling herself in the saddle. 'Not after all the trouble I've gone to. How do I look?'

He eyed her appraisingly. She had cut her dark hair into a mannish bob and wore the kind of jacket and trousers, and felt slippers, worn by Chinese men-servants.

'Put the hat on,' he ordered. Zoë tied on her round, flat coolie's hat. 'You look terrible,' he told her. 'Well, lead on, Macduff—or we won't be there before dark.'

They rode out of the town and up into the hills. The opium was laden on to three pack-ponies, driven by the same squint-eyed driver who had brought Zoë and Quentin to the school. He was, Quentin said, the one man he knew for the job who could be relied upon not to desert. He had sent for him specially, and promised him a small fortune to accompany them. The bells on the ponies jingled tunefully, and as the tracks grew stonier, the animals' hoofs slipped and stumbled. The air was cooler as they climbed higher, but it was still very warm. The pony-driver whistled and sang as he tramped along, to keep up his own spirits and to encourage his beasts, but Li Kim had fallen into a grim silence, and Quentin did not appear disposed to conversation.

'How far?' she asked him.

'Far enough.'

'Do you know the place where we're meeting him?'

'I know it.'

And that was all he would divulge, other than the single astounding item of information that Yang spoke English, having been educated by missionaries, who must have been sadly disappointed in their pupil.

After a while, a river, splashing down from the heights, joined the stony track and ran alongside it. The scenery invited canvas and easel, but Zoë was in no mood to appreciate its beauties. It was early evening before they reached a point on the road from which they could see an ancient Chinese *han* ahead of them.

It had probably been here, as a stopping-place for caravans, when the Mongols of Genghis Khan had swept down upon the Middle Kingdom. The pitched roofs of its inner buildings were only just visible above its outer walls of massive stone blocks. At the sight of it, Quentin unslung the rifle from his shoulder and settled it in the crook of his arm, and Kim followed his example. The pony-driver ceased his whistling and called his beasts to a halt, which they did in obedience to his voice, shaking their heads, their bells jingling faintly.

But their approach had already been heard. There was a sudden clatter, and a shower of dust and small stones rattled down from the hillside, and to Zoë's dismay, the turbaned scout she had seen before on the ridge rode out before them and signalled that he wished to parley.

It had not occurred to her that she might meet the same man again, and she wondered whether he might recognise her as the English woman he had watched ride along a country road on a bicycle. Viewed more closely, he had a face creased by a long deep scar across one cheek, and coarse Mongolian features. His eyes flickered rapidly over each member of the party. On Zoë they rested briefly, and she fancied that a hint of suspicion gleamed in them, before he returned his gaze to Quentin and addressed him at some length.

Quentin replied, indicating the surrounding hills. The scout shook his head and gestured widely with his rifle. Each side was assuring the other of good faith, a necessary ritual in which neither placed much confidence.

But the man seemed satisfied, and signalling them to follow him, led them through the gates of the *han* and into the courtyard. It was as if they had ridden through a time barrier. The ancient walls looked down on a wild, primitive scene, which had changed little in its essentials for six hundred years. The open fires that had been lit against the evening cool sent their flames leaping up to scorch walls already blackened by the fires that had warmed the silk and tea caravans of past centuries. The men who crouched around them, arguing, gesticulating, laughing, eating, playing age-old games of bone dice, might have stepped from the pages of her father's history-books. Only their ragged cotton uniforms, and here and there a modern rifle, generally very ill-maintained, marked any change.

The ponies and mules were stabled in one corner under an overhanging thatched roof, and it was towards these that their one pony-driver directed his beasts. Zoë coughed as she struggled to adjust to the atmosphere, thick with the smoke of the fires, with cooking smells, with the acrid smell of the animals and the rancid stench of grease and unwashed bodies.

Kim leaned forward and whispered, 'There are many more men here than Yang agreed.'

'That was to be expected,' Quentin murmured in reply. 'A good few seem to be drunk. As soon as it grows really dark, your father will move up with his men. So keep cool, don't look worried and take your time.'

The Mongol scout had entered the main building of the *han*, and now came out again and called to them, beckoning with one dirty hand for them to enter. They dismounted, left all the animals in the care of the pony-driver, and allowed the Mongol to conduct them inside and into the presence of the man they had come to meet.

As Eve had done earlier, Zoë felt a thrill of excitement run through her as they were ushered into the warlord's presence. Momentarily, it blotted out both worry and fear. It was followed, in Zoë's case, by an extraordinary initial feeling of disappointment and incredulity. She had imagined Yang as a huge, threatening, warlike personage. But the man who received them, seated and placidly drinking tea, was so wizened and shrunken that at first glance she would have assumed him to be of great age, even though she knew from Quentin that he was probably only in his forties.

Yang's body was so wasted that his head seemed too large. It was closely shaven, and the dry skin stretched over the bald cranium increased its skull-like appearance. He wore badges of rank on an army uniform, as would any regular officer, an affectation, no doubt, which pleased him. But any attempt at dignity it might have suggested was somewhat spoilt by a narrow wooden cylinder, pierced by tiny holes, that protruded from his filthy tunic. The Tiger of Nan-Ling was troubled by body fleas. The tube was a flea-trap. Tiny scraps of meat would be inserted in it, and the fleas, tempted by the smell, hopped and crawled into it through the holes, forsaking their human host. Once inside, they were unable to negotiate the tiny holes and make their escape.

Then Yang looked up. Never in her life had Zoë seen such evil little eyes as fixed themselves upon the new arrivals now: they held neither curiosity nor anger, still less welcome. Like a snake's eyes, they appeared black, shiny, lidless. They were alert and wary, yet dead to any emotion or passion. There was something completely inhuman about them. They belonged to a being who knew neither pity, love, happiness nor sorrow. It occurred to Zoë that the English expression 'Caught like rats in a trap', might here be termed like 'fleas in a trap'—and she hoped, uneasily, that Quentin, Li Kim and she were not the fleas. At Yang's side stood a heavily armed bodyguard—and the turbaned scout had entered behind them and guarded the exit.

The warlord silently stretched out a bony hand and indicated that they should be seated. When they had done so, an elderly man, by appearance the innkeeper, appeared from somewhere and nervously served them with tea in little pots with lids. It seemed that, for the moment at least, the niceties were to be observed. Yang sat motionless during the serving of the tea, studying each of them in turn. When he spoke it was to Quentin, but a movement of his desiccated hand indicated Kim.

'This is the son of General Li?' The voice was curious, very dry and creaky, and with a brittle edge to it. Zoë recalled how, as a child, she had walked on the dry heaps of leaves in the autumnal woodland, and listened to them crunch and crackle beneath her feet. Receiving confirmation of Kim's identity, Yang turned his shaven head slowly towards the young man. 'I remember your father. I knew him once, long ago, when I was a young man. Then your father was a great soldier, a Lion!' Yang's face contorted in what might have been a sardonic smile. 'But now I hear the Lion has grown old and toothless, no match for me!'

Angered at hearing his father so disparagingly described, and by such a human wreck as sat before them, Kim was moved to exclaim imprudently, 'My father is in excellent health, both of mind and body!'

'The Lion-cub wishes to growl,' Yang said scornfully, 'but only manages to squeak. But it is good that a son should defend the honour of his aged father. Filial duty is important, as the Sage teaches. It gains many good points for a man's spirit. You will greet your father from me, Lion-cub, when you see him again. *If* you see him again . . .' Yang turned back to Quentin. 'Well, barbarian, have you brought the gift you wish to offer to me?'

And for the first time, Zoë fancied that some trace of emotion showed in the reptilian eyes. Only very briefly, but it was there—anxiety, and greed.

'Have you brought your guests, the two ladies?' Quentin countered evenly.

'Oh, the women,' Yang said in disgust. 'If you have brought what I wished, then you can take your women. They are of no value. The younger one is comely, but the other is old and I cannot understand why you should want her back. Unless . . .' and to Zoë's surprise and discomfiture, the black eyes suddenly rested on her. 'Unless she is the mother of this young foreign man you have brought with you?'

'Yes,' Quentin said firmly. 'This is the lady's son.'

'Two dutiful sons,' Yang's shaven head nodded gravely. 'They say the young of today neglect their duty—but it is not so. I am pleased.'

'Old hypocrite!' thought Zoë, in distaste. A faint, prickling sensation touched the back of her neck. She glanced over her shoulder and saw that the turbaned scout was watching her, his eyes, narrow dark slits in his flat, weatherbeaten central Asian countenance, fixed on her. She forced herself to meet his gaze calmly and turned her head unhurriedly away.

'The opium you bring me as a gift—it is of good quality, and pure?' Yang demanded. 'It is not adulterated? I shall inspect it.'

'It would give us great pleasure if your guests, the two ladies, could inspect it also,' Quentin said smoothly, and he moved the rifle a fraction which lay across his knees.

'The guests of the Tiger of Nan-Ling are always comfortable,' Yang said. 'You need not fear. They are well.' He raised a bony finger aloft, pointing towards the ceiling. 'They are in an upper room, taking their ease.'

'I shall be honoured to show you the gift I have brought you,' Quentin said to him. 'But it would hardly be fitting that I should present it to you without your guests being there to see it.'

Yang considered the stalemate, and decided to resolve it. 'We shall all dine, barbarian. Afterwards, we shall exchange our gifts.'

They were joined at the table by the turbaned scout and the bodyguard, and the close proximity of these two persons, neither of whom seemed over-concerned with washing, did nothing to enhance the meal. Throughout, the turbaned man kept his eyes on Zoë, and eventually he muttered something into Yang's ear.

The warlord wiped his mouth on his sleeve. 'The young man speaks little,' he observed to Quentin, and nodding to Zoë. 'I have not heard a word from him.'

'He is young,' Quentin said calmly, 'and no doubt in awe at being in such company.'

Yang grunted and spat on the floor. 'It is well.' But he was clearly growing restive at the delay in getting his hands on the precious opium, and not in the mood to be sidetracked into discussions concerning anything else. 'Now, foreign devil,' he announced abruptly, 'we shall discuss my gift.'

His manner had changed over the last half-hour, and he seemed nervous and irritable, anxious to have their business concluded. It was growing late and dark, and possibly anxiety to inspect his booty for himself in good light had served to unhinge his brittle and unstable personality. There was a glitter in the cold black eyes which hinted at a far from normal mind.

'He is not to be trusted,' Li Kim whispered in Zoë's ear. 'But he trembles with desire to try the opium for himself. It is known that Yang chases the dragon.'

Zoë glanced questioningly at the two henchmen, but Kim hunched his shoulders, indicating that he did not know about them.

All at once, Yang ceased to speak in English, and Zoë suddenly found herself cut off from immediate knowledge of what was going on. Evidently he felt secure enough in his command of English for social small-talk —or perhaps he wished to display his learning—but he was not prepared to put himself at a disadvantage in negotiations by using any tongue but his own. Quentin was frowning in an effort to follow the rapid flow of discourse, and even Kim concentrated hard in order to keep up with what was evidently an unfamiliar dialect to him.

Zoë sat back and sighed. It was unbearably stuffy, and the meal sat uneasily on her nervous stomach. She glanced round. The bodyguard was picking his teeth, and staring vacantly into space. The Mongol scout had left the room. She frowned, wondering where he had gone. Curious to know, and also to see if she could discover somehow where the prisoners, whom they had still not seen, were kept, she got up and slipped out.

Back in the courtyard of the *han*, some of Yang's men, overcome by drink, had fallen asleep, slumbering in grotesque attitudes where they lay by the crackling fires. One or two groups were quarrelling, and a half-hearted drunken fight had broken out on the far side of the courtyard, coming to an abrupt end when one of the contestants stumbled and fell, howling, into the fire, from which he was rescued by his more sober companions. A bucket of unspeakable liquid, seized from a passing coolie who was emptying the latrines, was unceremoniously hurled over him and extinguished his smouldering clothing.

Zoë turned aside, a rising nausea in her throat, and met the squint-eyed gaze of their pony-driver, who sat by the *han* wall, guarding his beasts with the aid of a rifle Quentin had given him. He had been singing to encourage himself, and now, catching her eye and seeing her expression, he grinned and shrugged. Then his expression sharpened and grew wary.

Turning, she saw that the turbaned form of the Mongol scout had re-appeared and approached, carrying a basin of what looked like the cold remains of some kind of meat stew. He ignored them, and went to the pony lines, where he put the basin down in front of a stocky grey pony with a long, shaggy mane and tail, and hard little unshod hoofs. To Zoë's amazement, the animal pushed its muzzle into the dish and began to feed.

Years before, when her father had read to her of the Golden Horde, he had remarked that the Mongol warriors were said to have fed their horses on meat, adding that he himself thought it unlikely that a horse could be trained to do something so alien to its nature. But here, before her eyes, was a pony doing just that.

The scout looked satisfied at seeing his mount fed, and turned away, going back towards the inn. He had hardly gone, when a movement caught Zoë's eye, and what she had taken to be a bundle of rags in a corner unwrapped itself and took shape. Thin, stick-like arms and legs appeared, and a head, and a beggar-boy of about twelve years of age, certainly not more, began to creep towards the feeding pony, his eyes fixed hungrily on the dish.

The pony-driver sucked his front teeth and looked disapproving, but made no move to interfere as the thin hand stretched out cautiously and touched the rim of the dish. But the grey pony flattened its ears and snapped viciously, defending its dinner, and from behind them came a roar of anger. The Mongol scout dashed from the gloom, seized the child by the scruff of his neck, dragging him away from the horse-lines, and began to belabour him unmercifully.

Zoë, quite forgetting that on no account was she to

open her mouth, darted forward unthinkingly, grabbed the Mongol's sleeve, and shouted, 'Leave him alone!'

The scout threw the child aside like a handful of unwanted rags, and turned slowly. The pony-driver, realising what had happened, jumped up and came forward, holding his rifle in readiness. The Mongol's flat, scarred face moved slowly from side to side and up and down, assessing Zoë, his former suspicion glowing in his narrow eyes. Suddenly the glow became a gleam of recognition. He had remembered! She held her breath.

A shout from the door of the inn interrupted them and forestalled the scout. Quentin and Kim and Yang had all come out into the courtyard, Yang bobbing and weaving in a curious way, making quick little movements like a wary lizard. Without warning, a door flew open in the side of the inn and the bodyguard appeared, pushing in front of him Eve and Green Jade.

Both women, dusty, dishevelled and bewildered, were bundled into the courtyard, obviously having no idea of what was going on or what to expect. Then Green Jade caught sight of Kim, and giving a little cry of joy would have run forward, but was seized by the guard, who pulled her back with an ungentle hand.

'Thank God they are safe!' thought Zoë. 'And they *are* here.' She forgot the Mongol in an increased awareness of their collective danger, now that they were on the verge of possible success. Kim was muttering angrily beneath his breath, and fidgeting nervously with his rifle. She hoped that he would not be tempted to do something rash, having seen his beloved so roughly treated.

Quentin glanced at the two women, but gave no sign of relief or pleasure at seeing them safe. He and Yang went to the stack of unloaded opium, and the bodyguard slit open one of the packs. Yang inspected it, nodding feverishly, and appeared satisfied.

'Take my guests, your women, and go, barbarian!' he

ordered Quentin, waving them all away with his dry, mummified hand.

Immediately Quentin signalled to the pony-driver, who dragged their animals forward and they all scrambled hastily into the saddles. Green Jade and Eve were mounted on two of the pack-animals which had carried the opium, and the pony-driver vaulted on the back of the third.

'A pleasure to do business with you,' Quentin said courteously to Yang.

Yang, by now showing distinct signs of mental disturbance, twisting his bony hands and shaking his cobra's head to and fro, only muttered in response.

As their little band rode out of the courtyard in the dusk, passing between the flickering camp-fires and huddled groups of men, Eve leaned across from the saddle and peered at her nearest companion incredulously. 'Zoë—is that really you?'

'Yes, of course it is!' Zoë hissed, glancing about her uneasily. They were passing through the courtyard gates, which had been opened to allow them out. She had a most peculiar feeling that, somehow, it could not end like this. Glancing over her shoulder, she saw the distant figure of Yang, apparently giving some order, and a group of men who had been sitting by a fire got to their feet. At that point the gate was dragged shut and she could see no more.

Out in the darkness, possibly only half a mile away, was General Li and the men he was moving up under cover of night, waiting for a sign that the hostages and their rescuers were safe before he mounted his attack on the drunken bandits and their opium-obsessed leader. But to reach Li's troops, they had to descend a narrow hazardous path in total darkness. The pony-driver had gone ahead to mark out the route, and called back frequent warnings of obstacles.

Suddenly his warning call ended in a choking cry,

and the surrounding rocks became alive with living shapes.

Quentin gasped, 'That treacherous wretch, I thought he let us go too easily!' Then he yelled, 'Go!', and fired his rifle over the heads of the ponies which carried the women, so that the animals bolted into the darkness, away from the mêlée that had broken out all around.

Zoë's mount, seized with a kind of madness, plunged forward, head stretched out so low that it seemed as if nothing was in front of her saddle, no mane to grasp, only emptiness. Then it put a hoof into an unseen pothole, stumbled, and crashed on to its knees. Zoë pitched over the withers and landed with a bone-jarring crash on the stony ground.

As Zoë lay momentarily winded, the pony regained its footing and galloped off into the night. With difficulty, she managed to stagger to her feet, and stumbled forward in an attempt to follow, but a hand snaked out of the darkness, closing over her mouth, and in a single, horrifying instant, she became a prisoner.

A powerful sour stench of unwashed human body swept over her, and she knew, although she could not see who it was, that it was the Mongol. He must have tracked her, passing over the rocky terrain by night as easily as he would have done by day, like a hunting predator. Whatever ambush Yang had set up for the rescue party, the Mongol was pursuing his own particular quest. He suspected that the foreign 'boy' was the foreign woman he had seen before, and he meant to make sure.

Crushed against him in his repulsive grip, Zoë struggled in vain, almost overcome by the smell of sweat, dirt and horses. He kept his left hand clamped firmly over her mouth so that her head was held as if in a vice, ignoring her futile attempts to free herself, as his right hand tore at the front fastenings of her jacket, ripping it open. He thrust his hand inside, and she felt his loathsome touch on her skin as his fingers fumbled for and found her breast, closing on it in a painful grip.

She heard by her ear the man's hoarse chuckle of satisfaction. He had been right. This was a woman. In his glee, the hand he held over her mouth slackened its grip. Zoë seized her chance and sank her teeth deep into the flesh at the base of his thumb.

The Mongol let out a yell and snatched his hand away. Zoë twisted aside and stumbled blindly into the darkness. But at that moment she heard Quentin's voice, hoarse and desperate, shouting, 'Zoë!', and looking up, saw a familiar tall silhouette outlined against the moon and scrambling down the rocks above.

She screamed. 'Here!' as the scout turned and ran, vaulting into the saddle of the pony he had hidden near by. The sound of the pony's unshod hoofs thudded on the rocks. For a second, pony and rider were outlined against the skyline, very much as when she had first seen the scout on the road to Quentin's house. Then there was a crack from Quentin's rifle, and a spurt of yellow flame. The rider threw up his hands and pitched backwards. The pony, riderless, leapt forward and through the darkness came the sound of a heavy body rolling its way downhill, causing a small avalanche of stones and rock.

Fighting was still going on to the rear of them. Zoë staggered into Quentin's arms, throwing her own tightly about him, and sobbing.

He gave a strangled gasp, as if in pain, and muttered into her ear, as his hand caressed her cropped bare head clumsily, 'You're safe . . . General Li and his men are here. Everything is taken care of.'

And, with that, his hand fell away from her hair and he slid through her arms down to the ground, crumpling at her feet, motionless.

CHAPTER ELEVEN

THE WOUND had been caused not by a bullet, but by some kind of stabbing instrument, a large knife or a thrusting spear. It had passed through Quentin's right side, between his ribs, resulting in a two-inch gash at the point of entry out of which the blood flowed freely. General Li had led his men on to attack the *han* and lay his hands, at last, on the bandit warlord who had been so long his enemy. As a result, it was a very long time before they were able to get Quentin back to the house, and for the most time he was unconscious through loss of blood, aggravated by a cruelly jolting journey.

General Li himself had taken charge, organising a kind of litter balanced between two mules, but it was hardly the ideal way to transport any wounded man. By the time they had reached the house and examined the wound, the grey dawn was already creeping over the landscape, and the oil-lamps by the bedside burned low.

They were all gathered round the bed, Zoë and Eve, General Li and Kim, and an anxious Ah Ling. Quentin looked so pale that there seemed little difference between the colour of his skin and the bed-linen on which he lay. Even the bronzed suntan seemed to have faded. He looked what he was, a very sick man.

Eve said worriedly, 'If only we could be sure that the thrust has missed the vital organs.'

Zoë, pressing a linen pad to the wound to stanch the flow, whispered, 'Isn't there any doctor? I mean, not a Chinese one . . .' She glanced surreptitiously at the Li, as she spoke.

'None. When the Reverend Mr Morton was here, he used to do a little doctoring, and kept a medicine chest, but all the supplies he left behind were lost in the fire.'

Zoë removed the linen pad carefully. The wound looked clean, and was beginning to clot, but whatever had caused it would have been some uncleaned weapon, probably old, and the risk of infection had to be high. Moreover, thanks to her, they were without antiseptic. The possibility of gangrene froze her with dread, but it had to be faced.

'Whisky!' pronounced General Li unexpectedly, in English. It was, it transpired, the only English word he knew. He added an explanation in his own tongue, which Kim translated.

'My father says that, some time ago, Mr Farrell treated a man who had been badly cut with a knife, using whisky to wash out the wound. The wound did not become infected. My father thinks we should do the same.'

'There's bound to be whisky in the house!' Zoë exclaimed, seizing on this. 'Ah Ling?'

But Ah Ling was already on his way to fetch it.

They poured the whisky freely all over the injured area, and the smell of it made everything reek. Afterwards, Quentin claimed it was this which brought him round, either that or the fact that, as he described it, it made the wound sting as though a thousand wasps had attacked it. Whatever the cause, by the time they had bound up the wound he was conscious and muttering instructions to them faintly whilst they all told him, in two languages, to keep quiet.

'My father says,' Kim began, 'that we must leave you now, because we must return the lady Green Jade to her family. Also, he has to go to the town and make sure the captured men are well locked up. They will be executed. My father invites you both, honourable ladies, to view the execution of Yang. Mr Farrell too, of course, if he recovers in time to be present.'

'Thank you,' Zoë said hastily. 'We appreciate your

father's generous thought, but neither my sister nor I have a fancy to view an execution, even Yang's. Anyway, Mr Farrell can't be left.'

Quentin was restless, muttering something furiously. Zoë bent her head to his mouth and he whispered hoarsely, 'The opium, ask Li about it . . .'

'The opium will be destroyed,' Li Kim said firmly.

Zoë glanced at General Li, who looked bland. Possibly he hadn't understood, or perhaps he had not wished to. She hoped Kim would prevail upon his honoured parent to carry out the promised destruction. But the opium was a valuable commodity, and even an old stalwart like General Li, unexpectedly finding himself with a fortune on his hands, might be tempted to succumb to the prevailing corruption in the Chinese army.

When the Chinese party had left, the two women sat by the injured man's bedside, talking softly. He seemed to have fallen asleep. His complexion still had a grey tinge to it, which Zoë did not like at all, but all they could do was wait. He was a very strong man, and his own excellent health might prove the most effective medicine.

Eve sighed. 'I wish I had my spectacles. My eyes ache so.' She put her hand to her forehead.

'You must go and sleep,' Zoë urged. 'You've had a dreadful experience and must be exhausted. Go to bed straight away. I'll look in on you later, when I'm sure Quentin is all right.'

Eve looked from Zoë to Quentin and back again. 'I have often wondered,' she admitted shyly, 'whether —whether there was anything between you and Quentin.' She sounded apologetic. 'I couldn't help it. It was the way you looked at each other. I mean that no one ever looked at me like that. This may sound foolish, but it was as though you struck sparks off one another. Do you care for Quentin, Zoë?'

Zoë said quietly, 'Yes, I care.'

The three simple words had such a lost, hopeless sound to them that Eve leaned forward and took her sister's hand. 'He cares for you, too. I'm sure of it.'

'Not in the same way. Quentin lost the woman he loved, years ago. After that, the women in his life have been—a different sort of woman. He wasn't required to love them, only to make love to them, which is not the same. There is someone he cares about, but it isn't me, it's a child. All the love he has left in him is bound up in her.'

Eve shook her head. 'I can't advise you. I wish I could. But sometimes . . .' she hesitated. 'Sometimes, when we can't have what we want, we have to settle for what we can have.'

'That's not enough, if you love someone,' Zoë told her quietly. 'I couldn't bear to share any relationship with Quentin in which I loved him but he didn't love me in the same way. It would be the most miserable existence I could imagine.'

'I suppose you're right. I've never been in love,' Eve confessed. 'I always had my work, and I loved that. It's always been enough for me, but I don't think it's enough for you.'

When Eve had gone, Zoë sat down again by the bedside to watch over the sleeping man. In repose, he looked younger. The line of his mouth was softened, and she noticed for the first time that he had long, dark eyelashes, darker than his hair. The skin of his bare chest and shoulders was paler than his sunburned face and neck, and he wore a gold medallion on a thin chain that she had not noticed before. It must have been hidden under his shirt. She lifted it gently and looked at it curiously, wondering if it were Chinese. But it was a tiny case, with a watch-glass insert, of the kind in which mementoes of a loved one were kept, generally scraps of hair. This one held what looked like a few strands of fine gold thread. A baby's hair: his little daughter's. She

replaced it carefully, the tips of her fingers brushing his
bare skin which was warm and damp. That child, so
seldom seen, and to which he could never own, was the
linchpin of his life.

She felt no jealousy, only a great sorrow. Sorrow,
because Quentin could not have what he so much
wanted, and sorrow because she could not have him.
Neither of them, it seemed, could ever achieve their
heart's desire. Yet she loved him so much that it almost
made her ache. She loved him with all his imperfections,
his temper, his obstinacy. He was proud, and honest
and, in the truest sense of the word, honourable. It was
not the artificial honour of a military code or a social
convention. It was something much older, the honour of
the ancients, personal honour. A man can withdraw
from the world, but he cannot run away from himself.

'We all run from something,' Quentin had once told
her. 'Sometimes you can stay right where you are, and
still be running.'

She, Zoë, had been running away when she came to
China. At the time, she had not believed it, deceiving
herself. But it had never deceived him. He had seen a
young, warm and passionate woman, struggling to
mould herself into something she was not. As Eve so
rightly said, her work had always been enough for her,
but for Zoë it would never be enough. Not while this
man lived.

He looked peaceful, breathing easily. If the whisky
did the trick, and provided a good substitute antiseptic,
then rest and good nursing would bring him through.
And then?

She could not think about it now. Her mind was too
muzzy. She yawned and shook her head. She had not
slept in twenty-four hours—and what a twenty-four
hours they had proved! Her brain felt dead, and her eyes
heavy, her whole body ached with exhaustion. The
pillows of the bed offered an irresistible invitation, and

ten minutes' nap would do no harm. Zoë slipped off her shoes and curled up beside Quentin, falling instantly asleep.

When she opened her eyes, she was looking at the window, and seeing through it that the bright sun beat down upon the garden. She realised, horrified, that it must be mid-day. How could she have slept so long? What kind of a nurse did that? She turned over anxiously to look at the patient she was supposed to have been watching, and found that he was watching her.

She had no idea of how long he had been awake. He lay on his left side, facing her, one arm crooked behind his head, and showed no sign of fever. The blue eyes rested on her with an expression she could not quite fathom, but they were a clear, lucid blue. He smiled at her.

'How—how are you?' she faltered, sitting up.

'Weak as a baby, and my side is as sore as hell! But I'm all right. I'll survive. I'm as tough as old boots, and my guts—sorry—my inside is probably pickled in demon drink. You won't have to consult a geomancer yet, in order to locate a favourable burial-place.' He sounded weaker than usual, but in good humour.

In relief, she almost burst into tears. Looking away from him, she mumbled, 'I was afraid at first that you were going to die.'

'Well, it was a bad moment when some maniac leapt out of the night and stuck me like a pig. I didn't feel it too much at the time, and I was looking for you . . . But I knew he'd got me.' He stretched up a hand and brushed her cheek. 'Why are you crying? Because I'm all right?'

'No! And I'm not crying.'

'Ah, wishful thinking on my part. Male arrogance, you'd call it. I was flattering myself you were broken-hearted. Where are Green Jade and Eve?'

'I sent Eve off to bed. The Li family, father and son,

have taken Green Jade back to Wu Feng. They captured Yang and most of the men at the *han*; a lot of them were drunk and couldn't put up much resistance. General Li invited us all to see Yang decapitated, or whatever it is they plan to do to the poor wretch, but I declined.'

'Yang will be lucky to be decapitated. Probably something much nastier. Make sure that Li destroys that opium!' Quentin's voice grew stronger and more urgent.

'Kim will see to it, don't worry. He's very determined, and, you know, I think General Li has gained respect for his son, and is more inclined to listen to him. But none of this concerns *you*,' Zoë added firmly. 'You're to rest.'

'I'm not one for lying in bed—not alone, anyway. It was rather nice lying here and looking at you. You wouldn't care to come under this side of the sheet, would you?'

'You're supposed to be wounded!' she retorted, flushing.

'I still want you.' He shifted his weight on the pillows, and muttered, 'Ow!'

'You see? You're sicker than you think.'

'Rubbish! Come here, and I'll prove it.' He slid his arm round her waist.

'No! Behave yourself. You'll open up that wound and start it bleeding again.'

'Give me a kiss, anyway. Come on, comfort an injured man, can't you?' he wheedled.

Zoë hesitated, and bent over him tentatively. He moved more quickly than she anticipated, crooking his arm round her neck and pulling her down so that she sprawled over his bare chest. His mouth found hers, closing over it demandingly, and his hand grasped her cropped hair so that she could not escape. Neither did she want to escape. She surrendered willingly, oh, so willingly, to that insistent pressure, yielding to and answering it, every fibre of her being alive and wanting him.

Yet, within her, still remained the cold, certain knowledge that it was a terrible mistake.

'Don't, Quentin!' she whispered pleadingly, as soon as she was able to catch her breath.

'Why?' he returned in a low, husky voice. 'I want to . . . You want to . . .'

'You're injured, and the wound will . . .'

'It won't. Not if you do as I tell you.' He was pushing back the sheet.

There was a sharp knock at the bedroom door. Zoë gasped, and scrambled away from him, out of his grasp and off the bed. 'You're mad! I told you, no—and it's the middle of the day and the house is full of people!'

'Tell 'em to go away!' Quentin said irritably.

But Zoë pulled open the door. It was Ah Ling. 'Runner come from telegraph office, missee.' He handed her a crumpled envelope.

From the bed, Quentin called, 'What the devil is that? Bring it here!' He had pushed himself up on his left elbow, and held out his hand imperiously.

Zoë handed him the note. He tore it open, and scanned the words quickly. 'Tell the runner to send a message back that I'm coming,' he ordered Ah Ling.

'You can't go anywhere!' Zoë exclaimed.

In reply, he silently handed her the telegraphed message. It was from Canton, from Edward Linton. It read, *'Imperative you return Canton immediately'*.

'Is it a business matter?' she asked, puzzled.

'Damned if I know. No, I don't think so. Why should Teddy Linton start sending me cryptic messages on straightforward business matters? Urgent ones, at that! Unless a combination of heat and whisky has got to him at last.'

Zoë said quietly and reluctantly, 'Do you think . . . ?'

'Emily?' he replied in an expressionless voice. 'It doesn't look like a note demanding satisfaction. He might have found out, or she might have told him, out of

spite. I'll have to go to Canton and see what it's about.'
He looked up at her. 'Even at this distance, Emily
is managing to come between us, isn't she?' he said
bitterly.

Zoë shook her head. 'No, not Emily. It's something
else. Quentin, you can't go on that journey. You've lost
a lot of blood, and the wound is deep and won't knit
together for a long time.'

'I'll go tomorrow. I'll have got over the blood loss by
then, and the boat journey won't take anything out of
me.'

'There's a three-day pony ride before you get on that
boat.' She saw the familiar obstinate look close over his
face. 'Then I'm coming with you!' she said resolutely.
'You can't go alone.'

Quentin said warningly, 'Teddy Linton is a vicious
man, Zoë. Perhaps you ought not to be there.'

'I know what he is. He tried to seduce me, and I saw
that room.' Seeing his questioning look, Zoë explained,
'That morning, when we had to stay on in Canton
because I hadn't my Chinese papers, I went to their
bedroom to see if Emily was sick. It was in a terrible
state, bedclothes all over the place. She had a bruise on
her neck and seemed—numb, until she realised I was
there. Then hatred for me brought her to.' Zoë paused.
'I don't care if he is her husband. He had raped her. I
know it.'

Quentin picked up the telegraph message and
crumpled it in his hand. 'All right then, come. Lejeune,
the archaeologist, he's a Frenchman, an expert on
ancient artefacts. I sent those Tang figurines to him.
He's seventy, and one of the spryest men I've ever met
for his age. I'll beg his hospitality. He's often enough
enjoyed mine.'

She still believed Quentin was not fit enough, but
she had underestimated his determination and sheer

physical strength. Every yard of the pony ride was agony for him. His face ran with perspiration, and she could hear him swearing softly to himself every time the pony stumbled.

It was a great relief to be on a boat again, being carried swiftly, this time with the current, down river to Canton. The pony journey had tired Quentin and he was feeling the heat. He rested in the matting cabin during the first day afloat, and she sat by him, brushing away flies and insects, and fanning him to cool him. The crew thought that she was his wife, that was obvious. This boat was longer than the one by which they had come up-river. Its cabin was quite a big affair, capable of being divided into two sections by a hanging woven panel. By night, the mat curtain hung between the two sections of the cabin, but during the day it was taken down to make more space and let the air circulate more freely.

By the second day, Quentin had recovered from the exhaustion of the pony journey. The wound troubled him, however. The flesh, drawing together as it knitted, throbbed painfully, and the surrounding area was sore and tender. Zoë, changing the dressing on the evening of the second day, observed, 'It's healing much better than I expected. I know it hurts, but I was so afraid of infection.'

'Thank you, ma'am,' he said shortly. 'Yes, it's better, and yes, it hurts. But it's the least of my worries.'

'There's no point in worrying about the wretched Linton until we reach Canton,' she said in a practical voice, which was a disguise for a real feeling of anxiety on her own part.

'He's a devious rogue,' Quentin growled. 'Do you mind if I smoke? It will keep the insects away.'

'So long as you don't go to sleep with a lighted cigarette still in your hand. This boat is highly flammable with all those matting panels.'

'When I've finished, I'll throw the stub overboard, I

promise. Go and get some sleep.' He dismissed her gently, but very firmly.

Zoë scrambled back to her side of the matting curtain and tried to settle. Something whined about her head, a mosquito. She could smell Quentin's tobacco, and obviously so could all the insects which seem to have taken refuge in her section of the cabin as a result. She could not sleep. It was hot, the mosquito whined incessantly, she began to puzzle over Linton's message, to wonder whether Emily had done something rash, if the child was safe, if Quentin was still smoking or whether the smoke drifting through the mat curtain came from smouldering boat timbers, lit by an abandoned cigarette-stub. One thing which did not worry her was that Quentin might try to take any advantage of their shared sleeping-quarters. He had other things on his mind.

The wound was hurting. She could hear him draw in his breath sharply every time he moved on his cramped bed. Eventually he called softly, 'Zoë?'

She got up and crawled back through the curtain to sit beside him. 'I wish you'd stop worrying.' She took his hand in the darkness.

'I was wondering,' he said, 'if Emily had done a bunk. I don't quite see how she could, but she was always threatening it.'

'You're wondering if she would have taken the child, too.' She tried to sound calm. 'You—you'd be very unhappy if she did, wouldn't you?'

'I shall have to lose touch with Cara eventually,' he said dully. 'I know that.'

'Cara? Is that her name? Do you know, you're the only person I've ever heard call the child by her name. She was always just "Baby".'

After a moment he said, 'It's odd, the way things seldom work out as you want, and never as you expect.'

Zoë said softly, 'Yes, it's odd . . .'

'Ah, mademoiselle!' Monsieur Lejeune exclaimed. 'The lady who found the Tang figurines.'

Startled, Zoë protested, 'Our gardener found them.'

'No matter. I have them safe here. They are of great interest, and great value. Very fine pieces; but I understand from Monsieur Farrell that all the rest of the find is lost?' He shook his head and looked up at her hopefully, as if she might yet deny the loss. When she confirmed it, he looked despondent. 'A tragedy! It happens so often. In Egypt, where I worked some years ago, it is the same story. So much stolen, smuggled, lost . . . You know, a European museum would "give its eye teeth"—I believe the English expression is?—for the figures you found. If you do not wish to keep them for your private collection, I would venture to suggest, as a Frenchman, that the Louvre . . . But, naturally, you may prefer the British Museum.'

He was a small, spare man, so much dried up after many years of working in inhospitable climates that he looked as though he might last almost as long as some of the things he had unearthed. He had silvery, bushy hair, and small, bright, round eyes, like a sparrow's. The bungalow in which he lived, and to which he had welcomed them with enthusiastic hospitality, was crammed from ceiling to cellar with carvings, paintings, pottery, bronzes and furniture. To say nothing of porcelain. 'This is Ming,' he would say casually of a vase. 'It is a favourite period for western collectors, but by no means the finest. Now this is Sung . . .' So he chattered on, lost in his work.

Quentin left the archaeologist describing the arrangements of Tang burial-chambers to Zoë. He had an idea that Miss Hammond had intended to accompany him on his visit to Edward Linton, and the look of baffled frustration in her hazel eyes as he abandoned her, hopelessly locked into conversation with the enthusiastic Lejeune, afforded him a brief moment of amusement.

In truth, he was anything but amused. The gash in his side throbbed and smarted, and made it difficult for him to raise his right arm because that pulled on the angry flesh. As he walked through the crowded streets, full of early evening shoppers buying their bowls of steaming delicacies from the street vendors, the passers-by bumped against him. Once or twice the resulting spasm of pain sent blackness whirling about his head, and he hoped to hell he would not pass out.

He knew that Linton would be in his office at the warehouse at this time of day. The head clerk knew Mr Farrell, and allowed him through without hesitation. Linton, sitting over his accounts ledger and sucking an unlit cheroot, glanced up as the shadow of Quentin's tall figure fell across him.

'Got my message, I see.' He indicated the chair opposite, and stooping to one side, produced a whisky bottle from a cupboard in the side of his desk. 'Have a drink?'

Quentin said nothing, watching Linton pour out the whisky. The man looked pleased with himself, yet at the same time nervous. He spilled a little of the liquid on the top of the desk. Quentin, his left hand resting in his jacket pocket, leaned forward to pick up the glass in his right hand, and could not prevent himself from wincing.

Linton noticed it, and narrowed his bloodshot eyes speculatively. 'Have you been sick? You look a bit pale about the gills. Not picked up malaria, have you?'

Quentin said, 'No, I've got a hole in my ribs. I had a run-in with bandits.'

'Bad.' Linton shook his head.

'Yes. But it might have been worse. These had guns —brand-new, modern rifles—so recently acquired that they had hardly had time to get dirty and damaged yet.'

Some of Linton's self-confidence faded, but he gave

no other outward sign of alarm. He tossed back his own whisky and shook his head again. 'You've got a gun-runner operating in your area, old man.'

'Haven't I just . . .' Quentin replied softly. He leaned back. 'Why have you brought me down here, Linton?'

'A personal matter.' Linton set down his empty glass, put out a hand to the bottle, changed his mind and withdrew it. 'The fact of the matter is, my wife's run off with Hansen.'

'With *Hansen*?' Quentin could not control his surprise.

'You didn't expect that? No more did I—at first. Hansen is a psalm-singing humbug, but he always had an eye for Emily, and after you finished with her . . .' He allowed his voice to trail away, and a vicious look entered his mean little eyes.

'All right, I don't deny it,' Quentin said. 'But what has it to do with me now?'

'Because, my dear Farrell, there remains the question of the child!' Linton told him, not troubling to disguise his triumph.

Quentin caught his breath. 'The child's here?'

'Certainly. I've had to make a decision about her future. A busy man like myself, no wife about the place, it would be difficult for me to bring up a child—even if she were my own. But the missionaries run orphanages for the foundling babies the poor Chinese bring them or they find abandoned. I thought I might send the child to one of those. Spartan places, of course, but the missionaries take their duties seriously.'

'She isn't an orphan!' Quentin said in a low, tense voice.

'No,' Linton countered. 'She's a bastard brat of yours, and I won't raise her under my roof or let her mas-querade under my name!' He leaned back and studied his visitor, his sharp, shifty eyes marking Quentin's flushed countenance and ill-concealed agitation. 'Emily said, before she left, that you'd be willing to take the kid. Do you want her?'

'I'll take her,' Quentin said briefly. Linton gave away nothing, not even this unwanted child, and he knew it. 'What do you want in exchange?'

Linton smiled, almost affably. 'Well, now, I'll leave it to you. What will you offer for the child, her birth certificate and a properly made out and legal document signed by me, agreeing to your adopting her?'

Quentin moved slightly in his chair, which creaked, as he propped one foot up on the other knee in his habitual way.

The sight of the man whom he had imagined he held at his mercy making himself so comfortable, obviously discountenanced Linton, who added belligerently, 'Well?'

'I'll tell you,' Quentin said. 'You'll give me the child and the papers, and in return, I'll leave Canton with her, nice and quietly. I won't do as I was planning to do, which was to bring the authorities down here and get them to turn this warehouse of yours inside out. I don't like gun-runners and I don't like you. For the past year I've been running a check on the business you do. I've said nothing, for Emily's sake. But Emily has gone, and nothing stops me now. I know what's come in here, and what's gone out, officially and unofficially. The last time the *Empress of Cathay* docked at the wharf, you took delivery of twelve crates of industrial machine parts.'

'For the manufacture of cotton cloth,' Linton said promptly. 'The Chinese are thinking of modernising their production. They want some product cheaper and quicker to produce than silk. All the papers were in order for that shipment.'

'I dare say. But the factory on the packaging labels doesn't exist—except on paper. I've been out to the "site" of it. It's a burial-ground. Unless the Chinese are going to set up their looms among the ancestral tablets, there's precious little in the way of cotton goods going to be produced there. I've other examples. I've shipping dates, I've numbers of crates. You'll give me my daughter, Linton, or the whole lot goes to the relevant authorities here and in Hong Kong.'

'They won't listen to you, facts and figures or not!' Linton sneered. 'It's a regular business, running guns. I've government officials in my pay.'

'Not all; and none who is willing to risk his neck for you.'

Linton said softly, 'A man can come to grief, wandering about alone, here. I pay the men in this warehouse. They'll swear you never came in here.'

Quentin smiled thinly and slowly took his left hand out of his pocket. 'That's why we'll go out together, you and I, and conclude our business peaceably, and to our mutual satisfaction, elsewhere.'

Linton gazed, putty-faced, at the unwavering black muzzle of the revolver. He ran his tongue round his dry lips, and muttered, 'I've got your word? I give you the child, and you give me all the records you've made on my business?'

'I'll give you the records. But I'm not letting you go on running guns to your heart's content. You bring them in here, but you sell them up country. I have good contacts with the Chinese provincial officials, and I'll stop you, see if I don't.'

A malicious smile touched Linton's unattractive countenance. 'You can try. But there's revolution in the air, and everyone wants guns. Your Chinese officials will drink tea with you, be polite, promise . . . but they'll do nothing. You see, they need me.'

'I think that you're totally expendable,' Quentin told him softly. The muzzle of the revolver moved up slightly, towards the sweating man's forehead. 'Suppose, overcome by grief because your wife has left you,

you were to be discovered lying dead here on your desk, having blown out your own brains in despair.'

Linton swallowed and conceded defeat. 'I'll give you the child. Take the brat! I never want to see it again.'

Zoë had fallen asleep in a chair downstairs, waiting for his return. Dinner had been delayed for Quentin for an hour, but when he neither returned nor sent a message, she and her host dined without him. It was difficult to conceal her concern and she could not explain it to the archaeologist, since she herself did not know what Edward Linton had in mind.

Lejeune, chattering in his way about the food and archaeology—subjects which appeared of equal importance to him—was observant enough to mark her distress. Without warning, he reached across the table and patted her hand. 'Dear mademoiselle,' he said soothingly, 'I see you are worried about my friend, Farrell. You think he may be in some danger.' He held up his wrinkled hand to prevent her reply, and went on, 'But, you know, he is a very resourceful man, and used to looking out for himself. If he were not, he would not have survived all these years in China. He is also, in his own way, a ruthless man. I say this not in criticism but in admiration. He is a man who will have what he wants, in the end.' Lejeune smiled, and his button-bright little eyes twinkled at her merrily as though he knew some secret.

After dinner, he asked her to excuse him, and went to work in his study. So Zoë waited, growing hourly more anxious, until her eyelids closed, despite her best efforts to stay awake.

The sound of someone arriving at the house awoke her. She sat up with a start, grasping the arms of the chair, and saw that it was almost midnight. She could hear Quentin's voice, and Lejeune's, and then a female Chinese voice. Before she had time to go and investigate further, however, the door opened and Quentin came in. He was hatless and looked tired but triumphant, clasping in his arms a sleeping bundle, above which showed a crop of golden curls. Behind him, she saw the diminutive form and beaming face of the Lintons' ayah.

Hardly able to believe it, Zoë whispered, 'They have let you take the child!' She stared at him, unable to understand how such a thing could be.

Quentin returned the baby to the ayah's arms, and the woman scurried away with her. They could hear Lejeune's chuckling and making baby-talk in French. It sounded incongruous and quite unreal.

Quentin threw himself down in the chair opposite Zoë's, and automatically put a hand to his injured side. But if he was in pain, he was hardly conscious of it, so obviously did he float on a cloud of euphoria.

'Yes,' he said with quiet satisfaction. 'Linton has given me the child, her birth certificate and a document agreeing to my adopting her.' He saw how puzzled Zoë looked, and explained, 'Emily ran off with Hansen. You're surprised, and I must say it shook me. I wasn't surprised that Emily had left, but I was taken aback to learn it was with Nils Hansen. However, perhaps she'll be happy with him. I hope so.'

'What about Linton?' Zoë whispered.

'Hardly broken-hearted . . . more crowing in delight. The man's a rogue, running guns up country to bandits like Yang. I had proof, but was obliged to hand it over in exchange for Cara. It's not the end of the story, however. When I get back, I'll go to General Li and get the Chinese authorities moving on it. Somewhere along the line there has to be a Chinese middleman, and we can certainly lay our hands on him.'

Zoë, trying to absorb all of this, stammered, 'But what about Cara? Will you take her back with you?'

'Why not? The ayah is willing to come along, too.'

There was a pause, then Zoë said sincerely, 'I'm very

glad and very happy for you. I was so worried about that child.'

'Were you?' The blue eyes rested on her. Then Quentin said, in a changed voice, 'You know, Zoë, I've been thinking for some while that it's time I tried to make something more—more orderly out of my life. I've worked hard over the last ten years and built up a good business. I'm not poor. But my personal life has been a mess. I want it to be different.'

'If you really mean that, then it will be,' Zoë said.

'Hmm. Yes, but left alone, I tend to go off-target a little. I need someone to keep me on the path.'

'You have Cara now.'

'Cara's a twelve-month-old infant. She's a reason, but not a guiding hand. What I need, or rather the person I need, is you.'

Zoë felt the colour drain from her cheeks and was glad of the low level of lighting in the room which left her in semi-shadow. Quentin was sitting near an oil-lamp, and she could see his face clearly. He leaned forward, his expression questioning and earnest.

'Will you do it, Zoë? Take me in hand? Finish what you started? Because you did start it, you know, pouring away my whisky and reading me the riot act every time I stepped out of line.'

'You make me sound like a gaoler,' Zoë said, aghast.

'I was hoping that it might sound more like a wife.'

Zoë drew in her breath. 'You're asking me to marry you?' Her voice sounded oddly distant to her ears, as if it came from far away.

He said, rather hesitantly, 'Would you? I do need you, Zoë, and Cara needs a mother. You do care about Cara, don't you?'

Zoë's heart plummeted. The child—his concern was not with her, but with Cara. He didn't want a wife: he wanted a mother for the child. Zoë was available, and he had asked her.

She began to speak very slowly, picking her words carefully, trying to keep her voice from shaking and the awful pain in her heart from echoing in it. 'Yes, I care about Cara, and I know I could love her. I'll willingly help you to bring her up. But I won't marry you, Quentin. Cara began her life with one set of feuding parents, and the last thing she needs is another pair.'

He frowned. 'Why should we fight? I know we've skirmished in the past, but that was . . . If we were married, it would be different.'

'Would it? People are not different when they marry: they are the same as they were before. It wouldn't work out.'

It wouldn't, she was thinking, because I love you with every breath in my body, but you only have a fancy to have me around, running your house, bringing up your child, being there in your bed when you feel like it. She couldn't tell him any of this, so she said, her voice sounding increasingly stiff and unfriendly as the effort to hide the pain in it became greater and greater, 'You want a mother for Cara, that's natural. You've picked on me, and that's—flattering. It's also wrong.'

He was shaking his auburn curls vigorously. 'You've misunderstood, Zoë. It was a pretty wretched proposal, perhaps, but in unusual circumstances, and I can't help it if I can't provide a candlelit dinner and gipsy violins and go down on one knee! I'm not just looking for a mother for Cara.'

'So why didn't you ask me to marry you before?' she burst out sharply. 'Why this sudden desire for domesticity?'

Quentin said harshly. 'Because I had an idea, obviously a very stupid one, that we might be a family. Now I see it was the foolish dream of a man who has lived too long alone and too much out of touch with his own people. I suppose that damn school still fills your head, and offers you more than I can!'

He was hurt by her rejection, and angry. But she was growing angry, too, because had he really thought she would accept his proposal, just like that? She wanted to scream, 'You haven't spoken one word of love to me!' Somehow she managed to choke this back, and reply, 'Yes, I intended to return and help Eve to found a new school. I'll always be there when you want me, and when Cara wants me. But it won't be as your wife.'

'I see.' Quentin said stonily. 'I understand.' He took a deep breath. 'You won't mind waiting a few days in Canton before we start back? I have—some other business to see to here.'

'Yes, of course.' There was an expression on his face that almost frightened her, it indicated such a bottled-up fury. Because she was so unhappy and so much emotion was bottled up inside her, too, she burst out, 'You don't have to be angry about it! You've got what you wanted. You've always insisted on having what you wanted, haven't you, Quentin? No one has to stand in your way. You sent for Alice to come out East, you dallied with Emily when she took your fancy, you set your heart and mind on having the child, and you think you might just add me to that list! But I have a mind and feelings of my own, and I won't be yours on those terms.'

She was immediately sorry for all of it, especially the part about Alice, which had been a great tragedy in his life and one for which he had always nursed a secret feeling of responsibility. But pain made her cruel. He had no idea of how much he had hurt her, and she did not want to let him see it. But, at the same time, she felt an overwhelming urge to strike out at him in some way.

Quentin was deathly pale. He stood up and looked down on her, his blue eyes burning with a ferocity she could not have imagined. 'So that's it!' he said hoarsely. 'After all . . . after all the high-flown nonsense about feuding parents and the school, *now* the truth comes out. You always disliked and despised Emily, and you were jealous of her, too! I knew that, and I accepted it. But I never thought you were mean-spirited enough to take out your spite on the child! It's not because I'm asking you to mother *my* child that you've decided to stand on your dignity—it's because I've asked you to be a mother to Emily's! Cara is Emily's child, and you're not one to forgive her, or me, are you, Zoë?'

Horrified, she began, 'No, Quentin, that isn't . . .'

But he had stormed out of the room before she could complete her sentence.

CHAPTER TWELVE

A REFUSED PROPOSAL of marriage, no matter in what circumstances it is made, or for what reason, can only leave the unhappiest of situations between the two persons involved. Usually they can resolve some of the embarrassment and injury to feelings and self-esteem by avoiding one another, or, if such a thing is difficult, by one of them going away for a short spell. But in their case, as Zoë reflected miserably, she and Quentin were to be flung together on a two-and-a-half-week journey by river-boat and pony, in the closest circumstances and an unwished intimacy.

The first time she had made this journey with him, he had been a stranger of wild appearance and dubious reputation, whom she had found a highly disturbing companion but one with whom she was able to cope by keeping him at his distance, not entirely successfully. Now he was the man she loved, and had refused, and the thought of the trip up country together was agony to her.

It was without doubt the worst journey of her entire life. Quentin barely spoke to her. He sat under an awning on the deck and played with his baby daughter, and worried whether they would obtain fresh milk for her along the way. The ayah sat by, nodding and smiling like one of those toy mandarins with nodding heads which it sometimes amused Chinese craftsmen to carve. Zoë sat outside this little circle, longing to join it, fearing to offer, and ultimately excluded from it not by anything spoken, but by an invisible barrier which Quentin seemed to have built round himself.

With things in such a state, it was impossible even to

contemplate living under the same roof with him, passing days in unfriendly and reproachful silence. She explained matters to Eve, as briefly as possible, telling her only that Quentin had proposed and that she had refused him. Eve, obviously disappointed, nevertheless understood how her sister felt, and suggested that they should throw themselves on the hospitality of Wu Feng until such time as they could find another building to house a new school.

'So difficult,' Eve sighed. 'And so costly. Wu Feng has offered money, also the Li family and several other Chinese families who had daughters at the old school, but to find a suitable building won't be easy.'

Yet this was all that Zoë had now to occupy her days. It could not stifle the permanent ache within her, or fill the empty void in a life without Quentin. Not a waking moment passed, but she thought of him, and of Cara, and wondered what they were doing. She even entertained a wild hope that he might call and see them, but the days passed, and he did not appear.

It had all taken a fearful toll on her health and appearance. She saw that every time she looked in a mirror. The face which looked back was tired, pale and unwell. Her skin had begun to acquire that unhealthy ivory tinge which marked European women who were succumbing to an alien and difficult climate and way of life. She was going the way of Eve, and she knew it.

Eve could also see it, and her eyes mirrored her concern. Green Jade, too, was worried.

'Miss Zoë,' she said carefully one morning, as they tossed handfuls of food into the fish-pond in Wu Feng's garden. 'You know, many things I admire in English ways, and so does Kim. But in some things, I think Chinese ways are better.'

Zoë smiled faintly. 'What ways are those, Green Jade?'

'Well, you see,' she replied, concentrating very hard

on the fish. 'The marriage between Kim and myself has been arranged by go-betweens. I know that Kim and I would like to have been more involved ourselves. But it is sometimes very helpful to have a go-between. You see, there are not so many arguments and quarrels between the parties. If something is wrong, or you want to complain, you tell the go-between. The go-between brings the other person's answer. You have more time to think what you want to say, and to consider what the other person says.'

'Yes, I suppose that's true,' Zoë admitted, wondering where all this was leading.

'So,' said Green Jade firmly, 'I think that Miss Eve and I should act as go-betweens for a marriage between you and Mr Farrell. I think such a marriage would be very good. Miss Eve thinks so, and my father, and General Li. My father says that Mr Farrell should have a wife; a man cannot bring up a child alone. General Li says . . .' Here Green Jade looked a little flushed and whispered conspiratorially, 'He did not say it to *me*, but Kim heard it, and told me. You will not be offended, Miss Zoë? The General thinks it is not right that you should have lived in Mr Farrell's household, and now you have left it.'

'I'm not a runaway concubine!' Zoë said sharply. 'Green Jade, I know you mean well, but I must ask you not to mention this—this matter again. I suspect that you have heard some rumour that Mr Farrell and I might marry, but I assure you that it's quite unfounded.'

A wise, old-young expression crossed Green Jade's pretty face. 'That is because you did not have go-betweens, and tried to arrange this marriage yourselves.' She glanced at Zoë. 'Mr Farrell is coming to see my father tomorrow, and General Li and Kim also.'

Zoë turned aside, hoping the girl had not seen the effect this news had on her. So, he was coming here at last, and it was likely she would see him. Now that there was a real possibility of their meeting again, she panicked.

'I hope you will explain to your father, Green Jade, that I—I really can't see Mr Farrell. It would be very awkward.'

Green Jade looked obstinate. 'Mr Farrell is a guest.'

'So am I. And, Green Jade, neither you, nor any other person, is to mention the idea of marriage to Mr Farrell, do you hear? I absolutely forbid it.'

'I am only a lowly piece of silver in my father's household, an unworthy daughter,' said the girl smugly, in the manner of one who absolves herself from all responsibility. 'I cannot speak for my honoured parent, or for the brave and noble General Li.'

General Li arrived the following day, ahead of Quentin who, to Zoë's relief, had not yet put in an appearance. He was accompanied by his son, and a round-faced, pert and sharp-eyed damsel of about thirteen, whom any teacher would instantly identify as the kind guaranteed to cause mischief in a school-room anywhere in the world. This imp, Zoë learned, rejoiced in the singularly inappropriate name of Graceful Willow—and was Kim's sister. They all sat in the garden, Wu Feng and Madam Wu included, and partook of tea.

Madam Wu was a seldom seen lady who spoke no English, but who smiled a great deal. She was extremely shy, and conveyed her rare contributions to the conversation through Green Jade. It was clear that Wu Feng was as devoted a husband as he was a father, but Madam Wu's retiring nature and lack of contribution to family discussions had its origin, Zoë learned, in the fact that the poor lady had failed to produce a male child. Only the birth of a son would have given the unfortunate woman the right to make her voice heard with any authority. Now, despite her husband's affection and her charming and intelligent daughter, Madam Wu seemed anxious only to appear in the background. It was a situation which appeared to Zoë both heart-breaking and unacceptable. Yet like so many things in the Middle Kingdom, it had to be accepted.

At least Madam Wu had not suffered the humiliation of seeing her husband take another, and more fertile, wife, as he would have been entitled, and indeed, expected, to do. Wu Feng's loyalty to this self-effacing wife who had given him no son touched Zoë immensely, and raised the mandarin high in her estimation.

They sat and drank the tea beneath the peach trees, and Wu Feng himself graciously inspected the fruit and picked peaches for Green Jade and Graceful Willow in the manner of an indulgent father and relative. He also contrived, Zoë noticed, to slip a particularly fine peach into his ever-useful sleeve. A little later, she was charmed to see Wu Feng choose a moment when everyone else was busy talking, to present this prize peach to shy little Madam Wu, who dimpled at him affectionately.

It was all very domestic, peaceful and harmonious, when, without warning, Wu Feng produced a bamboo tube from his capacious sleeve, like a conjuror a rabbit. At the sight of it, Li Kim turned first white and then red, and looked as if he were about to faint.

'My future son-in-law,' said Wu Feng majestically, 'is a young man of truly remarkable talents. He has the courage of a lion, as we would expect of a son of his father, and he has achieved great success in his education. As if that were not enough, he is also a poet of great gift.'

'It is a wretched thing,' muttered the crimson Li Kim, breaking out in a cold sweat.

Wu made a graceful gesture, rebutting his modest denial, and turned to his daughter. 'It is to you, my child, that your bridegroom has addressed these flattering words. Therefore it is into your keeping that I give this golden flower of his talent.'

And at long last, Wu Feng handed Kim's love poem to Green Jade.

As cries of surprise, delight, thanks and denial (from Kim), of any claim to be a poet filled the air of Wu Feng's garden, Eve leaned towards her sister and whispered, 'Quentin is waiting in the house. Will you not go and talk to him?'

'In the house?' Zoë exclaimed in alarm, turning pale. 'I can't, Eve! Anyway, he doesn't want to see me.'

'But he does. There's something he has to tell you. Please, Zoë,' Eve touched her sister's hand. 'Won't you do it for me?'

Quentin was in Wu Feng's private study. The room, lined with books and western scientific journals, was in a cooling gloom, its windows all shuttered against the heat of the day. He looked up at the sound of her approach, and when she appeared in the doorway, there was an awkward moment of mutual embarrassment during which they looked at one another in a strained silence.

Then Quentin said, 'Thank you for coming.'

'I did it for Eve,' Zoë mumbled, and wished she hadn't, because it was hurtful and, in any case, not true. Though she had feared to meet him again, she had longed to see him. Sooner or later, too, she had to see him. In such a small community they could not have avoided one another indefinitely. She tried to pull herself together, and asked, more firmly, 'How is Cara?'

At the mention of the child he looked slightly obstinate. 'Doing pretty well. She holds on to furniture and pulls herself upright, trying to walk. I thought that babies crawled all over the place for months. The ayah says that Cara will be an early walker. I don't know much about babies.'

He was finding life difficult; Wu Feng had been right.

But Quentin would see it through, and he would not ask Zoë's help again. He was studying her critically and now said, with some concern in his voice, 'You look ill.'

He had been startled and dismayed at her altered appearance, but had not wished to let her see it. Now a fear gripped his heart that she was really sick.

He was relieved, though not entirely convinced, to hear her say, 'I'm all right, just a little tired.' And desperate, and lonely, but what's to be done about that?

Aloud, she asked, 'Did you manage to get on the track of the gun-runners?'

He twisted his face into a grimace and shrugged his broad shoulders. 'I went to see Li, if that's what you mean, and I've been hammering away at him and Wu today. In return, Li told me a story, and it's the only reply I'm likely to get. It was a tale from Chinese history concerning the Empress Wu. She was troubled with feuding generals, so she trained her cat to eat off the same plate as a pet parrot, and invited all the warlords to gather and view this scene of harmony between former enemies.' He paused.

'And what happened?'

'The cat bit off the parrot's head and ate the bird.'

'Is that true? What on earth did General Li mean?' Zoë demanded, startled.

'He meant that civil war is coming and internal strife, and no one can stop it. It's just as Linton said. All the generals want to buy guns, even Li himself. They won't stop Linton, they'll place orders with him.'

Zoë understood the bitterness and despair in his voice. A terrible time was coming, the shadow of revolution falling across a land he loved, and he could do nothing to prevent it.

'Was that what you wanted to tell me?' she asked gently. 'Eve said there was something.'

'No.' He shook his head. 'Something else. When we were in Canton, it was not only Linton who had a

surprise in store for me. There were some letters waiting, from England. I would have told you about them at
the time, only—we weren't seeing eye to eye, and I
thought you wouldn't want to know, so I let it go.' He
avoided looking at her flushed face, and rubbed his hand
jerkily over his untidy auburn hair.

It was such a familiar gesture, and one she loved so
much, that she wanted to cry. She wanted to take him in
her arms and say, 'I love you, and if you have troubles, I
want you to tell me about them, so that we can face them
together, not hide them away from me.' But he was a
proud man, and his pride had been hurt. He was as
prickly as a hedgehog, suspicious and defiant.

'One of the letters was from my family's solicitors . . .
and one from my father.'

'From your father?' It sounded rude, but she could not
help exclaiming the words. She knew that Quentin's
father had long ago disowned his black sheep of a son,
and they had not corresponded for years. What on earth
could have happened?

'It gave *me* something of a shock,' he said wryly. 'The
fact is, my elder brother—always a great man to hounds
—broke his neck on the hunting field last Christmas. No
one thought to tell me about it at the time—*I* was
already dead as far as any of my family was concerned!
But old Winters, the senior partner of the solicitors who
handle my family's business and affairs, has been at
pains to point out to my father that he now has no other
heir of his own blood but me. It's taken ages; but
Winters, who was always decent to me, I must say,
managed to persuade my father that it was time to seek a
reconciliation. So the old man wrote to me, at long last,
not very graciously, but fairly enough. He wants me to
go back. At first I thought, the devil I will. Why should I?
Then I began to think that I should go, because I've Cara
to consider now and her future, and the state of things
here. It's not going to be a place to bring up a child, and

in any case I should at least hear what the old man has to say to me, after all this time.'

Bitterness echoed in his voice, but Zoë was not deceived. Strange as it was to imagine Quentin anywhere but in his familiar Chinese surroundings, yet this was what he had longed for secretly during so many years in exile—his father's hand, stretched out in a wish for reconciliation.

'It's what you really wanted all the time, isn't it?' she asked dully.

He was leaving. He would go to England and she would never see him again. She could not pretend any longer, or disguise the tremor in her voice. She had often read of hearts breaking, and thought it a fanciful description, but that was exactly how it felt, a terrible pain in her heart, as if the end of the world had come, as perhaps the end of her world had.

She said wretchedly, 'You'll go away . . .' It was a simple statement of fact, yet expressed with such despair that he could not fail to hear it.

He stopped pacing up and down and came to stand before her. Something like hope flickered in his face, and then faded. 'Do you . . . mind?' His voice sounded hoarse and hesitant, and his demeanour almost shy, as if he were afraid to ask, and feared the answer.

Zoë whispered, 'Yes, I do mind.' Miserably, she added in a small, dead voice, like a lost child, 'I don't want you to go.'

'Is that true?' Quentin asked eagerly, then made an effort to control his voice. 'If it is true, Zoë, and if you really mean what I . . . pray you mean, then would you . . .' He hesitated again, and stumbled on before she could speak, 'I dare say this is stupid, but I suppose you couldn't . . . reconsider?' Then, in a rush, he burst out passionately, 'For God's sake, Zoë, say you'll come with me!'

'I don't think I could go on living here, without you,'

she said in the same small voice, and before the words had left her mouth, found herself suddenly swept up in his embrace, crushed against him.

'And I can't go on without you, Zoë!' he said earnestly. 'You're my compass and my guiding star, and I'm no damn good without you at all. I fell in love with you when we first travelled up river together, and you went bathing one afternoon, do you remember?'

'I remember,' she murmured, her head muffled against his chest.

He stroked her hair tenderly. It was beginning to grow again now, and she wore it in a glossy long bob, like a medieval pageboy. 'I saw how beautiful you were. Your hair looked to me then like one of those silk banners the Chinese fly at festivals. Afterwards, I saw you were courageous and loyal, and you represented everything I'd once had, and lost, and had thought I could never hope to get back again. I've done nothing but think of you, and dream of you and want you . . . oh, so much, you'll never know! But how could I tell you? Every time I tried, something went wrong, and we ended up at odds. I began to think that you must despise me so much that there could never be any hope for me. But you could never have despised me as much as I despised myself!'

'But I love you!' Zoë cried wildly, 'and I wanted you to say you loved me more than anything in the world!'

'I love you,' he whispered. 'I love you, Zoë, and I always shall.'

So they made the river journey for the last time, down to Canton, to be married by the Consul. Quentin's last act, before leaving, was to give his house to Eve. It would be a new school, new in more ways than one. Green Jade and Kim would help Eve to run it, a Chinese school for Chinese, on western lines, a novel idea and one revolutionary enough even for Kim.

Zoë parted from Eve with sadness, but knowing it was

right. This was Eve's life, which she had chosen, and for which she cared deeply. Zoë had chosen another.

Lejeune had gone away on an expeditionary dig, and left his best wishes and his bungalow at their disposal. The velvet night sky hung like a canopy above the sprawling, teeming city and above the ship, at anchor in the river, that would take them the next day on their long journey to the west.

Zoë pushed herself up on one elbow in the ornately carved Portuguese bed, brought many years before by Lejeune from Macao, watching Quentin, darkly silhouetted against the louvred shutters, and looking out between the slats at the night and the twinkling lights of the lanterns lining the wharf a short distance away.

'You'll miss China,' she said softly and a little sadly. 'You'll want to come back. If you ever want to return, you know I'll come too.'

Quentin shook his head and turned from the window. 'No, never.' He moved away, and began to pull off his clothes. The moonlight, falling in silver bars across the room, touched the bare skin of his naked body with luminous fingers. He stooped over the bed and said quietly, 'No one can ever go back, Zoë. There is no turning back.'

She could sense the heat from his body, and felt a strange trembling run over her of anticipation and longing, a union of the senses preceding a union of the flesh. She reached out her arms to encircle his neck and draw him down beside her. Feeling how warm and damp his skin was to the touch, and how tense the muscles beneath, she understood how apt was the ancient symbolism of Adam's rib, given to create Eve, for it was Man who planted life in the Woman, so that together they might discover the secret at the centre of everything, the fruit of the Forbidden Tree.

Outside, the crickets sang in the darkness. The moon cast its magic light on the curving pagoda roofs and ancient temples, awakening with its breath the carved lions at their gates and the temple guardians in the courtyards. The fountains rippled diamond showers into darkened basins so that the water sang melodiously. Somewhere, in the warm depths of the earth beneath, the Azure Dragon heard it, stretched his glittering scales and turned like a contented, somnolent cat at peace, knowing that the man and the woman lay together, and that all was well.

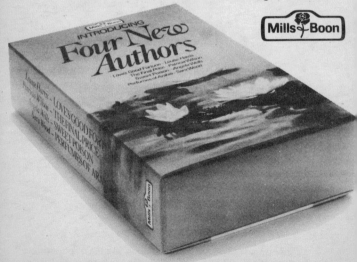